"What's your dream?" Meg asked Laury.

"If I tell you mine, will you tell me yours?"

"We will," agreed the girls.

. . . "If we're all alive ten years from now, let's meet. We'll see how many of us have gotten their wishes, or how much nearer we are to them," said Jo, always ready with a plan.

A Background Note about *Little Women*

Little Women takes place during the mid-1800s—a turning point in women's roles. Before the American Civil War, women were expected to serve their families as devoted daughters, wives, and mothers. "Proper" women dressed and behaved modestly. They wore full dresses, and pinned their long hair into buns. They rarely worked outside their homes, depending instead on their fathers or husbands for support. Married women did housekeeping and charity work. Unmarried middle-class women sometimes worked as governesses, living in wealthy families' homes and tutoring their children. Wealthy women organized social gatherings, and dabbled in art and music.

The Civil War disrupted many families. Husbands and fathers left their homes to fight. Three of every four soldiers died—many more from diseases than from bullets. Before antibiotics, infections spread easily, weakening or killing soldiers and civilians alike. Many women left their homes to volunteer as nurses. Others helped the war effort by knitting socks, sewing uniforms, and collecting and distributing supplies for the soldiers.

With so many men fighting and dying, women started doing "men's" work. For the first time, female authors felt free to write thrilling, daring, or even trashy stories about romance and crime. Some ambitious American women traveled to Europe to study art, where they hoped to earn fame as professional artists.

The mid-1800s offered American women opportunities as well as challenges. It was a time when women struggled to balance their roles as caregivers with their dreams of personal fulfillment. In other words, it was a time very much like today.

Louisa May Alcott

Little Women

Edited, and with an Afterword,
by Lisa Barsky

TP THE TOWNSEND LIBRARY

LITTLE WOMEN

TP **THE TOWNSEND LIBRARY**

For more titles in the Townsend Library,
visit our website: **www.townsendpress.com**

Copyright © 2009 by Townsend Press
Printed in the United States of America

0 9 8 7 6 5 4 3 2 1

Illustrations copyright © 2009 by Hal Taylor

Townsend Press Inc.
439 Kelley Drive
West Berlin, NJ 08091
cs@townsendpress.com

ISBN-13: 978-1-59194-113-2
ISBN-10: 1-59194-113-X

Library of Congress Control Number:
2008923251

Contents

Book Two

Afterword:

LITTLE WOMEN

Book One

Chapter 1

"Christmas won't be Christmas without any presents," grumbled Jo, lying on the rug.

"It's so dreadful being poor!" sighed Meg, looking down at her old dress.

"I don't think it's fair for some girls to have plenty of pretty things and other girls nothing at all," added little Amy.

"We've got Father and Mother and each other," whispered Beth, contentedly, from her corner.

The four young faces brightened at Beth's words. But then Jo reminded them sadly, "We don't have Father. And we won't for a long time."

Each girl added silently, "And perhaps we won't ever again." For their father was far from home, fighting in a dangerous war.

Nobody spoke for a moment. Then sixteen-year-old Meg broke the silence. She was the oldest of the four March sisters, and rather vain about her large eyes, soft brown hair, sweet mouth, and fair hands. "Mother said we shouldn't buy any presents this year because it's going to be a hard winter for everyone. We should be glad to sacrifice our own little pleasures to help those who are suffering in the army. But I'm afraid I just don't feel that way." There were so many pretty things she wanted!

Fifteen-year-old Josephine, who liked to be called "Jo," spoke next. She was very tall and thin, with legs as awkward as a colt's. Her sharp gray eyes seemed to see everything. At different times they could be fierce, funny, or thoughtful. Jo's hair was long, thick, and beautiful. But she usually pulled it back into a tight little bun so it would be out of her way. Jo hated having to dress, look, or act like a "young woman." But she loved to read. "We've each got a dollar," she began. "That's too little to help the army very much. Now, I don't expect gifts from anyone else. But I would like to buy a book for myself."

Thirteen-year-old Beth, rosy-cheeked and bright-eyed, wore a peaceful expression that was seldom disturbed. Quiet and shy, she seemed to live in a happy world of her own. "I was going to buy new piano music," she said, so softly that no one heard.

"Well, I'm going to buy a nice box of drawing pencils!" announced twelve-year-old Amy. Though the youngest sister, she thought of herself as a very important person. Blue-eyed, with yellow hair that curled at her shoulders, Amy always tried to act like a proper young lady

At that, Jo exclaimed, "Mother wouldn't want us to give up everything. So let's each use our money to buy what we want. We sure work hard enough earning it!"

"I know I do," complained Meg. "Teaching those children nearly all day long!"

"My job's a lot harder than yours," argued Jo. "Shut up for hours with a nervous, fussy old lady who's never satisfied. She pesters me and keeps me running around until I'm ready to jump out the window. Or cry."

"I know it's wrong to complain," Beth added softly. "But housework is the worst work in the world. It makes my hands so rough and stiff that I can't practice the piano."

"Well, I suffer the most!" exclaimed Amy. "I have to go to school with rude girls who tease me if I make a mistake. They laugh at my plain, hand-me-down clothes. And they make fun of my father because he isn't rich."

Meg, who was old enough to remember better times, sighed, "Don't you wish we had the money Papa lost when we were little? How happy and good we'd be if only we had no worries!"

"But, Meg. The other day you said we were much happier than the King children. You said they always fight, in spite of all their money," Beth reminded her gently.

"Well, I think we are. Even though we do have to work, we also make fun for ourselves."

At this, Jo sat up, put her hands in her pockets, and started whistling.

"Don't, Jo. It's so boyish!" scolded Amy.

"That's why I do it."

"Well, I hate rude, unladylike girls!"

"And I hate stuck-up, prissy misses!"

Beth, the peacemaker, sang out, "Birds in their little nests must all agree."

Meg started lecturing them both. "Really, Josephine. You're old enough to stop being a tomboy and start acting like a lady."

"I will not!" cried Jo, undoing the bun and shaking out her hair. "I hate having to grow up and be like Miss March—wearing long gowns and looking prim. It's bad enough to be a girl when I'd rather play boys' games and do men's work. I'm still disappointed that I wasn't born a boy. I'm dying to go fight with Papa instead of sitting here like a little old lady, knitting blue socks for the soldiers!"

"Poor Jo!" Beth said gently. "It's too bad, but it can't be helped. So try to be happy making your name sound boyish and playing 'brother' to us girls."

"As for you, Amy," Meg continued, "You're much too fussy and prim. I like your nice manners and your careful way of speaking. But when you try to be elegant, you end up sounding like a silly little goose."

"If Jo is a tomboy and Amy's a goose, then what am I?" asked Beth.

"You're a dear," answered Meg, for everyone loved Beth, who was the family "pet."

The sisters continued to knit, while outside the December snow fell quietly, and inside the fire crackled cheerfully. It was a comfortable room, though the carpet was faded and the furniture very simple. But it was filled with books, flowers, and a sense of peace.

The clock struck six. Having swept up the hearth, Beth put a pair of slippers in front of the fireplace to warm up. The sight of the old shoes cheered the girls, and they prepared to welcome Marmee, as they called their mother. Meg stopped lecturing and lit the lamp. Amy got out of the easy chair without being asked. And Jo forgot how tired she was as she held the slippers closer to the fire.

"They're completely worn out," observed Jo. "Marmee needs a new pair."

"I thought I'd get her some with my dollar," said Beth quietly.

"No, I shall!" exclaimed Amy.

"But I'm the oldest," began Meg.

Jo interrupted her. "I'm the man of the family now that Papa's away. He told me to take special care of Mother. So I'll provide the slippers."

"I know. Let's each get something for Marmee, and not get anything for ourselves," said Beth.

"You're so sweet!" exclaimed Jo. "What will we get?"

Looking at her own pretty hands, Meg announced, "I'll give her a nice pair of gloves."

"Good army shoes," Jo decided.

"Some nice handkerchiefs" said Beth.

"A pretty little bottle of perfume. She'll like it, and I'll still have some money left over to buy my pencils," added Amy.

"We'll go shopping tomorrow afternoon, and let Marmee think we're getting things for ourselves," suggested Jo. "But now we'd better rehearse our Christmas play."

When the sisters had finished acting out the scene, Beth applauded. "You write such splendid plays, Jo! You're a regular Shakespeare!" Beth believed that each of her sisters was a genius.

Suddenly a cheery voice greeted them from the doorway. "Well, dearies, how are you? How is your cold, Meg? Jo, you look exhausted." A tall, noble, motherly lady entered the room. She had a truly delightful "Can I help you?" look about her. The girls thought that the simple gray coat and old-fashioned hat covered the most wonderful mother in the world.

As they gathered around the table, Mrs. March said, with a particularly happy face, "I've got a treat for you after supper."

Like a streak of sunshine, a bright smile lit up each face, one after the other. Beth clapped her hands, forgetting that she was holding a biscuit.

Jo tossed her napkin in the air, shouting, "A letter! A letter! Three cheers for Father!"

"Yes, a nice long letter," said Mrs. March, patting her pocket as if it held a treasure. "He's well and thinks the winter will be easier than we'd feared. He sends his love, and a special message to you girls."

"I think it was wonderful that Father enlisted as an army chaplain—since he's too old and weak to be a soldier," said Meg.

Jo exclaimed, "How I wish I could go as a drummer—or a nurse, so I could help him!"

"It must be nasty to sleep in a tent and eat bad-tasting things and drink out of a tin mug," sighed Amy.

"When will he come home, Marmee?" asked Beth, her voice trembling.

"Not for many months, dear, unless he gets sick. And we won't ask him to come home until he isn't needed there anymore."

After dinner, Mother sat in the big chair, with Meg and Amy perched on its arms, and Beth close at her feet. But Jo stood behind them, so no one would see if she cried. In those hard times, most letters written by soldiers were very touching—especially ones sent by fathers to their families. This time, Father did not write about the terrible hardships, dangers, and homesickness he faced. Instead, it was a cheerful, hopeful letter. Only at the end did his heart overflow with fatherly love and longing for the girls at home.

"Give them all my dear love and a kiss. I think of them every day, and their love gives me great comfort. A year is a very long time to wait before seeing them. But we can all work to make sure that these hard days are not wasted. I know that the girls will remember all I said to them. And they will be loving children to you, and do their duty faithfully. So when I come back to them, I will be prouder than ever of my little women."

At that, Amy sobbed, "I'm so selfish! But I'll truly try to be better, so he won't be disappointed in me."

"We all will!" exclaimed Meg. "I think too much of my looks. And I hate to work. But I won't any more if I can help it."

"I'll try and be 'a little woman' instead of being so rough and wild," said Jo, thinking that it would be harder to control her temper than to fight a Southern rebel. "And I'll do my duty here instead of wishing I were somewhere else."

Wiping away her tears, Beth added, "And I must stop being afraid of people and envying girls with nice pianos." Determined to live up to Father's hopes, she went back to knitting with all her might.

"Everyone has burdens to carry," Mother said in her cheery voice. "But we must try to do good and be happy. That will help us find our way through our mistakes and our troubles. Why don't you see how much good you can do before Father comes home?"

"Yes, let's try to act good," said Meg thoughtfully.

"But even good actors need scripts to follow. What shall we do about that?" Jo asked.

"Look under your pillows Christmas morning," replied Mrs. March, "and you will find your guidebooks."

Then needles flew as the girls sewed sheets for Aunt March. The task was boring, but tonight no one grumbled.

At nine they stopped working and sang, as usual. Ever since they were little, the girls had sung "Twinkle, twinkle, little star" every night before going to bed. Beth, with her soft touch, was the only person who could get pleasant music out of the old piano. Meg had a voice like a flute. But Amy chirped like a cricket. And Jo's voice went its own way, never in tune with the melody. Their mother, though, was a born singer. The first sound every morning was Mother, singing like a lark. And the last sound at night was the same cheery sound. For the girls never grew too old for that familiar lullaby.

Chapter 2

Jo was the first one to wake up in the gray dawn of Christmas morning. No stockings hung by the fireplace. For a moment she felt as disappointed as she did when her stocking was so full of goodies that it fell down. Then she remembered her mother's promise. Under her pillow was a little book with a red cover. She knew that it would be a true guidebook for her.

Soon each of the girls found her own little book—one green, one white, and one blue. Inside each were a few words written by their mother, which made these gifts very precious in their eyes.

Downstairs, Old Hannah was preparing breakfast. She had lived with the family and worked in the house since Meg was born. So they thought of her more as a friend than a housekeeper.

When the girls ran down to thank Mother for their gifts, Hannah explained, "Some poor creature came a-begging, and your ma went right off to see what was needed. She's always giving away something!"

Suddenly the front door slammed and steps sounded in the hall. Instead of Mother, though, it was Amy, looking embarrassed.

"Where have you been, and what are you hiding behind you?" asked Meg.

"Don't laugh at me, Jo! But after talking about being good, I felt ashamed of myself for being so selfish. So I took all my money, and changed the little bottle of perfume for a big one." Amy looked so serious and humble that Meg hugged her, Jo complimented her for her generosity, and Beth found a flower to decorate the bottle. The girls added Amy's perfume to the basket of gifts and hid it under the sofa.

The front door banged again, and the girls ran to the table, eager for breakfast.

"Merry Christmas, Marmee! And many more of them! Thank you for our books!" they all called out.

"Merry Christmas, my daughters! But I want to tell you something before we sit down to eat. Not far from here lies a poor woman with a little newborn baby. Six children are huddled together to keep from freezing. They have no wood for a fire and nothing to eat. The oldest boy came here to tell me they were suffering from hunger and cold. My girls, will you give the Hummels your breakfast as a Christmas present?"

The girls were all unusually hungry, for they had been waiting an hour for breakfast. For a minute no one spoke. But then Jo exclaimed, "I'm so glad you told us before we started eating!"

"May I help carry the things to the poor little children?" asked Beth eagerly.

"I'll take the butter and muffins," added Amy, offering to give up the food she liked most.

Meg was already covering the pancakes, and piling the bread onto one big plate.

"I thought you'd want to help," Mrs. March smiled. "We'll all go. And when we come back, we'll have a simple breakfast of bread and milk."

So they carried their gifts to the poor, bare, miserable one-room house. It had broken windows, no fire in the fireplace, and torn sheets on the bed. There they found a sick mother, a wailing baby, and a group of pale, hungry children huddled under an old quilt, trying to keep warm. When the March women walked in, the Hummel children stared with wide eyes, and smiled with lips that were blue from the cold.

"Why, it's the good angels come to us!" the poor woman cried in joy.

"Funny angels—wearing hoods and mittens," said Jo, making everyone laugh.

In a few minutes, it really did seem that kind spirits had been at work there. Hannah made a fire and filled the broken windows with old hats and her own coat. Mrs. March tenderly dressed the little baby, and comforted the mother with hot cereal and promises of help. The girls fed the children, laughing and talking with them. And the children eagerly swallowed the food, like hungry little birds.

The Marches thought it a very happy breakfast, even though they didn't get any of it. And in all the city, there was no one merrier than the four hungry little girls who gave away their fine Christmas breakfasts, and enjoyed a simple meal of bread and milk.

"That's loving our neighbor better than ourselves," said Meg. "And I like it."

After they got home, Mother went upstairs to collect clothes for the poor Hummels. When she came back down again, Jo started prancing and shouting, "Three cheers for Marmee!" Beth played a cheerful march, Amy threw open the door, and Meg escorted their mother to the basket of gifts. Surprised and touched, Mrs. March smiled as she looked at the presents, her eyes full of tears.

They spent the rest of the day preparing for the evening's festivities. Because they were too poor to buy theater tickets, the sisters created their own productions. They made guitars out of cardboard and armor from tin can lids. They created a "gloomy woods" with a few potted plants and some green fabric on the floor. No boys were allowed, so Jo could enjoy playing all the male parts.

On Christmas night, a dozen girls piled onto a folding cot bed and watched the performance. During scene changes, the girls chatted and ate candy. At the end of the show, the audience clapped wildly.

But the applause stopped abruptly. The cot bed collapsed, and the audience tumbled under mattresses and blankets. Fortunately, the actors flew to their rescue. No one was hurt, but everyone laughed so hard they were breathless. Then Hannah appeared and announced, "Mrs. March would like to invite you ladies to come down to supper."

When the girls saw the table, even the actors were amazed. There were bowls of fancy ice cream, and plates full of cake, fruit, and chocolate candies. In the middle of the table were four big vases filled with flowers. The sisters hadn't seen anything that fine since the days when their family had money.

"Is it fairies?" asked Amy.

"Santa Claus," suggested Beth.

"Mother did it," smiled Meg.

"No, it was Aunt March. She must have had a sudden change of heart!" exclaimed Jo.

"All wrong," replied Mrs. March. "Old Mr. Laurence sent it."

"The Laurence boy's grandfather? What in

the world put such a thing into his head? We don't even know him!" exclaimed Meg.

"He knew my father years ago," explained Mrs. March. "And Hannah told one of his housekeepers about your 'breakfast party.' He's an odd old gentleman, but that pleased him. He said he wanted to express his friendly feelings toward my children by sending them a few little sweets in honor of the day. So now you have a feast at night to make up for your bread-and-milk breakfast."

"It was his grandson's idea, I'm sure of it," said Jo. "He's a fine fellow and I'd like to get to know him. But he's shy. And Meg's so proper she won't let me speak to him."

"You mean the people who live in the big house next door?" asked one of the girls. "My mother said that old Mr. Laurence is proud and doesn't like to mix with his poorer neighbors. He makes his grandson stay inside and study— except when he's horseback riding or walking with his tutor. The boy seems nice, but he never speaks with us girls."

"Once when our cat ran away, the boy brought her back. We talked over the fence—all about sports—and were getting along fine. But when he saw Meg coming, he walked away. I'm going to get to know him some day," announced Jo. "For he looks like he needs more fun in his life."

"I like his manners," Mother said. "And he seems like a perfect gentleman. So I don't mind your getting to know him if you have the chance. He brought the flowers himself."

"I've never had such a fine bouquet!" exclaimed Meg.

"They are lovely," said Mrs. March. "But Beth's roses are sweeter to me," she added, smelling the half-dead flower that Beth had given her.

Beth snuggled closer and whispered, "I wish I could send my bunch to Father. I'm afraid his Christmas isn't as merry as ours."

Chapter 3

"Jo! Jo!" Meg shouted as she ran into the attic. "Mrs. Gardiner invited us to her New Year's Eve dance tomorrow night!"

Jo looked up from the book she was reading. She loved curling up alone in the attic with a nice book, half-dozen apples, and the pet rat she called "Scrabble."

"Oh, if only I had a silk gown!" sighed Meg.

"Well, I'm sure our cotton dresses are nice enough for us," answered Jo with her mouth full of apple. "Yours is as good as new, but I burned a hole in mine when I was ironing it. What am I going to do?"

"You must sit still and keep your back out of sight. My new shoes are lovely, and my gloves will do, though they aren't as nice as I'd like."

"I spilled lemonade on mine and stained them. So I'll just have to go without gloves."

"Oh, but you must have gloves," Meg said. "You can't dance without them. If you don't have gloves, I'll be so humiliated!"

"Then I won't dance. Or I'll hold them

crumpled in one hand so no one will see the stain. Or—here's what we can do. We'll each wear one good glove and carry a bad one."

"But your hands are bigger than mine, and you'll stretch my glove terribly," complained Meg.

"Then I'll go without. I don't care what people say!" exclaimed Jo, going back to her book.

"OK. You may have my glove. Only don't stain it. And do behave nicely."

"Don't worry about me. I'll be as proper as I can. Now go and answer the invitation, and let me finish this wonderful story."

On New Year's Eve, Meg and Jo focused on the all-important business of getting ready for the party. Meg wanted to frame her face with a few curls. So Jo wound locks of her hair around little papers. She then set the curls with a hot iron.

"Are they supposed to smoke like that?" asked Beth.

"It's just the dampness drying," answered Jo.

"What a strange smell!" said Amy, admiring her own natural curls. "Like burned feathers."

Finally Jo set down the iron. "There, now. I'll take off the papers, and you'll see a cloud of little ringlets."

But as the papers came off, so did the hair. The horrified "hairdresser" laid a row of little scorched bundles on the table in front of her victim.

"Oh! Oh! Oh!" wailed Meg. "What have you done? I'm ruined! I can't go!"

"I'm so sorry. I always spoil everything," groaned poor Jo.

"It isn't spoiled," said Amy. "Just frizz it and tie it with a ribbon. It will look like the latest fashion."

"Serves me right for trying to be fancy. I wish I'd left my hair alone," cried Meg.

"So do I," said Beth, comforting her sister. "It was so smooth and pretty. But it will soon grow out again."

Finally the two girls were ready. Meg's high-heeled shoes were very tight and hurt her. But she would never admit it. And Jo's nineteen hairpins seemed to stick straight into her head, which was not exactly comfortable. But Meg thought that if they didn't look elegant, they'd just die!

As Meg and Jo went daintily down the walk, Mrs. March called after them, "Have a good time, dears! Don't eat much supper! Oh, and girls! Girls! Do you both have nice handker-chiefs?"

"Yes! Yes!" called Jo. Laughing, she turned to Meg, "I do believe Marmee would ask us about our handkerchiefs even if we were running from an earthquake!"

When they arrived at the Gardiner's house, Meg did some final primping. "Is my sash crooked? Does my hair look very bad?"

"If you see me doing anything wrong, just wink at me," said Jo, smoothing her hair.

"No, winking isn't ladylike. I'll raise my eyebrows if you do anything wrong, and nod if you're all right. Now, straighten your shoulders and take little steps."

"How have you learned to be so proper? I never can," sighed Jo.

Mrs. Gardiner, a dignified lady, greeted them kindly and led them to Sally, the oldest of her six daughters. But Jo didn't enjoy girlish gossip, and felt as out of place as a young colt in a flower garden. She carefully stood with her back against the wall, longing to join the boys who were talking about skating. But Meg's eyebrows went up in alarm at the idea.

Soon Meg was asked to dance. She moved so lightly in her tight shoes that no one suspected how much pain they caused her. For she suffered it with a smile.

Jo panicked when she saw a tall, redheaded boy approaching, afraid he might ask her to dance. She slipped behind a curtain, planning to peep out and enjoy herself in peace. Unfortunately, another shy person had chosen the same hiding place. Suddenly she found herself face to face with "the Laurence boy."

"Oh, dear!" Jo exclaimed, backing away.

"Don't mind me," the boy laughed. "Stay if you like."

"I won't disturb you?"

"Not a bit. I only came here because I don't know many people, and I felt rather strange."

"So did I. Please don't go away," said Jo. "Unless you'd rather."

So the boy sat down again and stared at his feet, not knowing what to say.

Finally Jo said, trying to be proper, "I think I've had the pleasure of seeing you before. You live near us, don't you?"

The boy looked up and laughed at Jo's "lady-like" formality. "Next door," he answered.

Then Jo laughed, too, and said heartily, "We had such a good time with your Christmas present!"

"Grandpa sent it."

"But it was your idea, wasn't it?"

Instead of answering, the boy asked rather stiffly, "How is your cat, Miss March?" He tried to look serious, but his dark eyes sparkled with fun.

"Very well, thank you, Mr. Laurence. But I am not Miss March. I'm only Jo," replied the young lady.

"And I'm not Mr. Laurence. I'm only Laury."

"Laury Laurence. What an odd name."

"My first name is Theodore, but I like Laury better."

"I hate my name, too. So girlish! I wish everyone would call me 'Jo' instead of 'Josephine.'"

"Don't you like to dance, Miss Jo?" asked Laury, looking as if he thought the name fit her.

"Only if there's lots of room to move around. Here I'm afraid of knocking something over, or stepping on someone's toes. Don't you dance?"

"Sometimes. But I don't know any American dances. You see, I've been going to a boarding school in Switzerland for a long time."

"Oh, tell me all about it! I love to hear people describe their travels!"

Soon they were chatting like old friends. At one point they peeped out at the dancers, and Laury asked the name of the young lady in the pretty shoes.

"It's my sister Meg, and you knew it! Do you think she's pretty?"

"Yes. She's so fresh and quiet, and she dances like a lady."

Jo enjoyed hearing her sister praised by this tall, good-looking, very polite boy. She memorized every word to repeat later to Meg.

"I suppose you're going to college soon? You're always cracking the books—I mean, studying," Jo said.

"Not for a year or two. I won't be sixteen until next month."

"How I wish I was going to college!"

"I hate the idea! Nothing but studying and playing pranks."

"What do you like?"

"Living in Italy. And enjoying myself in my own way."

Jo wanted very much to ask what his own way was. But then, with a fine little bow, the young man invited her dance.

"Oh no. I can't. I told Meg I wouldn't because . . . "

"Because what?"

"You won't tell?"

"Never!"

So Jo explained about the hole in her dress. Then she added, "You can laugh if you want."

But Laury didn't laugh. Instead he said very gently, "Don't worry. We can dance in the hallway, and no one will see us. Please come."

Jo thanked him and gladly went—though when she saw her partner's nice white gloves, she wished she had two neat gloves of her own.

Suddenly Meg appeared, looking pale. She signaled to Jo, and Jo followed her reluctantly.

"I've sprained my ankle," Meg moaned in pain. "That stupid high heel turned under me. It aches so much I can hardly stand. How will I ever walk home?"

"I knew you'd hurt your feet with those silly shoes. I'm sorry."

"Well, a carriage would cost too much. And I

can't stay here all night because Sally already has some girls staying with her. I'll just have to wait till Hannah comes, and then try to limp home."

"I'll ask Laury. He'll go," said Jo.

"Goodness, no! Don't let anyone know. Just bring me a cup of coffee and let me know as soon as Hannah comes."

Jo picked up a cup of coffee from the dining room table and immediately spilled it. Now the front of her dress was as bad as the back. Then she ruined Meg's glove by using it to mop her dress.

"Can I help you?" asked a friendly voice. And there was Laury, with a cup of coffee in one hand and a dish of ice cream in the other.

"I was trying to get some coffee for Meg, who is very tired. But someone bumped into me and now I'm a mess," Jo answered.

"I'm sorry," said Laury. "Well, I was just looking for someone to give this to. May I take it to your sister?"

Jo led the way to where Meg was sitting. As if he was used to waiting on ladies, Laury pulled up a little table. Then he brought another cup of coffee and dish of ice cream for Jo. He was so kind that even Meg agreed he was a "nice boy."

By the time Hannah appeared, they were having so much fun that Meg had forgotten about her ankle. When she got up, she cried out in pain and had to catch hold of Jo. Then she said, "It's nothing. I turned my foot a little. That's all." And Meg limped upstairs to get her coat.

In the upstairs room, Hannah scolded, Meg cried, and Jo was at her wits' end. Finally, Jo decided to take things into her own hands. She ran downstairs and asked one of the servers if he could get her a carriage. Overhearing her, Laury came up and offered his grandfather's carriage, which had just come for him. "Please let me take you home. It's right on my way."

Jo told him about Meg's accident, and gratefully accepted the offer. Laury sat up front with the driver, so the girls were able to talk in back without being heard.

"I had a fabulous time. Did you?" asked Jo, letting down her hair.

"Yes. Till I hurt myself. Sally's friend Annie Moffat asked me to come spend a week with her and Sally in the spring, when the opera comes to town."

"I saw you dance with the boy I ran away from. Was he nice?"

"Oh, very!"

"Well, Laury and I couldn't help laughing at the way he danced. He looked like a grasshopper in a tornado!"

"That's rude, Jo. So what were you up to, hidden away there?"

When they got home, they thanked Laury warmly and said goodnight. Then they crept into the house, hoping not to wake up anyone. But the instant the door creaked, two sleepy but eager voices begged, "Tell about the party! Tell about the party!"

Jo had brought home some candies for her younger sisters, which Meg said was very improper. After talking about the most thrilling events of the evening, the girls went off to bed.

Jo brushed Meg's hair and rubbed ointment onto her swollen ankle. Meg said, smiling, "I really feel like a fine young lady—coming home in a fancy carriage and having a 'maid' wait on me."

"I don't think fine young ladies enjoy themselves any more than we do—in spite of our having burned hair, old gowns, one glove apiece, and tight shoes that sprain our ankles when we're silly enough to wear them."

Chapter 4

"*O*h, dear," sighed Meg, the morning after the party. "How hard it is to go back to work. Those four children are so cranky and spoiled."

"I wish it was Christmas or New Year's all the time. Wouldn't it be fun?" Jo answered, yawning.

"We wouldn't enjoy ourselves half as much as we do now. But it's so nice to have little suppers and bouquets, and go to parties and drive home in a carriage. I envy girls who get to do such things."

"Well, we can't. So instead of grumbling, let's do our work as cheerfully as Marmee does hers. Aunt March is such a burden for me to carry. But if I stop complaining, it won't seem so heavy."

Everyone was grumpy at breakfast. Beth had a headache and lay on the sofa, trying to comfort herself with the cat and three kittens. Amy was upset because she hadn't finished her math homework, and she couldn't find her boots. Hannah was in a bad mood because she had stayed up too late. And Mrs. March was trying to finish a letter that needed to be mailed right away.

Jo complained, Meg scolded, Beth cried, and Amy whined because she couldn't remember how much nine times twelve was.

"Girls, girls, do be quiet one minute!" begged Mrs. March, crossing out the third mistake in her letter.

There was a moment of silence. Then Hannah stalked in, placed two hot muffins on the table, and stalked out again. No matter how busy or grumpy Hannah might be, she never forgot to make them. The two older girls called them their "muffs" because they kept their hands warm on their way to work, since they had no real mittens.

"Get over your headache, Bethy!" called Jo, as she and Meg left for work. "Goodbye, Marmee! We're little devils this morning, but we'll be regular angels when we come home!"

Meg and Jo always looked back before turning the corner. For their mother was always at the window, smiling and waving. They could never have gotten through the day without that. For whatever their mood, the last glimpse of that motherly face warmed them like sunshine.

"Call yourself a little devil if you like, but don't call me one!" Meg mumbled wearily.

"You're just miserable because you can't always sit in the lap of luxury," Jo laughed. "Poor dear. Just wait till I make my fortune. Then you shall delight in carriages and ice cream and high-heeled shoes and roses and red-headed boys to dance with!"

Meg laughed in spite of herself. And they parted for the day, each trying to be cheerful in spite of the wintry weather, hard work, and personal sacrifices.

A few years ago, their father had lost everything trying to help a friend in trouble. So the two oldest girls begged to help support the family. Their parents agreed, thinking it might help them develop independence and strength of character.

So both girls went to work with good will—which in the end can overcome most obstacles.

Meg took care of the four youngest King children. She rarely complained. But sometimes she envied the older King sisters. For they had beautiful gowns and bouquets, went to concerts and plays, and spent precious money on silly things. Meg remembered when her own family had money, and she longed for luxuries. She had not yet learned how "rich" she was in the things that make people truly happy.

Jo worked as a companion for her Aunt March, a childless and cranky old lady who had trouble walking and needed someone to wait on her. Something about Jo's frank manner and expressive face appealed to Aunt March. And in her heart, Jo rather liked the spirited old lady.

But what she really liked was Aunt March's large library filled with fine books. Whenever Aunt March took her nap or had visitors, Jo hurried to this quiet place. But like all happiness, her reading pleasures never lasted long. For as soon as she reached the heart of a story or a moment of great suspense, a shrill voice called, "Josy-phine! Josy-phine!" Then Jo had to leave her paradise to wind yarn, wash the poodle, or read boring essays with her aunt.

Jo longed to read, run, and ride as much as she liked. Her ambition was to do something wonderful with her life. But her quick temper, sharp words, and restless spirit were always getting her into trouble. Her life was a series of ups and downs, both funny and sad. But earning money to support herself made her happy—in spite of that annoying "Josy-phine"!

Beth was too shy to go to school. So her father taught her at home until he went away to fight in the war. That's when her mother began devoting all her skill, time, and energy to the Soldiers' Aid Societies. So Beth faithfully tried to study on her own and to help Hannah take care of the home. Beth spent her long, quiet days alone, but she was never lonely. For her little world was filled with the pets and dolls who were her imaginary friends. Still a child a heart, Beth set up a hospital for all the dolls that her sisters had outgrown, damaged, or thrown away.

She cherished the dolls she rescued, nursed, and cared for tenderly.

Beth loved music dearly, and she patiently practiced playing the Marches' squeaky old piano. Sometimes, when she was all alone, she cried because she couldn't take music lessons or have a piano that would stay in tune. But nobody saw her wipe the tears off the yellowed piano keys. And nobody—not even Aunt March—offered to help her. Beth never asked for anything, because the only reward she ever wanted was to be loved.

Beth sang like a lark as she worked, and she never gave up hope. Day after day she said to herself, "I know I'll get my music sometime if I'm good." Shy people like Beth sit quietly in corners until they're needed. They live so cheerfully for others that no one notices the sacrifices they've made—at least, not until their sweet sunshiny presence vanishes, leaving silence and shadow behind.

Amy's greatest burden in life was her nose. It wasn't big or red. But it was rather flat. And all the pinching in the world could not make it fine. Amy longed to have a nose like a Greek goddess, so she drew hundreds of handsome noses to console herself. Amy had a real talent for drawing, and loved copying flowers, designing fairies, and illustrating stories. Her teachers complained that she covered her math worksheets with animals.

But she was always pleasant and well behaved. Her classmates admired her elegant manners and her ability to read French without mispronouncing more than two-thirds of the words. Amy liked to tell people gracefully, "When Papa was rich, we did such-and-such."

Everyone spoiled Amy, and she was becoming rather selfish. But having to wear her cousin's hand-me-down clothes kept her from becoming too vain. As an "artist," Amy's eyes hurt whenever she looked at the plain purple dress that she had to wear to school.

The two older girls loved each other dearly, and "played mother" to their younger sisters. Meg took special care of Amy. And shy, gentle Beth confided her thoughts only to Jo.

That evening, as the family sat sewing together, each girl told about her day.

Jo told how Aunt March had scolded her for reading a thrilling romance instead of boring essays. But then later Jo caught Aunt March finishing the romance on her own. "She could have such a pleasant life if only she chose to!" said Jo. Then she added, "I don't envy her, though, in spite of her money. For rich people have as many worries as poor ones."

"That reminds me," said Meg, "of how upset the Kings were today. Their oldest son did something terrible, and Mr. King sent him away. I felt so sorry for them, and was glad I didn't have any wild brothers to disgrace the family by doing wicked things."

"I think being disgraced in school is worser than anything bad boys can do," said Amy, as if she were wise from years of experience. She then told how her friend Susie Perkins was scolded in front of the entire class for drawing a cartoon of their teacher. "After that, I didn't envy Susie's lovely gold ring. Not even millions of gold rings could make me happy after being so humiliated."

"Today at the fish store, I saw something I liked," said Beth, as she tidied Jo's messy sewing basket. "A poor woman asked if she could clean fish in exchange for fish to feed her children. The owner said 'no.' But then Mr. Laurence hooked a great big fish on the end of his cane and held it out to the woman. She was so glad and surprised that she took the fish right into her arms, and thanked him over and over. Wasn't that good of him?"

Then the girls asked their mother for a story. Mrs. March smiled. "Once upon a time, there were four girls. They all had enough to eat and drink and wear. They had pleasant activities, kind friends, and parents who loved them dearly. Yet they were not satisfied. 'If only we had this,' they'd say. Or, 'If only we could do that.' They forgot how much they already had, and how many things they could actually do.

"One day they asked an old woman for a magic spell that would make them happy. She answered, 'When you feel unhappy, just think about your blessings and be grateful.'

"Being sensible girls, they followed the old woman's advice. Soon they were surprised to see how well off they were. One girl found out that money can't protect rich people from shame and sorrow. Another discovered that, even though she was poor, she was much happier than a grumpy, frail old lady who couldn't enjoy her luxuries. The third girl realized that good behavior is more valuable than gold rings. And the fourth learned that it's less unpleasant to prepare dinner than to have to beg for it.

"So they all agreed to stop complaining, and enjoy what they already had. They would try to deserve their blessings rather than risk losing them completely. And I believe the girls were never disappointed or sorry about taking the old woman's advice."

Chapter 5

To Jo, the fine stone mansion next door to the March house seemed like an enchanted palace, full of treasures that no one enjoyed. She felt sorry for Mr. Laurence's grandson, who seemed lonely and shy. One snowy afternoon, she noticed him gazing wistfully down from his window. Below him, Beth and Amy were having fun throwing snowballs at each other in the Marches' garden.

Poor boy, thought Jo. *All alone and sick on this dreary day.* That's when she made up her mind to visit the Laurence boy.

After seeing Mr. Laurence drive off, Jo tossed up a snowball to catch the boy's attention. "Hello, there! Are you sick?"

Laury opened the window and called out hoarsely, "I'm starting to feel better, thank you. I've had a bad cold, and I've been stuck inside for a week."

"I'm sorry. But don't you have fun reading?"

"They won't let me read because it might give me a headache."

"Can't somebody read to you?"

"Grandpa does a little. But my books don't interest him. I could ask Brooke, my tutor. But I hate to keep bothering him."

"Well, then. I'll come and read to you if my mother will let me."

A few minutes later, Jo appeared, with a covered dish in one hand and Beth's three kittens in the other. "Mother sends her love, and said she'd be glad if I could be of some help. Meg wanted me to bring some pudding she made. Amy decorated it with flowers from her favorite geranium. And Beth thought her cats might comfort you. I knew you'd laugh, but she really wanted to do something for you, too."

Laughing about the kittens helped Laury forget his shyness. "How kind you are! Now, let me do something to entertain you."

"No, I came to entertain you. Shall I read aloud?" asked Jo, looking eagerly at some nearby books.

"Thank you, but I've already read those. If you don't mind, I'd rather talk," answered Laury.

"Well, I can talk all day if you get me started. Beth says I never know when to stop."

"Is Beth the one who stays at home? The pretty one is Meg, and the one with curly hair is Amy, I believe?"

"How did you know that?"

Laury blushed, but then admitted frankly, "I can't help looking over at your house. You always seem to be having such good times. Please forgive my rudeness. But when you leave the curtain open, it's like looking at a picture with all of you gathered around the table. Your mother's face looks so sweet, I can't help watching it. I don't have a mother, you know," said Laury, turning away so Jo wouldn't see the tears in his eyes.

Feeling rich in home and happiness, Jo gladly offered to share her family with Laury. "We'll leave the curtain open, and I give you permission to look as much as you like. But I'd rather you came over to visit us, instead. Mother's splendid, and would do you heaps of good. Beth would sing to you if you begged her to. And Amy would dance. Meg and I would keep you laughing, and we'd have jolly times. Wouldn't your grandpa let you?"

"I think so, if your mother asked him. He's very kind, though he doesn't look that way. You see, Grandpa lives among his books and doesn't pay much attention to the outside world." Then, changing the subject, Laury asked, "Do you like your school?"

"Don't go to school. I'm a businessman—I mean, a businessgirl. I take care of my great-aunt. And a dear, cranky old soul she is, too."

Jo explained about the fidgety old lady, her fat poodle, the parrot that spoke Spanish, and the library that delighted her. Then she told how a proper old gentleman once came to win Aunt March's love. But then the parrot plucked off the gentleman's wig. At that, Laury laughed till the tears ran down his cheeks.

Jo was delighted to find out that Laury loved books as much as she did, and had read even more than she.

"If you like books so much, come down and see ours. Grandfather is out, so you don't have to be afraid," said Laury, getting up.

"I'm not afraid of anything!" declared Jo, with a toss of her head.

"Why, I don't believe you are!" exclaimed the boy in admiration.

When they got to the library, Jo clapped her hands with delight. "What richness!" Jo sighed. "Theodore Laurence, you ought to be the happiest boy in the world!"

"A fellow can't live on books," said Laury, shaking his head.

Then the doctor arrived, so Laury had to leave Jo alone in the library.

Jo looked closely at a portrait of the boy's grandfather. Thinking out loud, she said decidedly, "No, I'm sure I don't have to be afraid of him. He's got kind eyes, even though his mouth is stern. And he looks terribly strong-willed. He's not as handsome as my grandfather, but I definitely like him."

"Thank you, ma'am," said a gruff voice behind her. And there, to Jo's great dismay, stood old Mr. Laurence.

Jo blushed. She thought about running away. But that would be cowardly. So she decided to stay and try to get out of the mess as best she could.

After a terrible pause, the old gentleman said abruptly, "So you're not afraid of me, eh?"

"Not much, sir."

"And you think I'm less handsome than your grandfather?"

"A little, sir."

"And I have a very strong will, have I?"

"I only said I thought so."

"But you like me in spite of that?"

"Yes, I do, sir."

That answer pleased the old gentleman. He gave a short laugh and shook hands with her. "You've got your grandfather's spirit. He was a fine man, my dear. But more important, he was brave and honest, and I was proud to be his friend."

"Thank you, sir," said Jo, feeling quite comfortable now.

"And you have come here because—?" the gentleman asked sharply.

"Well, sir, your grandson seems a little lonely. We're only girls, but we'd be glad to help if we can. For we haven't forgotten the splendid

Christmas present you sent us," Jo explained eagerly.

"Well, that was the boy's idea. But how is the poor woman?"

"Doing nicely, sir." And Jo started talking very fast, explaining how her mother had convinced some rich friends to help care for the Hummel family.

"So your mother's doing good for others— just like her father. Please tell her that I'd like to come and see her some day."

Laury was surprised to find Jo comfortably chatting with his intimidating grandfather. And Mr. Laurence was pleased to see his grandson looking happy and energetic.

Then Laury took Jo to their greenhouse. It seemed like a fairyland to Jo—blooming walls and hanging vines in the middle of winter. Her new friend happily cut the finest flowers until his hands were full. "Please give these to your mother. Tell her that I very much like the 'medicine' she sent me."

Then they joined Mr. Laurence in the large living room. There stood a grand piano that captured Jo's full attention.

"Do you play?" she asked Laury.

"Sometimes," he answered modestly.

"Please play for me. I want to hear it so I can tell Beth."

As she listened, Jo's respect and admiration

for Laury grew. He played extremely well, and Jo wished Beth could hear him. She praised him so much that he blushed.

Then his grandfather interrupted her abruptly. "That's enough, young lady. Too many compliments aren't good for him. He plays well, but I hope he will do well in more important things. Thank you for coming, and I hope you'll come again. Please give my respects to your mother. Good night, Doctor Jo."

Mr. Laurence shook her hand kindly. But he looked as if he was not pleased.

As Laury led Jo to the door, the boy shook his head. "It wasn't anything you did. It's just that he doesn't like to hear me play."

"Why not?"

"Someday I'll tell you. You will come again, I hope?"

"If you promise to come see us when you're better."

"I will."

"Goodbye, Laury!"

"Goodbye, Jo. Good night!"

After Jo told about her afternoon, the Marches agreed to visit their neighbors as a family. Mrs. March wanted to talk about her father with the old man who hadn't forgotten him. Meg longed to walk in the greenhouse. Beth sighed for the grand piano. And Amy was eager to see the fine pictures and statues.

Jo asked her mother why Mr. Laurence didn't like to have Laury play the piano.

"I'm not sure. But I think it's because Laury's mother was a musician. She was a lovely Italian lady, who was a very good person. But the old man, who is very proud, did not approve of the marriage. He was so angry that he never saw his son again. Laury's parents both died when he was a little child, so his grandfather brought him home from Italy.

"The boy's musical skill must remind Mr. Laurence of the woman he disliked. He probably worries that his grandson may want to become a musician. I suspect that the boy isn't very strong, and so his grandfather may be a bit overprotective."

"How romantic!" exclaimed Meg. "Maybe that's why he has such handsome black eyes and lovely manners! That was such a nice thing to say about the 'medicine' Mother sent him."

"He was only thanking her for the pudding," Jo said flatly.

"Don't be stupid, child! He was talking about *you*, of course. You don't know a compliment when you get one," said Meg, acting as if she knew all about romance.

"That's nonsense," answered Jo. "Laury's a nice boy, and I like him. And I won't have you spoil my fun with silly stuff about compliments. We must all be good to him because he doesn't have a mother. He can come see us, can't he, Marmee?"

"Yes, Jo. Your friend is very welcome in our home."

Beth hadn't heard a word. She was too busy dreaming about the wonderful grand piano. "Maybe that house will be like a palace of happiness for us," she whispered.

"But first we have to get inside," said Jo, looking forward to the challenge.

Chapter 6

Before long, nobody except timid Beth was afraid of old Mr. Laurence. The Marches soon forgot their pride. They stopped worrying that they could never return the Laurences' favors. For the Laurences thought that Mrs. March's motherly welcome, the girls' cheerful company, and the family's humble home were far more valuable than anything money could buy.

The new friendship grew like grass in the spring. The young people put on plays, went skating, and had merry little parties. Laury studied less and enjoyed people more. Meg walked in the greenhouse whenever she liked. Jo devoured books in the library. And Amy enjoyed the artwork.

But Beth, though longing to play the grand piano, was afraid to enter the "palace of happiness."

Somehow Mr. Laurence learned about her fear and found a way to fix the problem. On one of his visits to the March home, he started talking about music—the great singers he'd seen, and the fine organs he'd heard. Beth was so fascinated that she left her corner and crept nearer and nearer to Mr. Laurence. Pretending not to notice her, Mr. Laurence said, as if the thought had just occurred to him, "You know, Mrs. March, my grandson hasn't been practicing his music lately. Do you think one of your girls might run over and play the piano now and then—just to keep it in tune?"

Before Mrs. March could answer, Mr. Laurence went on, with an odd little smile, "They wouldn't need to see or speak to anyone. And I'd be shut up in my study at the other end of the house. Of course, it's all right if they don't want to come."

Suddenly, Beth took Mr. Laurence's hand and said, "Oh, yes, sir. They do want to. Very, very much!"

The old gentleman bent down and gently kissed her. His voice shook when he said quietly, "I once had a little granddaughter, with eyes like yours." Then away he went, in a great hurry.

The next day, Beth sneaked into the Laurences' living room, as quietly as a mouse. After making sure that no one would hear her, she finally dared to play. As soon as her fingers touched the keys, Beth forgot her fear. For the music, like the voice of a beloved friend, gave her great delight.

After that, she slipped into the room nearly every day. She never knew that Mr. Laurence opened the door to his study so he could listen. She never suspected that the sheets of music that mysteriously appeared on the piano were placed there for her pleasure.

One day, Beth decided to sew a pair of slippers for Mr. Laurence to thank him for his kindness. Mrs. March bought Beth the material, and her sisters gladly helped her. They enjoyed giving Beth whatever she wanted because she rarely asked for anything. When Beth finished, she wrote a short, simple note, and smuggled them into the gentleman's study before he got up.

Beth waited to see what would happen. One day passed, and then part of a second. When she hadn't heard anything, she began to fear she'd offended her cranky old friend. But on the second afternoon, when Beth returned home from an errand, her sisters called to her, "Here's a letter from the old gentleman. Come quick and read it!"

Beth hurried into the living room. She turned pale with delight and surprise when she saw the letter—lying on top of a new little piano.

"For me?" gasped Beth, feeling faint.

"Yes, all for you, my dear!" said Jo. "Isn't he the dearest man in the world? Go ahead and open the note. We're dying to know what it says."

"You read it, Jo. Oh, it's too lovely!" Beth hid her face, overwhelmed by the gift.

Dear Miss March,
    I have had many slippers in my life. But never ones as perfect as yours. You have chosen my favorite colors, and they will always remind me of the gentle person who gave them to me. I always pay my debts. So please allow me to send you something that once belonged to the little granddaughter I lost.
    With hearty thanks and warm wishes, I remain your grateful and humble friend,
                                    James Laurence.

"You'll have to go and thank him," Jo teased, never imagining that Beth would ever dare to do so.

"Yes, I will. And I guess I'll go now, before I get frightened thinking about it."

To everyone's amazement, Beth walked straight over to Mr. Laurence's study and knocked on the door. A gruff voice called out, "Come in!" Without giving herself time to think, Beth went right up to him and held out her hand. "I came to thank you, sir, for . . ." But she didn't finish. Remembering that he had lost the little girl he loved, she put both arms around his neck and kissed him.

If his roof had suddenly flown off, the old gentleman would not have been more shocked. But he was so touched and delighted that he hugged her back. And from that moment, Beth stopped being afraid of him, and started talking to him as if she'd known him all her life. For love can chase away fear. And gratitude can conquer pride.

Chapter 7

*O*ne day, Amy sighed, hoping her sisters would hear. "I wish I had a little of the money that Laury spends on his horse."

"Why?" asked Meg kindly.

"I'm really in debt. I owe at least a dozen pickles, and I can't pay for them."

"Pickles?" asked Meg, trying not to smile, since Amy looked so serious and worried.

"You see, all the girls are buying them. And unless you want to seem mean, you've got to do it, too. If one girl likes another, she gives her a pickle. If she's mad at her, she eats one in front of her face and doesn't let her have a bite. They take turns treating. I've had lots, but haven't been able to return the favor."

So Meg gave Amy enough money to buy two dozen delicious pickles. As soon as Amy got to school, she hid them in her desk. Her teacher, Mr. Davis, did not allow food in the classroom. And he said that he'd beat the next person found "breaking the law."

But word spread among the girls that Amy March had 24 pickles in her desk. Katy Brown, hoping to have one, immediately invited her to her next party. Mary Kingsley let her wear her watch until lunchtime. Jenny Snow offered to give Amy the answers to her math homework. But Amy remembered Jenny's nasty remark that "Some people's noses aren't so flat they can't smell other people's pickles and ask for them." So Amy sent Jenny a quick note saying, "You don't have to be so nice all of a sudden, for you're not getting any of my pickles!"

That morning, a visitor to the school noticed and praised the beautiful maps that Amy had drawn. This hurt Jenny's pride even more. So she went up to Mr. Davis's desk, and informed him that Amy March had pickles in her desk.

Maybe Mr. Davis had drunk too much coffee that morning. Or maybe his arthritis was bothering him. In any case, he rapped on his desk with his ruler and demanded sharply, "Young ladies. Your attention, please!"

Instantly the buzz of voices stopped, and all fifty pairs of eyes looked up obediently.

"Miss March, come to my desk. And bring all the pickles you have in your desk."

Amy quickly brought up all the pickles and laid them out on his desk. But Mr. Davis hated the smell of the popular pickle. "Now take those disgusting things and throw them out the window."

Angry and ashamed, Amy obeyed. The other

girls sighed, as their hopes flew out the window with each plump and juicy treat. Some glared at Mr. Davis. Others sent him appealing looks. One pickle-lover burst into tears.

"Young ladies, you remember what I said to you a week ago. I won't allow my rules to be broken. Now, Miss March, hold out your hand."

Amy was too proud to cry or beg. So she set her teeth, threw back her head in defiance, and let him whip her hands with his ruler. It was the first time in her life that Amy had been hit. Until then, she'd always been guided by her parents' love, not by humiliation. Now the disgrace she felt hurt much more than the blows.

"You will now stand at the front of the room until lunchtime."

That was horrible enough. But even worse, Amy knew she'd have to tell her family and face their disappointment.

So for the next 15 minutes, the proud and sensitive girl suffered a shame and pain that she never forgot.

When it was lunchtime, Mr. Davis said, "You can go now, Miss March."

Without a word to anyone, Amy snatched her things and left the school—for what she decided would be "forever."

Amy was in sad shape when she got home. Mrs. March tried to comfort her daughter, but was upset herself. Meg cleaned the cuts on Amy's hand with soap and tears. Beth felt even her kittens couldn't help such terrible grief. Jo angrily suggested that Mr. Davis should be arrested without delay. And Hannah pounded the mashed potatoes as if they were Mr. Davis himself.

Just before classes ended the next day, Jo appeared at the school. She walked grimly up to the teacher's desk, delivered a letter from her mother, collected all of Amy's belongings, and left in disgust.

That evening, Mrs. March said, "Yes, you can have a vacation from school. But I want you to study every day with Beth. I don't approve of punishing people by hitting them. I don't like Mr. Davis's teaching methods, and I don't think the other girls are a good influence. I shall ask your father's advice before I send you to another school."

"Great! It makes me so mad to think of all those lovely pickles I lost!" whined Amy.

"Well, I'm not sorry you lost them, for you broke the rules and deserve some kind of punishment," answered her mother. "You're getting rather conceited, my dear. You have many fine qualities and talents. But you don't need to show them off. Real talent and goodness are never overlooked for very long. And even if they are, you should be satisfied just knowing that you have them and by using them well. For conceit spoils talent, and modesty has great power."

"I agree!" said Laury, who was playing chess in a corner with Jo. "Why, I know a girl who has a special talent for music. She composes wonderful little things when she's alone. But she's so modest that she'd never believe how good they are."

"I'd like to know that girl," sighed Beth. "Maybe she could help me with my music."

"Oh, but you *do* know her," said Laury, with a twinkle in his eyes. "And she helps you more than anyone else ever could."

When Beth realized he was talking about her, she blushed and hid her face.

And because Laury had praised Beth so kindly, Jo let him win the game of chess.

After Laury had gone, Amy asked, "Laury's talented. But he's not conceited, is he?"

"Not at all. That's why we like him so much," Mrs. March answered.

"I see. So it's nice to do things well, but not to show off."

"Talents will be noticed if they're used modestly. You don't need to brag about them," explained her mother.

Jo laughed. "That would be like wearing all your hats and dresses and jewelry at the same time—just to show people you've got them!"

Chapter 8

One Saturday afternoon, Amy found out that Jo and Meg were going to the theater with Laury. She begged to go with them, and finally Meg agreed.

But Jo protested. "If Amy goes, then I won't. And if I don't go, Laury won't like it. And since he invited only us, it would be very rude to go and drag in Amy. I should think she'd hate to push herself where she isn't wanted."

When Amy insisted and began putting on her boots, Jo scolded, "You're not going with us. So you might as well just stay where you are."

Sitting on the floor with one boot on, Amy began to cry. Laury called up to them, so the two girls had to hurry downstairs, leaving their sister wailing. As they left, Amy called downstairs in an angry, threatening voice, "You'll be sorry for this, Jo March! You just wait and see!"

"Nonsense!" Jo called back, slamming the door.

The play was wonderful. But Jo's pleasure had a drop of bitterness in it, for the fairy queen's yellow curls reminded her of Amy. Between acts, Jo amused herself wondering what her sister could possibly do that would make her "sorry for this."

When they got home, Amy was reading in the living room and didn't even look up from her book. In Jo's room, everything seemed to be in its place. So Jo decided that Amy had simply forgiven and forgotten.

But Jo was wrong. The next afternoon she couldn't find the book of fairy tales she'd been writing. She burst into the living room, demanding breathlessly, "Has anyone taken my book?"

Meg and Beth looked surprised, and right away said "no." Amy poked the fire and said nothing.

"Amy, you know where it is!" Jo cried, grabbing Amy by the shoulders.

"I don't know where it is now, and I don't care."

"Then you'd better tell me what you do know, or I'll make you do it!" Jo threatened, giving Amy a slight shake.

"Scold as much as you like. You'll never see your silly old book again!" cried Amy.

"Why not?"

"I burned it up."

"What! The little book I've been working on—writing and rewriting—and planning to show Father when he gets home? Have you really burned it?" said Jo, turning very pale.

"Yes, I did! I told you I'd make you pay for being so mean to me yesterday."

Overwhelmed by grief and anger, Jo started shaking Amy. "You wicked, wicked girl! I'll never be able to write it again! And I'll never forgive you as long as I live."

Then Jo stormed out of the room to deal with her anger alone.

When Mrs. March came home and heard what had happened, she helped Amy see how wrong it was to destroy her sister's book. Jo had been patiently revising her stories for several years, putting her whole heart into her work, hoping to make them good enough to publish. She had just made a final version and destroyed all the old copies.

Beth mourned as though one of her kittens had died. Meg refused to defend her little sister. Mrs. March looked upset and stern. And Amy, who regretted her action more than any of them, felt that no one would love her until she'd asked Jo's forgiveness.

When Jo appeared for dinner, she looked grim and unapproachable. But Amy gathered all her courage and asked, very meekly, "Please forgive me, Jo. I'm very, very sorry."

"I shall never forgive you," Jo answered sternly, and then ignored Amy entirely.

When it was time to sing before bedtime, Beth and Jo were silent. Amy broke down and cried. Meg and Mother tried to sing cheerfully. But everyone felt out of tune.

As Mrs. March gave Jo her goodnight kiss, she whispered gently, "Don't let the sun go down upon your anger, my dear. Forgive each other, help each other, and begin again tomorrow."

Jo wanted to place her head on her mother's shoulder and cry away her grief and anger. But she thought tears were a sign of weakness, and she still wasn't ready to forgive. And since Amy was listening, Jo muttered, "It was a horrible thing to do, and she doesn't deserve to be forgiven."

Nothing went well for Jo the next day, either. It was a bitterly cold morning. Jo accidentally dropped her precious muffin in the street, and Aunt March was even more demanding than usual. When Jo got home that afternoon, Meg was irritable, Beth looked miserable, and Amy kept making remarks about people who tell everyone else to be good, but then refuse to accept apologies.

So Jo decided to go skating with Laury. *He's always so kind and jolly. He'll be able to put me in a good mood,* she thought, and off she went.

Amy whined to her sisters, "But Jo promised to take me the next time they went skating. And the river won't freeze again this year."

"It's hard for her to forgive the loss of her

precious little book," explained Meg. "But go after Jo. Wait till Laury gets her in a good mood. Then just give her a hug, or do something kind. I'm sure she'll be friends again with all her heart."

"I'll try," said Amy. She got her ice skates and ran after Jo and Laury.

Jo heard Amy approach. But she turned her back on her sister and started out on the ice. Laury never saw Amy, because he skated on ahead to make sure the ice was solid. As Laury disappeared around the bend, he shouted back, "Keep near the shore, Jo! It isn't safe in the middle."

Jo heard, but Amy was too far away to hear. Jo glanced over her shoulder and thought, *I don't care whether she heard or not. Let her take care of herself.*

Far behind, Amy started out from the shore. She wanted to skate on the smoother ice in the middle of the river. Something in Jo's heart made her turn around, just in time to see Amy throw up her hands and go down. A sudden crash of rotten ice, the splash of water, and a desperate cry made Jo's heart stand still with fear. She stared, terror-stricken, at the little blue hood floating above the black water.

Then Laury rushed swiftly past her, shouting, "Bring a rail from the fence. Hurry!"

Laury calmly stretched out flat on the ice.

He held Amy's head above water until Jo dragged over a rail. Then together they pulled out the child, who was more frightened than hurt. They wrapped their coats around Amy and hurried her home—shivering, dripping, and crying.

Once Amy was sleeping comfortably, Jo thought about how that golden head might have been swept away forever. Guilt-ridden, she whispered to her mother, "Are you sure she'll be all right?"

"Yes, dear. She's not hurt. And you were sensible to cover her and get her home quickly," Mrs. March replied.

"Laury did all that. What I did was turn my back on her. Mother, if she'd died, it would have been all my fault!"

Crying her heart out, Jo confessed everything. "It's my awful temper! I try to cure it, but then it breaks out worse than ever. Oh, Mother, what shall I do?" cried poor Jo, in despair.

"Keep trying, dear. And never think it's impossible to conquer your faults," said Mrs. March. Placing Jo's head on her shoulder, she kissed her cheek so tenderly that Jo cried even harder.

"You can't imagine how bad my temper is! When I lose it, I get so wild that I could hurt someone—and even enjoy it. I'm afraid someday I'll do something so horrible that it will ruin my life and make everybody hate me. You've got to help me, Mother!"

"I will. But instead of crying so bitterly, try to remember what happened today. Make up your mind that you'll never do anything to feel that way again. You know, I used to lose my temper just like you."

"But you're never angry, Mother!"

"I've been trying to cure my temper for forty years. But all I can do is control it. I get angry nearly every day of my life. But I've learned not to show it. And I still hope someday to learn not to feel it—even it takes me another forty years."

Knowing that her mother had a fault like hers and was trying to fix it made it easier to live with her own. Now Jo became more determined than ever to cure it—though forty years of work seemed like a very long time to a 15-year-old girl.

"Mother, I've noticed that sometimes you fold your lips tightly together and leave the room—like when Aunt March complains or someone bothers you. Is that because you're angry?" asked Jo, feeling closer to her mother than ever before.

"Yes. I've learned to stop the hasty words before they get past my lips. If I think I can't, then I go away for a minute and give myself a little shake."

"But the sharp words fly out of my mouth before I've had a chance to think them through. And the more I say, the worse I get, till I start to enjoy hurting people's feelings. Tell me how you do it, Marmee, dear."

"My good mother used to help me. But I lost her when I was only a little older than you. I was too proud to confess my weakness to anyone else. So for years I had to struggle alone. Then your father came into my life, and I was so happy that I never got angry. But then we became poor, and I hated to see my four little daughters wanting things we couldn't have. I'm not naturally patient, so the old trouble started up again."

"Poor Mother! What helped you then?"

"Your father, Jo. He never loses patience. He never doubts or complains. He works so cheerfully and hopefully that I wanted to do the same. He showed me that I needed to set a good example for my little girls. It was easier to try for your sakes than for my own."

"I will try, too, Mother. But you must help keep me from lashing out at others. I used to see Father sometimes put his finger on his lips. That's when you'd fold your lips tightly and go away. Was he reminding you then?" Jo asked.

"Yes. I asked him to help me, and he never forgot," she answered.

Noticing her mother's eyes filling with tears, Jo asked anxiously if she'd hurt her feelings by speaking so openly.

"My Jo, you may say anything to your mother. For it is my greatest happiness to feel that my girls trust me and know how much I love them. But speaking about Father reminded me how much I miss him, and how I must keep his little daughters safe and good."

Amy stirred and sighed in her sleep. Jo leaned over her and whispered, "Yesterday, I let the sun go down on my anger. Today I refused to forgive you. And if it hadn't been for Laury, tomorrow might have been too late."

As if she'd heard, Amy opened her eyes and held out her arms with a smile that went straight to Jo's heart. Neither said a word. But they hugged each other close. And everything was forgiven and forgotten in one heartfelt embrace.

Chapter 9

"$\mathcal{I}$t's such lucky timing that those King children are sick with the measles," said Meg, as she packed her bag with her sisters' help.

"And so nice of Annie Moffat not to forget her promise to have you come visit her. Two weeks of fun will be absolutely splendid!" added Jo.

"I wish all of you could come. You've been so kind about lending me your things and helping me get ready."

"What did Mother give you out of the treasure box?" asked Amy.

"A pair of silk stockings and that pretty fan. I wanted to wear the violet silk gown, but there isn't enough time to make it fit. So I'll have to be satisfied with my old cotton dress."

"It'll be perfect for the big party," said Amy. "You always look like an angel in white."

"It doesn't have a low neck, and it doesn't sweep enough. But it will have to do. And Laury promised to send me flowers. Of course, my hat is out of fashion. And I'm disappointed about my umbrella. I told Mother I wanted one that was black with a white handle. But she forgot and bought one that was green with a yellow handle. It's well made, so I shouldn't complain. But I know I'll feel ashamed of it, compared with Annie's silk umbrella with a gold handle."

"Then exchange it," suggested Jo.

"I wouldn't do anything that silly, for it might hurt Marmee's feelings. But I'd be so happy if I could have real lace on my dresses."

"But just the other day you said you'd be perfectly happy if only you could go to Annie Moffat's," observed Beth, in her quiet way.

"So I did! Well, I am happy. But it seems as if the more one gets, the more one wants."

Mrs. March was reluctant to let Meg spend so much time with the wealthy Moffats. She was afraid that Meg would come back more dissatisfied than ever.

In fact, the more Meg saw of Annie Moffat's pretty things, the more she envied her and longed to be rich. In comparison, Meg thought her own home seemed barer than ever, and her work harder than before. That made Meg feel like a poor, helpless victim—in spite of the silk stockings and treasured fan.

Meg charmed the Moffats, and she was flattered by their attention to her. Annie's older sisters seemed like such very fine young ladies. As the girls dressed for the party, Meg noticed them glancing at her old cotton dress, with pity in their eyes.

The maid brought in a box of flowers that had just arrived. "They must be for Belle," said Annie. "George always sends her some."

"They are for Miss March," explained the maid, handing her the flowers. "Here's a note."

"What fun!"

"Who are they from?"

"Didn't know you had a boyfriend!"

The girls fluttered around Meg, surprised and curious.

"The note is from Mother, and the flowers from Laury," Meg answered simply. Then she slipped the note into her pocket as a reminder not to give in to envy, vanity, and false pride.

That evening, Meg was enjoying herself very much. She loved to dance, and everyone was very kind. But then she overheard Mrs. Moffat and Annie gossiping about Meg and Laury.

"Sallie says they are quite close. And the old man adores them. What an opportunity! Wouldn't it be great if one of the girls married into the L. family?"

"I'm sure that Mrs. M. has figured out a way to make that happen."

"Poor thing! Meg would be so attractive if only she wore something more stylish. Do you think she'd be offended if we offered her a dress for Thursday night?"

"She's proud. But I don't think she'd mind if we lent her a decent dress. Especially if that dumpy-looking cotton one just happens to get torn tonight."

Meg was glad when the evening was over and she was in bed. Angry and disappointed, she cried a lot and slept very little. She resented her friends, and was ashamed of herself for not standing up to the Moffats.

The next morning, Meg's friends seemed to treat her with more respect. She was flattered, but did not understand why. Then Annie's older sister Belle explained, "Meg, dear, I've sent your friend, Mr. Laurence, an invitation to Thursday's party."

Meg blushed, but decided to tease the girls. "You are very kind. But I'm afraid he won't come."

"Why not, darling?" asked Belle.

"He's too old."

"My child, what do you mean? How old is he?"

"Nearly seventy, I believe," answered Meg, trying to look serious.

Belle exclaimed, laughing, "Of course we meant the young man!"

"Oh, but Laury's only a little boy."

"About your age."

"Oh, no. Much nearer my sister Jo's. I'll be seventeen in August," said Meg casually.

"But it's very nice of him to send you flowers," said Annie, pushing Meg to say that Laury was her boyfriend.

"Yes. He often sends flowers to all of us. My mother and old Mr. Laurence are friends, you know. So it's quite natural that we children should play together," explained Meg, hoping to end the discussion.

"Such an innocent child," sighed Belle, looking at Meg with pity and shaking her head.

Then Mrs. Moffat stepped into the room. "I'm going shopping. Anything you girls want?"

"No, thank you," answered Meg, though there were many things she wanted. "I'll wear my old white dress again if I can fix the tear in it."

"Why mend your dress when I can lend you a sweet blue silk one that I've outgrown?" asked Belle. "Do let me dress you up in style. I'd love to do it. I could turn you into a regular little beauty—like Cinderella going to the ball."

Meg couldn't refuse such a kind offer. Nor could she resist a chance to be turned into a "little beauty."

On Thursday evening, Belle and her maid curled Meg's hair and put on lipstick. They squeezed Meg into a low-cut dress so tight that she could hardly breathe. They slipped on bracelets, high-heeled shoes, and a corsage. Then Belle smiled with satisfaction, like a little girl who had just dressed up a new doll.

The other girls admired Belle's work, and

called Meg "a little beauty."

"You don't look a bit like yourself," Sallie said, trying not to care that Meg looked prettier than she. "But Belle did a good job."

When Meg walked into the party, she discovered that fine clothes attract certain kinds of people and gain their respect. Young ladies who had ignored her before were suddenly treating her kindly. Young gentleman who had only glanced at her before now walked over and told her silly, but flattering things. And old ladies watched and gossiped about her.

Meg felt strange, and the tight dress made her side hurt. But she pretended that she was acting the part of a fine lady. She was flirting with her fan and laughing at the feeble jokes of a young gentleman trying to be witty, when suddenly she stopped. Across the room stood Laury. He bowed and smiled at her. But his honest eyes showed his disapproval. Suddenly she wished she had on her old cotton dress.

Then she saw Belle nudge Annie. They glanced at Meg, and then at Laury, and then started giggling.

Silly girls. Trying to put romantic thoughts into my head, thought Meg, as she crossed the room to shake hands with her friend.

"Jo wanted me to come," Laury explained, "and tell her how you looked."

"And what will you tell her?" asked Meg.

"I shall say I didn't recognize you. You look so grownup and unlike yourself that I'm quite afraid of you."

"How silly of you! The girls dressed me up for fun, and I rather like it. Wouldn't Jo stare if she saw me?"

"Yes, I think she would," Laury answered seriously.

"Don't you like me this way?" asked Meg.

"No, I don't," he answered honestly, but without his usual politeness.

"Why not?" she asked, anxiously.

"I don't like fuss and feathers."

Hurt and embarrassed, Meg walked away, saying, "You are the rudest boy I ever saw."

As she stood at a quiet window trying to calm down, Meg overheard one of the young gentlemen say to his mother, "They are making a fool of that little girl. I wanted you to meet her, but she's nothing but a doll tonight."

"Oh, I'm so ashamed of myself," sighed Meg, too upset to notice that they were playing her favorite waltz.

She stood there, half-hidden by the curtains. Then someone touched her. Turning, Meg saw Laury. He bowed and held out his hand. "Please forgive my rudeness, and come dance with me. I don't like your gown. But I do think you are absolutely splendid."

Meg smiled and gave in. Then she whispered,

"Be careful you don't trip on this silly skirt. I was a fool to wear it."

Away they went, dancing gracefully and twirling merrily together. After their small quarrel, they felt even more comfortable with each other.

"Laury, would you do me a favor, please?" Meg asked.

"Of course."

"Please don't tell them at home about my dress. They wouldn't understand, and Mother would worry."

Laury gave her a look that asked, "Then why did you do it?"

Meg answered his look. "I'll tell them myself and confess to Mother how silly I've been."

"Then I promise I won't tell. But what should I say when they ask me?"

"Just say I looked pretty and was having a good time."

"I can honestly say that you look very, very pretty. But are you really having a good time?"

"No," Meg whispered. "I only wanted to have a little fun. But I found out that this kind of fun isn't worth it. And now I'm getting tired of it."

"Here comes Ned Moffat. What does he want?" asked Laury, frowning.

"I promised I'd dance with him. What a bore!" sighed Meg.

During dinner, Laury noticed that Meg was

drinking champagne with Ned and his friends. The boys were, in Laury's opinion, behaving like fools. Like a brother looking out for one of his sisters, Laury went over to Meg and whispered in her ear, "You'll have a splitting headache tomorrow if you drink much of that. I wouldn't, Meg. And you know your mother wouldn't like it."

"But I'm not 'Meg' tonight. I'm just 'a doll' that does all sorts of crazy things. Tomorrow I'll put away my 'fuss and feathers' and be good again," she answered, trying to sound merry.

"Then I wish it was already tomorrow," muttered Laury, walking off.

For the rest of the evening, Meg danced and flirted, chattered and giggled—just like the other girls. But somehow she didn't enjoy herself as much as she'd expected. She was sick all the next day. By the time she went home on Saturday, she felt she'd "sat in the lap of luxury" long enough.

"Home is a nice place, even though it isn't splendid," said Meg on Sunday evening, after Amy and Beth had gone to bed.

"I'm glad to hear you say so," said her mother. "I was afraid your home would seem dull and poor after two weeks in a mansion."

Meg paused, and then said, "Marmee, I want to confess."

"Should I leave?" asked Jo.

"Of course not," Meg answered. "Don't I

always tell you everything? I'm so ashamed of what I did, but I want you to know."

So Meg told Mother and Jo about how the girls had flattered her into looking like "a doll."

"Is that all?" asked Jo.

"No. I drank champagne and tried to flirt and was altogether horrible."

"I have a feeling there's something else," Mrs. March suggested gently.

So Meg told about the gossip she'd over-heard—that Mrs. March wanted a daughter to marry Laury for his money.

Jo saw her mother tightly fold her lips together. Then Mrs. March spoke. "Never repeat such foolish gossip. And forget it as soon as you can. I'm sorry I let you spend time with such well-meaning, but thoughtless people."

"Don't be sorry, Mother. For I've learned not to be such a silly girl, though I must say I enjoyed being praised and admired," confessed Meg, half-ashamed.

"There's no harm in enjoying praise—as long as it doesn't become your only goal in life or make you do foolish things. Learn whose praise is worth having. And gain the admiration of good people by being modest as well as pretty, Meg."

Jo listened—interested, but not understanding fully. She felt that in the past two weeks her sister had grown up. Now Meg was drifting away from her into a world she couldn't enter.

"Mother, do you have 'plans' for us, as Mrs. Moffat said?" Meg asked.

"Yes, my dears. I have a great many plans. But I suspect that mine are different from Mrs. Moffat's. I am ambitious for you—but not to marry rich men just because they're rich, or to live in splendid houses which are not homes because they don't have love. Money is necessary and precious. When it is used well, it can be a noble thing. But I never want you to think it's the most important prize to try to get. I'd rather you married someone poor who loves you and makes you happy, than lose your dignity and self-respect."

"Belle says that poor girls don't stand a chance," Meg sighed.

"Then we'll just be old maids," Jo said firmly.

"You're right, Jo. Better to be happy old maids than unhappy wives—or change your values just to get husbands," Mrs. March added. "Give it time. For now, learn to make this home happy, so later you'll know how to create a happy home. And if you choose not to leave home, then you'll also be happy living here. Remember, my girls, Father and I are always ready to help you. And we hope and trust that our daughters—whether married or single—will be good and decent people."

"We will, Marmee! We will!" both girls promised with all their hearts.

Chapter 10

After reading *The Pickwick Papers*, by Charles Dickens, the girls decided to create their own secret society. They called it "The Pickwick Club," or the "P.C." for short.

Each girl pretended to be one of the characters in *The Pickwick Papers*. Meg was Samuel Pickwick, the club's kind, protective president. Jo played the part of Augustus Snodgrass, poet and editor of the paper. Beth played the loving Tracy Tubman. And Amy was Nathaniel Winkle, who was always trying to do things he couldn't do.

The girls' club met "secretly" in the Marches' attic every Saturday night. At each meeting, they read articles they'd written for their weekly newspaper, *The Pickwick Portfolio*.

One Saturday that spring, Meg, as president, read an original poem by "Augustus Snodgrass":

We all are here in perfect health.
None gone from our small band.
Again we see each well-known face
And shake each friendly hand.

A year has gone, and still we meet
To joke and laugh and read.
O may someday our written words
To fame and glory lead!

At the close of the meeting, the "president" read the weekly report of its members' behavior:

Meg—Good

Jo—Bad

Beth—Very Good

Amy—OK

Everyone applauded. Then Jo stood up and said, "Mr. President and Gentlemen, I would like to propose that we allow Mr. Theodore Laurence to become an honorary member of the P.C."

"We'll have to take a vote," said the president.

Beth and Jo voted "yes." But Meg and Amy disagreed. "This is a ladies' club," Amy explained. "We wish to be private and proper."

Meg said anxiously, "I'm afraid he'll laugh at our newspaper and make fun of us."

Then Jo stood up and said, very seriously, "Sir, I give you my word as a gentleman. Laury won't do anything of the sort. He does so much for us. The least we can do is offer him a place in our club and welcome him if he comes."

This made Beth stand up and say decisively, "Yes. We ought to do it, even if we are afraid. I say he should be allowed to come—and his grandpa, too, if he wants."

The girls were stunned by Beth's speech. When they took a second vote, all four members shouted, "Yes!"

So Jo said, "Well, then, there's no time like the present." She threw open the closet door, and out stepped Laury, trying hard not to laugh.

Meg scolded, "How could you, Jo!" and tried to frown.

But then Laury bowed to Meg and said, in his most charming manner, "Mr. President and Ladies—I beg your pardon, Gentlemen—allow me to introduce myself. I am Samuel Weller— your president's humble and devoted servant. On my honor, I will never deceive you again."

Accepting his gracious apology, Meg bowed kindly.

Then Laury continued. "As a token of my gratitude, I have set up a 'post office' in the hedge between our gardens. It's an old birdhouse that's now vacant. The roof can be opened and closed with a key. Letters, articles, books, and packages can be passed back and forth between us. I hope it will be helpful for the mails—as well as for the females, if I may use that word."

The post office, or "P.O." as they called it, was wonderful. Many things passed through it—tragedies and neckties, poetry and pickles, garden seeds and long letters, music and ginger-bread, invitations and scoldings—and even some puppies. The old gentleman joined the fun, and sent little gifts, funny telegrams, and mysterious messages. Once Mr. Laurence's gardener sent a love letter to Hannah. The girls laughed when they found out—never dreaming how many love letters would pass through that little post office in the years to come.

Chapter 11

"The Kings are off to the seashore, and I'm free! Three months of vacation!" Meg exclaimed as she walked into the house one warm June afternoon.

Looking exhausted, Jo said from the sofa, "And Aunt March went off to her country house today! I was afraid she'd ask me to go with her. But Plumfield is about as merry as a graveyard. So as soon as she got into the carriage, I turned and ran."

"So how are you going to spend your vacations?" asked Amy.

"Sleep late and do nothing," answered Meg. "Rest and relax as much as I like."

"Not me," announced Jo. "I'm going to improve myself by reading heaps of books—that is, when I'm not having fun with Laury."

"Then let's not do our lessons, either, Beth," suggested Amy. "We'll just play all day, like Meg and Jo."

"As long as Mother doesn't mind," answered Beth. "I want to learn some new songs. And my poor dolls have outgrown all their old clothes."

"May we, Mother?" Meg asked Mrs. March, who sat sewing in her favorite chair.

"You may try your experiment for a week, and see how you like it. I think that by Saturday night you'll find that all play and no work is as bad as all work and no play."

The next morning, Meg slept late, but found out that breakfast didn't taste as good when she had to eat it all alone in a messy kitchen. Jo spent the morning on the river with Laury, where she got a terrible sunburn. Beth started several projects, but left them all unfinished and played the piano instead. Amy put on her best dress and sat outside drawing, hoping someone would notice her. But no one appeared except a spider, and the grass stained her white dress.

Mrs. March and Hannah added the girls' chores to their own, so the household continued to run smoothly. But the days seemed to get longer and longer, while the girls' tempers got shorter and shorter. Meg ruined some of her dresses by trying to make them look more fashionable. Jo read so much that her eyes hurt, and she became restless and sick of books. Amy became bored and cranky, because nobody can draw all the time. And Beth was upset because everyone in the house seemed upset.

But no one admitted being tired of "rest and relaxation." So on Saturday, Mrs. March decided to let the girls take care of themselves

She gave Hannah the day off, and announced that she would sleep late and then go out. "I've never enjoyed housekeeping. So today I'm going to take a vacation. I'm going to read, write, visit friends, and amuse myself."

So Jo announced that she would cook lunch for her sisters, and she invited Laury to join them. But on her way to the kitchen, she found Beth crying in the living room. Pip, the canary, lay dead in his cage.

"It's all my fault," sobbed Beth. "I forgot to feed him, and he starved to death. Oh, Pip! How could I be so cruel to you?"

"Don't cry, Beth," said Jo. "We'll have a funeral this afternoon, and we'll all attend it."

Before she left the house, Mother checked on the girls and comforted Beth. Then, as their mother's gray hat disappeared around the corner, the girls felt a strange sense of helplessness.

Their helplessness turned to despair when Miss Crocker appeared at the door. She was a little old lady who gossiped about everything she saw. The girls disliked her, but felt sorry for her because she was poor and had few friends. So they invited her to join them for lunch.

Jo worked hard to prepare a fancy meal. But she knew nothing about cooking. As she placed the food on the table, she was tired and worried. She knew that Laury was used to fine dining. And she knew that Miss Crocker would tell everyone about the meal.

Poor Jo watched as each dish was tasted and then left on the plates. She was confident, though, that everyone would enjoy the fruit course. The strawberries she'd bought were a little underripe, but she'd covered them with sugar and heavy cream.

Miss Crocker tasted hers, made a face, and quickly drank some water. Amy took a heaping spoonful, then hid her face in her napkin and rushed out of the room.

"What is it?" exclaimed Jo.

Meg answered, "Salt instead of sugar. And the cream is sour."

Suddenly Jo remembered grabbing a box and pouring it over the berries without looking. And she'd left the cream out on the counter all morning. She blushed and was about to burst into tears. Then, noticing the merry look in Laury's eyes, Jo saw the funny side of the situation. She laughed until tears ran down her cheeks. And so did everyone else, even Miss Crocker. So for lunch they ended up having bread and butter—and a good laugh.

After lunch, Laury dug a grave in the garden, and they buried little Pip. Laury took Amy on a carriage ride to try to cheer her up, since the soured cream had put her in a bad mood. The three older girls went to work, cleaning and putting things back in order.

After Mrs. March came home, they all gathered on the porch.

"What a horrible day this has been!" groaned Jo.

"Shorter than usual, but really awful," said Meg.

"Not a bit like home," added Amy.

"It can't be like home without Marmee and little Pip," sighed Beth, looking at the empty cage.

"I'm here, dear, and I'll get you another bird tomorrow if you like," began Mrs. March. "Are you satisfied with your experiment, girls? Or would you like another week of it?"

"No!" they all cried out.

"So you think it's better to have a few duties and live a little for others?"

"Mother, did you do this just to see how we'd manage?" asked Meg.

"Yes. I wanted you to see how everyone's comfort depends on each person's doing her share of the work. Now you know what happens when everyone thinks only of herself. Even when Hannah and I did your chores, you didn't seem very happy. Don't you think that helping others and working hard makes leisure time more pleasant when it comes?"

"We do, Mother! We do!" exclaimed the girls.

"Remember that work keeps us from being bored or getting into trouble. It's good for health and spirits. And it gives us a sense of power and independence."

"We'll work like bees," said Jo. "And love it, too. I'll learn to cook."

"I'll make Father's shirts instead of fussing over my own things," Meg offered.

"I'll do my lessons every day," announced Beth.

"And I'll work on my vocabulary," added Amy, who was always getting her words mixed up.

"Then I'm quite satisfied with the experiment. But don't go to the other extreme and work like slaves. Set aside time for both work and play. Make each day useful and pleasant. And use your precious time well. Then you'll enjoy your youth, and you'll have few regrets when you grow old. Your life will become a beautiful success, even if you're poor."

"We'll remember, Mother!" And they did.

Chapter 12

*I*t was Beth's job to check the "post office" every day and deliver the "mail." One day in July she came inside with her hands full.

Beth handed Mother a flower from Laury.

She gave Meg one glove and a German song she'd asked to have translated. "I think Mr. Brooke did the translation, for this isn't Laury's handwriting," said Meg with surprise. "And I don't understand why only one glove was returned. I'm sure I left both gloves there by accident."

Mrs. March glanced at her daughter. Meg was looking pretty and womanly, but she was still innocent about romance.

Laury sent Jo a silly-looking men's hat with a very wide brim. She'd complained to him that the fashionable little ladies' hats didn't protect her face from burning in the sun. "I told him that if I had one, I'd wear it," explained Jo. "And I will—just for fun!"

Mrs. March sent Jo a letter, in which she praised her progress in controlling her temper. Reading it, Jo's eyes filled with tears, for she didn't think anyone had noticed or appreciated her efforts to be good.

Amy got a box of chocolates and a picture she'd wanted to copy.

Beth got a note from Mr. Laurence, who was now her close friend. He invited her to play for him later that afternoon.

Laury sent an invitation to all the girls. He was arranging a picnic lunch with Ned and Sallie Moffat, and the Vaughns, who were visiting from England. Kate Vaughn was older than Meg, and could help chaperone. The twin boys, Fred and Frank, were Jo's age. And Grace was nine years old. Laury also wrote that Mr. Brooke would be there to keep an eye on things.

Beth was worried, but agreed to go as long as Jo didn't let any boys talk to her. "I love you for trying to overcome your shyness. I know it isn't easy, and that encouragement helps," Jo praised Beth, smiling at her mother.

"Let's do twice as much work today, so we can play tomorrow without feeling guilty," added Jo.

The next day, Laury greeted his guests. "Welcome to Camp Laurence! Let's play a game of croquet before it gets too hot."

The English team was losing. Then Jo noticed Fred Vaughn cheat.

"We don't cheat in America," Jo said angrily. "But you can if you choose."

Fred answered with an insult, and hit Jo's ball into the bushes.

Jo opened her mouth to say something rude, but instead went off to look for her ball. She spent a long time in the bushes, but then returned looking cool and calm.

Jo patiently worked to catch up. But the English team was about to win. Fred shouted that she might as well give up. Instead, Jo carefully hit the ball through the goal and won the game.

Laury whispered to Jo that he'd seen his guest cheat, and was sure he'd learned his lesson. And Meg said privately, "He really pushed you, Jo. But I'm glad you were able to control your temper."

Then Jo helped prepare lunch, using the cooking she'd recently learned.

At the table, Laury handed Jo a bowl of berries. "Would you like some salt for them?"

Jo laughed and answered, "I prefer spiders, thank you." And she fished out two that had drowned in the cream.

After lunch, they all took turns making up stories. Mr. Brooke told the first one. It was about a knight who was hired to tame a good king's young horse. Every day he looked everywhere for the beautiful face he'd seen in his dreams. Finally he saw the lovely face in a ruined castle. Inside the castle, four princesses were held captive. He wanted to set them free, but he was too poor to buy their freedom.

Each person added to the story. Finally it was Laury's turn. He told how three of the princesses had sewn their way to freedom—all except the one he loved. "The knight tried to climb over the hedge that kept her from escaping. But the bushes grew higher and higher. So, patiently, he broke one twig at a time until he'd made a hole in the hedge." He paused, and then added, "Now I'll let Mr. Brooke tell you how it turns out."

But Mr. Brooke seemed to be daydreaming. Laury threw acorns at him and finished the story by saying, "I guess the princess gave him a flower so the knight could open the gate."

Then Kate suggested that they play "truth or dare." Laury got the short straw, so he had to answer first.

"Who are your heroes?" asked Jo.

"Grandfather and Napoleon," Laury replied.

"Which lady here do you think is the prettiest?" asked Sallie.

"Meg."

"Which one do you like the best?" asked Fred.

"Jo, of course. What silly questions."

When it was Fred's turn to answer, Laury whispered to Jo, "Let's give it to him."

So Jo asked, "Didn't you cheat at croquet just now?"

After they pushed him to be honest, Fred finally admitted, "Well, yes, a little bit."

At the same time, the three oldest sat apart, talking. Kate was drawing. Meg watched her. And Mr. Brooke sat with a book in front of him, but he wasn't reading it.

"You draw so beautifully! I wish I could draw," said Meg, with both admiration and regret.

"Why don't you take lessons?" suggested Kate.

"I don't have time."

"I suppose your mother wants you to study music instead. But can't your governess teach you?"

"I don't have a governess."

"Oh, so you go to a private school?"

"I don't go to school at all. I am a governess myself."

"Oh, indeed!" said Kate, looking down her nose at Meg.

Mr. Brooke looked up and said quickly, "Young ladies in America love independence as much as their ancestors did in 1776. They are admired and respected for supporting themselves and their families."

After an awkward silence, Mr. Brooke asked Meg if she enjoyed the German song.

"Oh, yes! It was very sweet. And I'm grateful to whoever translated it for me," Meg said, her face brightening.

"Don't you read German?" asked Kate, with a look of surprise.

"Not very well. My father taught me a little, but he's away now. I don't have anyone to teach me."

"Well I'm a tutor who loves to teach. Why don't you try reading this?" Mr. Brooke smiled and placed his book on Meg's lap. "They're German love poems."

Meg read aloud, while Mr. Brooke leaned over and pointed to each word with a long blade of grass. Meg read with such feeling that she didn't notice the odd look in Mr. Brooke's eyes.

"Excellent!" said Mr. Brooke, ignoring her many mistakes, and looking as if he did indeed love to teach.

Kate shut her sketchbook and stood up abruptly. "I guess someone who's a governess herself doesn't need me to chaperone her."

After Kate walked away, Mr. Brooke said cheerfully to Meg, "I guess workers like you and me are better off in America than in England."

Meg answered, "Even if I don't like what I do, at least I get satisfaction from working. I only wish I liked my work as much as you like yours."

"You would if Laury were your student. I'll miss him next year."

"He's going away to college?" she asked.

"Yes. And as soon as he leaves, I'll join the

army. I'm needed there. I have no family and no one who cares whether I live or die," Mr. Brooke said rather bitterly.

"Laury and his grandfather would care a lot. And we would all be very sorry if you got hurt," Meg said.

"Why, thank you," Mr. Brooke began, looking cheerful again.

Then Ned interrupted their conversation. "How can you be so cruel to me?" he whispered to Meg. "You've been avoiding me all day."

"I didn't mean to," Meg answered. But in fact she was still upset about what happened at the Moffats' party.

At the same time, Grace Vaughn was telling Amy about her pony, and about all the fine ladies and gentlemen who ride with her in the park.

"How charming!" said Amy. "I hope someday I shall go abroad. I'd so love to see Rome."

Beth noticed that Frank was sitting alone. He'd hurt his leg and was unable to run with the other boys. So she walked over and asked him, in her shy, yet friendly way, "Can I do anything for you?"

"Talk to me, please," the boy answered. "I'm bored, sitting all by myself."

Beth panicked. But she felt so sorry for him that she forgot she was afraid of boys. Soon Frank was laughing for the first time in a long while.

At the end of the day, Kate watched the four sisters leave and observed, "You know, American girls are really very nice once you get to know them."

"I quite agree with you," said Mr. Brooke.

Chapter 13

Laury was sitting in the garden one early September afternoon. He was bored and grumpy. Having wasted the day doing nothing, he wished he could live it over again. From the corner of his eye, he saw the March girls walk up the hill and into the woods. Each was carrying a bag, and all looked very determined.

Laury followed them, hid behind some bushes, and watched. *What a pretty sight!* he thought to himself. Meg was sewing daintily, looking as fresh and sweet as a rose. Jo was knitting army socks and reading aloud to her sisters. Amy was sketching some ferns. And Beth was gathering pinecones to make into pretty decorations.

Then Beth noticed Laury. She smiled at him.

Laury came out from the bushes and asked, "May I join you, please?"

Meg frowned, but Jo answered right away. "Of course you may. We would have asked you before, but we didn't think you'd enjoy being part of our 'Busy Bee Society.'"

"I enjoy everything I do with you. But if Meg doesn't want me, I'll go away."

"I don't object, as long as you do something useful. It's against the rules here to be lazy," answered Meg.

"Thank you. I'll do anything, for it's dull as the desert at home. Shall I sew, read, gather cones, draw, or do them all at the same time?"

"Finish reading this story while I knit the heel," ordered Jo.

"Yes'm," Laury answered meekly.

"You see," Jo explained, "we've decided not to waste our summer vacation. So each of us has picked a task to work on with gladness. Sometimes we bring our work here and have nice times. You see, up here, we can look into the distance and dream about the future."

"What's your dream?" Meg asked Laury.

"If I tell you mine, will you tell me yours?"

"We will," agreed the girls.

"Well, I have so many dreams it's hard to choose just one. But my favorite is to travel around the world, and finally settle down in Germany. I'd like to become a famous musician, and do what I enjoy. And I'd never have to bother about money or business. What's yours, Meg?"

"I'd like to live in a lovely house, full of fancy food, pretty clothes, pleasant people, and heaps of money. I'd have so many servants that I'd never have to work at all. Instead, I'd spend my time helping other people."

"But wouldn't you need a man to help run

your mansion?" Laury asked, grinning.

"Yes, but Meg would require a splendid, wise, good husband, along with some angelic little children," teased Jo.

"I only said 'pleasant people,'" Meg murmured, blushing. She looked across the river with the same hopeful expression as Mr. Brooke, when he told the story of the knight.

"I'd have a magic pen, and become rich and famous," announced Jo. "I want to write something wonderful, so people won't forget me after I'm dead."

"Now that I have my little piano, all I wish is for all of us to stay healthy and for all of us to be together," said Beth.

"I have ever so many wishes," said Amy. "But most of all I want to go to Rome and be the best artist in the whole world."

"If we're all alive ten years from now, let's meet. We'll see how many of us have gotten their wishes, or how much nearer we are to them," said Jo, always ready with a plan.

"I'll be so old," exclaimed Meg. "27!"

"You and I will be 26, Laury," said Jo. "Beth will be 24, and Amy 22!"

"I hope I'll have done something by then I can be proud of. But I'm so lazy."

"Mother says all you need is a reason to work hard. She's sure that once you have one, you'll do splendidly."

"Is she? Then I will, if only I get the chance!" exclaimed Laury, with sudden energy. "Grandfather wants me to go to college and become a businessman, like he was. But I'd rather be shot! I'd like to break away and do what I want, like my father did. But then who would stay with the old gentleman?"

"Just go and have your own adventure!" urged Jo.

"That's wrong, Jo," scolded Meg. "Don't take her bad advice, Laury. Do your best at college. When your grandfather sees that you're trying to please him, I'm sure he'll treat you fairly. There's no one else to stay with him and love him. And you'd never forgive yourself if you left without his permission. Be like good Mr. Brooke, and do your duty. Then you'll be rewarded with love and respect."

"What do you know about Brooke?" demanded Laury, irritated by Meg's lecture.

"Only what your grandpa told us. How Mr. Brooke took good care of his mother until she died. And how he didn't take a job in Europe because he wouldn't leave her alone. And now he supports the old woman who helped nurse his mother. And he never tells anyone, but is wonderfully gracious and patient and good."

"That he is!" agreed Laury. "If ever I do get my wish, I'll do anything I can for good old Brooke."

"Then you can start now by not driving him crazy," said Meg sharply.

"And how, Miss Meg, do you know about that?"

"I can always tell by his face. If you've been good, Mr. Brooke looks satisfied and full of energy. When you make trouble for him, he looks gloomy and walks slowly, as if he wished he could do a better job."

"So you keep track of my behavior by watching Brooke's face, do you? I've seen him bow and smile as he passes your window. But I didn't know he was sending you reports about me. I guess I'll just have to be a better student for you."

"I didn't mean to lecture you. I just don't want you to do something you'll regret later. You're so kind to us that we think of you as our brother and tell you just what we think. Please forgive me," Meg said gently.

"No, I'm the one that should apologize," said Laury. "I've been in a bad mood all day. I do like having you tell me when I'm doing something wrong."

That evening, Laury listened as Beth played for Mr. Laurence. He watched the old man, who sat with his gray head on his hand, thinking of the dead child he'd loved so much. Remembering what Meg had said, Laury made up his mind. "I'll stay with the dear old gentleman as long as he needs me, for I am all that he has."

Chapter 14

$\mathscr{J}$o was very busy in the attic that October. Sitting on the old sofa, she scribbled away till the last page was filled. She signed her name and threw down her pen, exclaiming, "There! I've done my best. If it's not good enough, I'll have to wait till I can do better."

Lying back on the sofa, Jo read the manuscript carefully, making a few last-minute changes. Then she picked up a second manuscript, put both in her pocket, quietly crept downstairs, put on her jacket and hat, and sneaked out the back door. She walked out to the road, got on a bus, and rolled away into town, looking very merry and mysterious.

Once in town, she walked quickly until she reached the building she was looking for. Outside were several signs, including a large one for a dentist's office. Jo stepped into the doorway, looked up the dirty stairs, and then turned and ran back into the street. She did this several times. Finally, Jo pulled her hat down over her eyes and walked up the stairs, looking as if she were about to have all her teeth pulled out.

From across the street, a dark-eyed young gentleman watched with great amusement. He said to himself, "That's just like her to come here on her own. But if she has to have a tooth pulled, she might need some help getting home." So the young man put on his coat and hat, and waited for her just outside the building.

Ten minutes later, Jo came running out the door, looking as if she'd been through a terrible ordeal.

The young gentleman followed her, and asked, "Was it painful?"

"Not very."

"It was quick?"

"Yes, thank goodness!"

"Why did you come alone?"

"I didn't want anyone to know," she explained.

"That's strange. So how many did you have out?"

Suddenly Jo understood his confusion. The young man thought she'd been to the dentist, not the newspaper office. She'd hate having her teeth pulled out. But she'd love having both her stories "come out"—in print, that is.

Instead of clearing up the misunderstanding, Jo burst out laughing. "I'd like to have two come out, but I won't know till next week."

"Why are you laughing? You're up to something, Jo," said Laury.

"So are you. What were you doing up in that pool hall?"

"Begging your pardon, ma'am. I wasn't at the pool hall. I was in the gym downstairs, taking a lesson in fencing."

"I'm glad of that."

"Why?"

"You can teach me. And then we can act out the fencing scene in *Hamlet*."

Laury laughed. "Is that the only reason you said you were glad?"

"No. I hope you never spend time in places like pool halls. Because then you'll go more and more often, and waste time and money, and act like Ned Moffat and those other awful boys," said Jo, shaking her head.

"So now I've got to act like a saint!" Laury said, annoyed by Jo's lecture.

"No. Just be a simple, honest, respectable boy, and we'll never desert you. I hear people say that money can tempt people to do bad things. Sometimes I wish you were poor so I wouldn't have to worry about you."

"So you worry about me, Jo?"

"A little. Especially when you're in one of your moods. You have such a strong will that if you started doing bad things, it would be hard to stop you."

"Are you going to preach at me all the way home?"

"Of course not. Why?"

"Because I have something interesting to tell you."

"What is it?" asked Jo.

"It's a secret. But I'll tell you mine if you tell me yours."

"I gave two of my stories to a newspaper editor," whispered Jo in his ear.

"Hooray for Miss Josephine March, the great American author!" shouted Laury, clapping his hands.

"Shhh. Nothing will come of it. But I had to try anyway. Please don't tell anyone. I don't want anyone else to be disappointed."

"Why, Jo, your stories are ten times better than the junk that's published every day."

Jo's eyes sparkled with pleasure, knowing that her friend believed in her, no matter what the newspaper editor thought. But she didn't want to get her hopes up.

Then Jo demanded, "So what's your secret?"

"I know where Meg's other glove is." And Laury whispered three words in Jo's ear.

"In his pocket!" she exclaimed, both shocked and upset.

"Yes, isn't that romantic?"

"No," gasped Jo. "It's disgusting. It's ridiculous. It won't be allowed."

"But I thought you'd be pleased."

"At the idea of somebody taking Meg away from us? No way," Jo said, looking upset.

To cheer her up, Laury suggested that they race each other down the hill. As Jo darted away, her hat blew off, her hairpins scattered on the road, and her loose hair flew all around her face.

When they reached the bottom of the hill, Jo threw herself onto a pile of leaves. "Be an angel, Laury. Go back and pick up my things, please," she asked.

Jo tried to fix her hair, hoping no one would see her. But someone did. Unfortunately, it was Meg.

"What in the world are you doing?" asked Meg.

"Gathering leaves," Jo said sheepishly, scooping up a handful.

"And hairpins," added Laury, throwing a bunch into Jo's lap. "They grow on this road, Meg—along with straw hats."

"You've been running, haven't you, Jo?" Meg scolded. "How could you! When will you stop romping around like a boy?"

"Not till I'm old and stiff, and have to use a cane. Don't try to make me grow up before I'm ready, Meg. It's hard enough having you change all of a sudden."

For the next two weeks, Jo's sisters wondered why she was acting so strangely. As soon as the mail arrived, she rushed to the door. She was rude to Mr. Brooke. And she kept looking sadly at Meg.

Then one Saturday, Jo ran into the house with a newspaper and pretended to read it.

"Anything interesting there?" asked Meg.

"Only a story, but I doubt it will be very good," Jo answered.

"Why don't you read it out loud to us?" Amy suggested.

"What's the title?" asked Beth.

"'The Rival Painters.'"

"Sounds interesting. Read it," said Meg.

Jo cleared her throat, took a deep breath, and began to read. The girls listened closely, for the story was romantic and tragic.

"I like the part about the beautiful painting," said Amy, when Jo had finished.

"I prefer the part about the lovers. Isn't it funny that the author used some of our favorite names?" said Meg.

"Who wrote it?" asked Beth, carefully studying Jo's face.

Jo put down the paper and announced, "Your sister."

"You?" exclaimed Meg, dropping her sewing.

"It's very good," said Amy, seriously.

"I knew it! I knew it! Oh, Jo!" Beth beamed, and ran to hug her sister.

"Well, I never!" exclaimed Hannah.

"I'm so proud of you, dear," said Mrs. March.

Then Jo explained that the editor liked both her stories. But he never paid beginning writers. Once the stories were published, other editors might notice them and, as she improved, pay her for her work.

"I showed the stories to Laury, and he said they were very good. So I'm going to write more, and Laury's going to help me get money for them. I'm so happy, for I hope someday my writing will help support myself and the family."

Jo stopped to wipe away the tears in her eyes. What she wished for most was to be independent and to earn the praise of the people she loved. And this seemed to be the first step toward making that dream come true.

Chapter 15

"*N*ovember is such an unpleasant month," sighed Meg, one gray afternoon as she worked in the garden.

"But if something pleasant happens, then we'll think it's a delightful month," said Beth, who took a hopeful view of everything—even November.

"Not likely. All we do is work, work, work," Meg complained.

"Just wait ten years," said Amy, sculpting little figures out of clay. "Jo and I are going to make a fortune and share it all with you."

"I'm grateful, but I don't have much faith in ink and dirt," sighed Meg.

Laury came over and invited the girls to go for a ride in his carriage. But Meg said "No, thank you." She and her mother agreed it would be best if she didn't spend too much time alone with the young gentleman.

When Mrs. March came home, the girls told her they still hadn't received their weekly letter from Father.

Then a telegram arrived for Mrs. March. She

read it, turned pale, and fell back into her chair as if the piece of paper had sent a bullet to her heart. Jo took the telegram from her mother and read it out loud:

Mrs. March:
Your husband is very ill.
Come immediately.
S. HALE
The Military Hospital
Washington D.C.

Suddenly the whole world seemed to change. The sky grew strangely dark. The girls gathered around their mother, feeling that all their happiness and support was about to be taken away.

Mrs. March stretched out her arms to her daughters. She said in a tone they never forgot, "I'll go right away. But it may already be too late. Oh, children, children, help me bear it!"

For several minutes, they tried to comfort each other with words of hope, and then broke into tears. Finally Hannah spoke. "Instead of wasting time crying, I'll go and get your things ready, ma'am."

"She's right, girls," said Mrs. March, trying to pull herself together. "There's no time for tears. Be calm, and let me think."

Mrs. March sat up, pale but steady. She put away her grief in order to think and plan for them. "Jo, give me that pen and paper. I'll write Aunt March and ask to borrow money to pay for the train."

Jo tore a blank sheet from her book of stories. She knew how much her mother hated to ask for money, and wished she could do something to help.

"Laury, would you please take this note to Aunt March? And send a telegram saying that I'll take the next train, early tomorrow morning? Jo, go to the storerooms and tell Mrs. King I won't be able to work there for a while. On the way, get these things. I must be ready to nurse your father myself, since war hospitals don't have enough supplies. Beth, go ask Mr. Laurence if we could have these other things. I'm not too proud to beg for Father. Amy, tell Hannah to get down the black suitcase. And Meg, come help me find my things, for I'm feeling a little overwhelmed."

Everyone scattered like leaves in a gust of wind. And the quiet, happy household was suddenly broken apart by a single piece of paper.

Mr. Laurence hurried back with Beth, bringing much more than Mrs. March had asked for. He promised to watch over the girls while their mother was away. And he offered everything he could—including his own clothing. He even offered to escort Mrs. March on this long, sad journey. But Mrs. March could not accept the offer, because the old gentleman was too weak for such a trip. Seeing how worried she looked, Mr. Laurence frowned, thought for a while, and then suddenly disappeared.

A few minutes later, the doorbell rang. Meg was surprised to see Mr. Brooke. "I'm very sorry to hear your news, Miss March," he said, in a kind, quiet tone that she found soothing. "I came to offer to escort your mother on the trip. Mr. Laurence has some errands for me to do in Washington, and I would like to be of service to her there."

Seeing Meg's face light up with gratitude was thanks enough for Mr. Brooke. "How kind you are!" she said, squeezing his hand. Then something in his brown eyes made her drop his hand and turn away.

Soon Laury returned with an envelope from Aunt March. In it was the money and a note that said, "I told you all along that he shouldn't have joined the army. Maybe next time you'll take my advice." Mrs. March put the money in her purse and the note in the fireplace. She folded her lips together tightly, and then went back to getting ready.

By the end of that afternoon, everything was ready. But still Jo had not returned. The Marches began to worry, so Laury left to find her. Then Jo walked into the room. She looked both merry and fearful, both satisfied and sorry. She placed a roll of dollar bills in front of her mother. With a little choke in her voice, she said, "This is my contribution toward helping Father and bringing him home."

"My dear Jo, where did you get it? Twenty-five dollars! I hope you haven't done anything wrong?"

"No. I didn't beg, borrow, or steal. I only sold what was my own."

Jo took off her hat. Everyone gasped in dismay, for all her beautiful hair was gone.

Jo rubbed her short, boyish haircut, trying to look as if she liked it. "I was getting too vain about my hair. Now it feels so light and cool, I may never let it grow back. Besides, it might help my brains air out."

"My dear, I understand how gladly you gave up your 'vanity' for your love. But I'm afraid you might regret it someday," said Mrs. March.

"No, I won't!" declared Jo, relieved that her mother wasn't mad at her. "But I have to admit that it felt strange to see my dear old hair lying on the table. It almost seemed as if I'd had an arm or a leg cut off. The barber let me keep a long lock of hair. I'll give it to you, Marmee, just to remember the glorious past."

Mrs. March placed the wavy brown lock in a little box, right next to the short gray one she'd kept as a reminder of Father. She could only say, "Thank you, dear," before her voice broke with emotion.

At ten o'clock, they all gathered around the piano. Beth played one of Father's favorite songs. But they broke down, one by one, until Beth had to finish it alone.

They kissed their mother quietly, and then went off to bed. Soon Beth and Amy were asleep. Meg lay awake, thinking the most serious thoughts she'd ever had in her short life. Then she heard a muffled sob from Jo.

"What is it, Jo? Are you crying about Father?"

"No, not now."

"What is it, then?"

"It's my—my hair!" she cried, trying to smother the sobs in her pillow.

"I'm not sorry," Jo continued. "I'd do it again tomorrow if I could. It's only the silly, vain part of me that's crying. I just needed to grieve a little bit for the one thing about me that was beautiful. But why are you awake?"

"I'm too worried to sleep," Meg answered.

"Then think about something pleasant, and soon you'll fall asleep."

"I tried to, but that only made me feel more awake."

"What were you thinking about?" asked Jo.

"Handsome faces. Especially eyes—brown eyes."

Jo laughed, and Meg soon fell asleep, thinking about her own dream for the future.

It was midnight when a silent figure glided from bed to bed—smoothing blankets, fluffing pillows, and stopping to look tenderly at each sleeping face. Then, as Mother took one last look out at the night sky, the moon suddenly broke out from behind the clouds. It seemed to whisper in the silence, "Take comfort. Behind the clouds there is always light."

Chapter 16

In the cold gray dawn, the sisters waited anxiously for the carriage that would take their mother to the train station. They said little, trying to hold back the tears. Finally their mother spoke. "Children, Hannah will take care of you, and Mr. Laurence will protect you as if you were his own. Don't grieve or worry while I'm gone. Just do your work as usual, for work can be a source of comfort. Hope and keep busy. And whatever happens, remember that you are loved."

"Yes, Mother," the girls answered.

"Meg, dear, be careful and watch over your sisters. Be patient, Jo, and don't do anything rash. Write to me often, be brave and helpful, and try to cheer up everyone. Beth, comfort yourself with your music and do all your chores. And you, Amy, help as much as you can and be obedient."

Then Laury and his grandfather arrived with Mr. Brooke, who looked strong and kind.

"Goodbye, my darlings!" whispered Mrs. March, kissing each face one more time. Then she and Mr. Brooke hurried into the carriage.

As they rode away, the sun came out, shining on the group like a good sign. The last thing the travelers saw were four bright faces, smiling and waving their hands. Standing behind them, like bodyguards, were old Mr. Laurence, faithful Hannah, and devoted Laury.

Mrs. March turned to Mr. Brooke and said, "How kind everyone is to us!"

"I don't see how they can help it," he replied, with so much warmth and respectful sympathy that Mrs. March couldn't help smiling.

The girls then sat down to breakfast, looking mournful.

"I feel as if an earthquake has struck," said Jo.

"It seems as if half the house is gone," added Meg.

Beth was too upset to speak. Instead, she pointed to a pile of clothing that Mother had just mended—trying to take care of them even as she hurried to get ready herself. Suddenly, in spite of their efforts to be brave, they all broke down and cried bitterly.

"Now, my dear young ladies," Hannah said, "remember what your ma said. Come have some hot chocolate. I've made it as a special treat."

"'Hope and keep busy' will be our motto," said Jo, feeling more cheerful as she sipped the chocolate.

As Meg and Jo left with their hot muffins,

they looked back sadly at the window where they were used to seeing their mother's face. It was gone. But Beth remembered, and there she stood, nodding and smiling at them.

As they parted ways, Jo told Meg, "I hope the King children won't make trouble for you today."

"And I hope Aunt March won't lecture and complain. By the way, Jo, your hair looks very boyish and nice," answered Meg gently, trying not to chuckle at the curly hair that looked so silly on her tall sister.

Every day, Mr. Brooke sent a report about the girls' father. Mr. March was very ill, but his wife's tender care was already helping him get better. Everyone was eager to write back. Meg wrote on pretty pink paper, and told her mother how busy everyone was. Jo scribbled messages about how hard she was working to control her anger, and included silly little poems to cheer up her father. Beth sent them pressed flowers and all her love. Amy complained that Laury was treating her like a child even though she was almost a teenager. Then she added that she was studying every day. Hannah wrote about managing the house. Laury sent funny notes. And Mr. Laurence offered to send money or anything else they needed.

Chapter 17

After a week, the girls began falling back into their old ways. They didn't forget their motto. They just felt they needed a break after all that hoping and keeping busy.

So instead of doing chores, Meg spent her time writing long letters to her mother. Jo went back to reading and writing stories. And Amy spent her days sculpting clay.

Only Beth did her duties—and some of her sisters', too. Finally, one day Beth asked her older sisters to take their turn visiting the Hummels. "I've been there every day, caring for the children while Mrs. Hummel is at work. But the baby is sick, and I don't know what to do for her. She's getting sicker and sicker, and I think you or Hannah should go. Besides, my head hurts, and I feel really tired."

The sisters promised to go tomorrow, and went back to the things they preferred doing. So Beth filled a basket with food for the children, put on her coat, and went out into the chilly air. It was late when she came back, and no one saw her creep upstairs and shut herself in her mother's room.

Half an hour later, Jo walked into the room to get something. There she saw little Beth, looking upset, with red eyes and a bottle of medicine in her hand.

"What's wrong?" cried Jo.

But Beth waved her away, saying, "Have you already had scarlet fever?"

"Yes. Meg and I both had it. Why?"

"Oh, Jo, the Hummel baby died in my arms! When Mrs. Hummel came with the doctor, he said it was scarlet fever. He was angry because no one had called him sooner. But Mrs. Hummel said she couldn't afford to pay him, so he said he'd treat the other children for free. Then he told me to go home and take this medicine right away, or I'd get scarlet fever, too."

"Oh, Beth! I should have gone. If you get sick, I'll never forgive myself! If only Mother were home!"

Jo felt Beth's forehead, looked in her throat, and said sadly, "I'm afraid you're going to have it, Beth. Meg and I won't get it again. But we can't let Amy get near you, or she could catch it."

Jo told the others what had happened. "As soon as we get one problem under control," she muttered, "along comes another."

Since Mrs. March was away, Hannah took charge. She called for Dr. Bangs. She told Jo and Meg to stay home so they wouldn't spread the illness to anyone else. She ordered Amy to live with Aunt March until Beth was well again. But Amy refused, saying she'd rather have scarlet fever than live with Aunt March.

That's when Laury walked in. Amy told him the whole story, sobbing, "It's so boring at Aunt March's, and she's so grumpy."

"It won't be boring if I come visit every day," suggested Laury.

"Will you really come every single day? And take me out in the carriage?"

"I promise on my honor as a gentleman."

"And take me to the theater? And bring me home the minute Beth is well?"

"The very second."

"Well, then—I guess I'll go."

"Good girl!" said Laury, patting her on the head. This annoyed Amy, who thought Laury was treating her like a little child.

After examining Beth, Dr. Bangs said she would probably have a mild case of scarlet fever, and he ordered Amy to leave the house immediately.

When Jo, Amy, and Laury showed up at her house, Aunt March "welcomed" them in her usual cranky way. "What do you want now?" she demanded sharply, peering at them over her glasses. Her parrot, sitting on the back of her chair, called out, "Go away!"

After Jo told what had happened, Aunt March scolded, "That's what you get for hanging around poor people. I'll let Amy stay here as long as she doesn't cry or get sick, which I'm sure she will."

Noticing that Amy seemed about to burst into tears, Laury poked the parrot until it called out, "Bless my buttons!" That made Amy laugh instead.

"Any news of your father?" asked Aunt March.

"Father's doing much better," answered Jo.

"Well, I'm sure he'll get worse again," declared Aunt March, still annoyed that he hadn't followed her advice. "He's always been rather weak."

"Gonna die! Gonna die! Goodbye! Goodbye!" squealed the parrot, as Laury poked it again.

"Be quiet, you disrespectful old bird!" scolded Aunt March.

"Be quiet, you disrespectful old bird!" the parrot echoed back.

Jo and Laury left, trying not to laugh at the parrot's last speech. Left alone with Aunt March, Amy tried to be brave. But then the parrot screamed at her, "Go away! Go away!" And Amy burst into tears.

$\mathscr{B}$eth became much sicker than the girls expected. The fever made her body shake, and she became delirious. She didn't recognize the familiar faces around her, and she called for her mother in a hoarse, broken voice. Jo grew frightened, and Meg wanted to write to her mother about what was going on. But Hannah was in charge now, and Hannah saw no need to add to Mrs. March's worries. Then a letter arrived, saying that Mr. March had gotten worse and wouldn't be coming home for a long time.

The days seemed dark now, and the house sad and lonely. The sisters' hearts were heavy, for the shadow of death hung over the once happy home. Meg realized how rich she had been in those precious things that money can't buy—love, protection, peace, and health. Jo learned that Beth's unselfishness was more valuable than talent, worth, or beauty. Amy longed to come home and do those chores she used to hate. Laury haunted the house, feeling helpless. And Mr. Laurence couldn't bear to look at the piano Beth used to play. Everyone missed Beth—from the butcher to the neighborhood children to poor Mrs. Hummel. They sent all sorts of gifts and good wishes. The Marches were surprised to discover how many friends shy little Beth had made.

The first of December felt like the dead of winter. A bitter wind blew, and the snow fell fast. That morning, Dr. Bangs looked at Beth and shook his head sadly. He turned to Hannah, "If Mrs. March can leave her husband, tell her she should come home right away."

Jo paled, and then rushed out into the storm to send her mother a telegram. After she returned, Laury appeared with a letter, which said that Mr. March was improving again. Jo was thankful, but her face was so full of grief that Laury asked, "What is it? Is Beth worse?"

"The doctor said that Mother should come home right away—before Bethy—" Tears streamed down poor Jo's cheeks. "Beth is my conscience, and I can't give her up. I can't! I can't!"

Laury wanted to say something tender and comforting, but he couldn't find the right words. So he stood silently beside Jo, gently stroking her head.

It was the best thing he could have done. For Jo felt his unspoken sympathy. She'd tried to act bravely and keep herself from crying. But now she lowered her head, and cried out her despair

Finally, Laury spoke. "Poor girl. You're worn out. But here's something that will cheer you up."

"What is it?" cried Jo.

"I telegraphed your mother yesterday. Brooke answered that she'd be here tonight. Grandpa and I thought your mother would never forgive us if Beth—well, if anything happened. So I got Grandpa to let me send a telegram, even though Hannah said not to. Your mother's train gets in at 2 this morning, and I'll go pick her up at the station."

Jo flew out of her chair, threw her arms around Laury's neck, and cried out joyfully, "Oh, Laury! Oh, Mother! I'm so glad!"

Laury wasn't sure how to react. At first he patted Jo's back, then kissed her on the cheek. Suddenly Jo realized what was happening, and gently pushed him away. "Oh, don't. I didn't mean to throw myself at you. But you were such an angel that I couldn't help flying at you. How can I ever thank you?"

"Fly at me again. I rather liked it," said Laury, with a twinkle in his eye.

"No, thank you. Go home and rest, for you'll be up all night."

When Jo told everyone the good news, Hannah looked relieved, and Meg smiled for the first time in two weeks. But Beth lay still, unconscious, feeling neither hope and joy, nor doubt and danger. The once rosy face looked empty, the once busy hands weak, and the once smiling lips dry and cracked.

All day, Jo and Meg watched over Beth and waited, hoping. All day the snow fell, the bitter wind raged, and the hours dragged by slowly. The doctor stopped in and said that around midnight there would probably be some change—for better or for worse. When the clock struck twelve, the house was still as death. Weary Hannah had fallen asleep, and only the wailing of the wind broke the deep silence. An hour went by, and nothing happened, except that Laury left for the train station. Another hour, and still no one came. The girls were haunted by fears of accidents along the way, or something tragic in Washington.

Some time after two, Jo noticed a change in Beth. The flush of the fever and the look of pain were gone. The little face looked pale, but peaceful, completely at rest. Fearing the worst, Jo kissed the damp forehead and softly whispered, "Goodbye, my Beth. Goodbye!"

Hannah woke up, hurried to the bed, and looked at Beth. "The fever's turned. Her skin's damp, and she's breathing easy."

Then the doctor arrived, smiled, and said, "Yes, I think the little girl will pull through this time. Keep the house quiet, let her sleep, and when she wakes up, give her this medicine."

Meg and Jo held each other close, with hearts too full of joy for words. Looking out at the fresh snow, sparkling in the early morning light, they thought the world had never looked so beautiful. "It looks like a fairyland," said Meg, relieved that their long, sad vigil was done.

And then, from the first floor, they heard Laury's joyful whisper, "She's home, girls! She's home!"

Chapter 19

*W*hile these things were happening at home, Amy was having a hard time at Aunt March's house. For the first time in her life, she realized how much her parents and sisters loved her and spoiled her.

Although she would never admit it, Aunt March did, in fact, care about her nephew's four children. And she found Amy much better behaved than Jo. So she decided to train Amy as she had been trained 60 years ago. But Aunt March's endless rules and lectures made Amy feel like a fly trapped in the web of a very strict spider.

Every morning, Amy had to polish the old-fashioned silver teapot and spoons until they shone. She had to comb the cranky little lap dog, who snarled and yelped at her the whole time. She had to feed Polly the parrot, who pulled her hair and spilled his food as soon as she finished cleaning its cage. All day long, Aunt March ordered Amy to run up and down the stairs to get little things she wanted. Then Amy had to do her own lessons perfectly. She had to read aloud to the old lady, and listen to Aunt March's incredibly dull stories about her youth. Amy tried to look obedient, but inside she felt like rebelling.

Fortunately, old Esther, the maid, amused Amy with stories of her childhood in France. And she showed Amy the beautiful jewels that Aunt March hid away in secret places.

"I wish I knew where all these pretty things will go when Aunt March dies," Amy wondered out loud.

"To you and your sisters," Esther answered. "I witnessed her will."

"Oh, how nice! But I wish she'd let us have them now. It's not good to put things off," Amy observed.

"You're too young to wear such fine things. But the first one to marry will have the pearls. And I think she may give you that little blue ring because of your good behavior and charming manners."

"Oh, I'll be a lamb if only I can have that lovely ring! It's so much prettier than Susie Perkins' gold ring! I guess I do like Aunt March after all," said Amy, trying on the ring.

From that day on, she obeyed every one of Aunt March's orders. And the old lady was pleased with herself for having trained the girl so well.

Soon Amy forgot about herself and her selfish motives for being good. Instead, she tried to think of others, keep cheerful, and be satisfied just knowing she was doing the right thing—even though no one noticed or praised her for it.

In an effort to be very, very good, Amy decided to write her own will—even though it hurt to think about giving up her little treasures. But if she became ill and died, she wanted her things to be divided justly and generously.

One day, with Esther's help, she wrote out this important document. Esther signed it, and Amy decided to ask Laury to be the second witness.

She then amused herself by trying on some fancy old dresses that Aunt March had stored away in an upstairs room. Amy paraded around the room, sweeping up her long skirts, pretending to flirt with her fan, and trying not to trip on her high-heeled shoes. The parrot followed her, squawking, "Kiss me, dear!"

She didn't hear Laury walk into the room. Trying not to laugh out loud at the little girl playing "dress up," Laury politely knocked on the wall.

Amy twirled around Laury, and then invited him to sit down. "I want to consult with you about a very serious matter," she said. She showed Laury her will, and asked him to make sure that it was legal. "You know, life is uncertain, and I don't want any bad feelings about my property."

"What put that idea into your head? How did you find out that Beth was giving away her things?"

"What's this about Beth?"

"I'm sorry. I thought you knew. Beth felt so ill one day that she told Jo she wanted to give her piano to Meg, her cats to you, and her poor old dolls to Jo, who would love and take care of them. She was sorry she had so little to give. So she left locks of her hair to the rest of us, and her best love to Grandpa."

Amy frowned for a moment, and then said, "I'd like to add to my will that I want all my curls cut off and given to my friends—even though it will ruin my looks."

Laury added it, smiling at Amy's great sacrifice. Then he entertained her for the next hour, and listened to her complaints and stories about living with Aunt March. When it was time for Laury to leave, Amy whispered, with trembling lips, "Is Beth really in danger?"

"I'm afraid so. But we must hope for the best." And Laury put his arm around her, comforting her in a brotherly way.

Amy's heart ached, and tears streamed down her cheeks. Not even a million blue rings could make up for the loss of her gentle little sister.

Chapter 20

$\mathscr{W}$hen Beth finally woke from that long, healing sleep, the first thing she saw was her mother's tender face. She smiled, nestled closer to her mother, and fell asleep again, too weak to wonder at anything.

Feeling as if a heavy burden had been lifted from them, Meg and Jo closed their weary eyes and finally slept soundly. Mrs. March would not leave Beth's side, like a guard watching over a treasure that had been lost, but now was found.

Laury rushed to tell Amy the good news. Aunt March was so touched that she actually wiped away a tear and never once said, "I told you so." Amy set aside her own impatience to see her mother, and never even thought about the little blue ring. She behaved so well that Laury thought her "a fine little woman." Polly squawked, "Good girl! Bless your buttons!" Then Aunt March took Amy aside and gave her the little blue ring.

Amy saw how tired Laury was. So instead of asking him to take her out to enjoy the bright wintry day, she persuaded him to stay and rest on the sofa. To Amy's surprise, Aunt March closed the curtains so Laury could sleep more comfortably.

Amy was busy writing a long letter to her mother, when suddenly Mrs. March appeared at the door. Amy joyfully led her mother to a little room, where they could be alone together. After a while, Amy saw her mother glance at her hand and smile. "I wanted to tell you about this, Mother. But I forgot. Aunt gave me the ring today. She kissed me, put it on my finger, and said she was proud of me and would like me to stay here forever. Can I keep it, Mother?"

"It's very pretty. But I think you're too young to wear such fine jewelry, Amy."

"I'll try not to be vain. I like how pretty it is. But I also want to wear it as a reminder."

"Of Aunt March?" asked her mother, laughing.

"No. To remind me not to be selfish. I've been thinking a lot about my faults, and being selfish is the worst one. Be†h isn't selfish, and that's why everyone loves her and feels so bad at the thought of losing her. People wouldn't feel as bad if I got sick. And I don't deserve it, either. But I'd like to be loved and missed by a great many friends. So I'm going to try and be as much like Beth as I can. Maybe this little ring will help me remember."

"I'm not sure how much the ring will help. But you may wear it, dear, and do your best. Half the battle is a sincere wish to improve. Now I must go back to Beth. Keep up your spirits, little daughter. Soon we'll have you home again."

That evening, while Meg was writing to their father, Jo slipped quietly into Beth's room. "I want to tell you something, Mother," Jo whispered.

"About Meg?"

"How did you know?"

"That Moffat boy hasn't been here, I hope?" asked Mrs. March sharply.

"Oh, no. I would have slammed the door in his face if he had. Remember when Meg left a pair of gloves at the Laurences' house, and only one was returned? Well, Laury told me Mr. Brooke had kept the other glove. He said that he liked Meg, but he didn't want to tell her so, because she's so young and he's so poor. Isn't that perfectly awful?"

"Do you think Meg likes him?" asked Mrs. March, anxiously.

"How would I know? The only thing I know about love and such nonsense is what I've read in books. In novels, girls blush, faint, and generally act like fools. Meg's too sensible to do anything like that!"

"Then you think Meg isn't interested in John?"

"Who?" asked Jo, staring.

"Mr. Brooke. I call him 'John' now. He's been so devoted to poor Father that we've both grown very fond of him."

"Oh, dear! Now you'll let Meg go and marry him. How sneaky to go helping you, just to get your permission to marry Meg," Jo said angrily.

"My dear, it was Mr. Laurence that asked John to go with me. He's been open and honorable about Meg, and he's told us he loves her. But first he wants to earn enough money to give her a comfortable home. He is truly an excellent young man. But I will not allow Meg to get engaged so young."

"I knew something was wrong, but it's worse than I imagined. I just wish I could marry Meg myself, and keep her safe in the family."

Mrs. March smiled, but then said seriously, "Jo, I've confided in you, and I don't want you to say anything to Meg. When John comes back, I'll have a chance to see them together. Then I'll have a better idea of how she feels about him."

"She'll see those handsome eyes that she keeps talking about. And then she'll go and fall in love. And that'll be the end of peace and fun and cozy times together. I can see it now! They'll be all lovey-dovey, and we'll have to stay out of their way. Brooke will somehow come up with the money, carry her off, make a hole in the family, break my heart, and everything will be horrible. I wish we were all boys. Things would be so much simpler! Send him away, Mother, so we can all be happy together again—just as we always used to be."

"Jo, it's natural and right that all you girls should go to homes of your own. But only when you're old enough. Your father and I have agreed that Meg will not make any commitments until she's at least 20. If Meg and John truly love one another, they can wait three years to test their love."

"Wouldn't you rather she married a rich man?" asked Jo.

"Money is a good and useful thing, Jo. I hope my girls will always have enough, but never be tempted by too much. I'm not ambitious for my girls to have great wealth or status. It's fine if love and kindness bring fame and fortune. But I know from experience that true happiness can be found in a simple little house, where money is earned by honest, hard work. Doing without some things helps you enjoy the pleasures you have. And the love of a good man is worth more than all the money in the world."

"I agree, Mother. But I'm disappointed about Meg. For I'd planned to have her marry Laury and be wealthy. He's rich and generous and good, and he loves us all. It's too bad that Brooke has spoiled my plan."

"Don't meddle with your friends' hearts, Jo.

Or you may ruin your friendships."

"All right. But I hate to see things all mixed up when it would be so easy to fix them."

"Fix what?" asked Meg, as she crept into the room. She handed Marmee the letter she'd written to Father in case she wanted to add anything.

Mrs. March glanced at the letter and handed it back. "Beautifully written, Meg. Please add that I send my love to John."

"You call him 'John'?" asked Meg, smiling innocently.

"Yes. He's been like a son to us, and we are very fond of him," answered Mrs. March, looking carefully at her daughter's face.

"I'm glad, because he is so lonely."

Mrs. March thought to herself, feeling both sadness and satisfaction, "She doesn't love him yet. But soon she'll learn."

Chapter 21

*M*other's trust in Jo made her feel important. But at the same time, Jo was upset and worried that she might lose Meg to Mr. Brooke. Laury suspected that Jo had a secret, and he was determined to pry it out of her. Even though Jo refused to tell, Laury finally guessed that it had something to do with Meg and his tutor. Angry that no one trusted him with the secret, Laury made up his mind to seek revenge.

Over the next few days, mysterious letters for Meg appeared in the little "post office." Meg seemed troubled. She blushed often, slept little, and generally kept to herself.

Then one day, Meg read a letter and gasped, "Oh, Jo! How could you do this to me!" She hid her face in her hands, crying as if her heart were broken.

"Do what? What are you talking about?" answered Jo, bewildered.

"You wrote the letters, and that awful Laury helped you. How could you be so rude, so mean, so cruel to both of us?"

"If that wicked boy did anything to hurt you,

Meg, I'll go right over and—"

"Quiet, Jo!" Mrs. March commanded. "Now Meg, tell me the whole story."

Meg explained that she'd been getting love letters that she thought were from Mr. Brooke. At first they'd made her feel important, but then they started talking about marriage.

"What did you say to him then?" asked Mrs. March.

"That I was too young, that I didn't want to keep secrets from you, and that he must first speak with Father. I was very grateful for his kindness, and would happily be his friend. But nothing more—not for a long while."

Mrs. March looked pleased, and Jo felt relieved.

Then Meg continued. "But then I got this letter from John—I mean, Mr. Brooke—written in a very different style. He said he'd never sent any love letters, and was sorry that my sister Jo had played such a mean trick. He was very kind and respectful. But I'll never again be able to look him in the face!"

Meg sobbed, and Jo stomped around the room, calling Laury names. Then suddenly Jo stopped, grabbed the notes, and looked at them closely. "I don't believe Brooke wrote any of these letters. Laury wrote them all, and he kept your answers. He was mad at me because I wouldn't tell him my secret."

"What secret?" asked Meg.

"I'll handle this, Jo" interrupted Mrs. March. "You go and get Laury. I want to get to the bottom of this, and put a stop to such hurtful pranks."

After Jo left, Mrs. March gently told Meg how Mr. Brooke really felt about her. "Now, dear, how do you feel about him? Do you love him enough to wait till he can provide a home for you? Or would you rather not make any commitments right now?"

"Lately I've been so scared and worried. I don't want to have anything to do with love and marriage for a long time—perhaps never. If John doesn't know anything about this nonsense, please don't tell him. And don't let Jo and Laury say anything."

Mrs. March wanted to speak with Laury alone. For the next half hour, the girls heard them talking in the living room, while Jo stormed up and down the hall. But they never knew what was said. Finally, Mrs. March asked the girls to join them. Laury looked so sorry that Jo wanted to forgive him right away.

Laury assured Meg that Brooke knew nothing of the joke. "I'll never tell him, as long as I live," Laury promised. "Wild horses couldn't drag it out of me. I'll do anything to show you how sorry I am. Please forgive me, Meg," he begged, looking very much ashamed of himself.

Meg accepted his humble apology, although she said it was "a very ungentlemanly thing to do." Jo said nothing, still trying to harden her heart against him.

But as soon as Laury had gone, Jo wished she'd been more forgiving. Finally, she decided to visit him, with the excuse of returning a borrowed book. But when she arrived, the housekeeper said that Laury had just had an argument with his grandfather, and both were still too angry to talk to anyone.

"I'll go and see what's wrong," said Jo. "I'm not afraid of either of them."

Jo went straight up to Laury's room and knocked briskly on the door.

"Stop knocking, or I'll open the door and make you stop!" the young gentleman yelled out in a threatening voice.

Jo immediately knocked again. The door flew open. Jo rushed past Laury, dropped dramatically to her knees, and said with great humility, "Oh, do please forgive me for being so angry. I came to beg your forgiveness and make it up to you."

"Oh, it's all right. Get up, Jo, and don't be a goose," he answered.

"Why, thank you. I shall. Might I ask what's wrong? You look like a thundercloud."

"Grandfather shook me by the shoulders," Laury growled indignantly. "If it had been anyone else, I'd have—"

"But I often give you a shake, and you don't seem to mind," Jo said, trying to calm him down.

"Yeah, but you're a girl, so it's fun. But I won't allow another man to treat me like that!"

"Why did he shake you?"

"Just because I wouldn't tell him why your mother wanted to see me. I promised her I wouldn't tell anyone. So of course I couldn't break my word as a gentleman."

"Couldn't you find some way to reassure your grandfather?"

"Not without bringing Meg into it. Besides, he should trust me, instead of treating me like a baby. He's got to learn that I can take care of myself and that I don't need anyone to tell me how to behave!"

Jo sighed. "So how will you work things out with him?"

"Well, he should apologize. And he should believe me when I say I can't tell him what this fuss was about."

"Now, Laury, be sensible. You can't stay in your room forever."

"I don't plan to. I'll run away. Once Grandpa misses me, he'll change his mind."

"I'm sure he will. But you really shouldn't worry him like that."

"Don't lecture me, Jo. I'll go to Washington and stay with Brooke. It'll be fun."

Jo sighed. "I wish I could run off, too."

"Why not? Let's do it, Jo. I've got enough money. We'll leave a note saying we're all right. Then we'll surprise your father and Brooke. It will do you good."

For a moment, Jo looked as if she would agree. She was tired of being cooped up for so long, taking care of Beth. She longed for a change—for freedom and fun. But then when she looked through the window at her old house next door, she shook her head with sorrow. "If I was a boy, we could run away together and have a wonderful time. But since I'm a girl, I must be proper and stay home."

"I knew Meg would refuse to go along. But I thought you had more guts."

"Quiet down, you bad boy. Think about your own sins, and don't tempt me to be more wicked than I already am." Then Jo added seriously, "If I get your grandpa to apologize for shaking you, will you give up this idea of running away?"

"Yes. But you won't be able to," answered Laury. Even though he really wanted to make up with his grandfather, he still felt he'd been treated unfairly.

"If I can handle the young Laurence, I can handle the old one," Jo muttered.

Jo went straight to the library door and knocked firmly. Suspecting that Jo wanted to do more than just return a book, Mr. Laurence demanded gruffly, "What's that boy done now? I can't get a word out of him."

"He did do something wrong," Jo explained. "But we forgave him, and we all promised not to say a word because it might hurt someone."

"So the boy was protecting someone else, rather than himself? Then I'll have to forgive him. He's a stubborn fellow and hard to manage."

"So am I," answered Jo. "But sometimes a kind word will control me better than all the punishments in the world."

"You think I'm not kind to him?" asked Mr. Laurence, sharply.

"Oh, no, Sir. You're sometimes too kind. And then you're a bit too quick to punish him when he does something wrong," Jo said, hoping she wasn't being too bold.

To her relief and surprise, the old gentleman said, "You're absolutely right, girl. I am! I love the boy. But sometimes it's hard to put up with his behavior."

"But if you don't work things out, he'll run away," Jo said, hoping to help Mr. Laurence be more patient with his grandson.

Suddenly troubled, Mr. Laurence glanced at the picture of a handsome young man that hung over his desk. It was Laury's father. Instead of obeying the old man's orders to stop seeing the woman he loved, he'd run away, married her, and never again saw his father.

Jo felt sorry she'd upset the old man. So she turned her warning into a joke. "You know, ever since I cut my hair, I've thought about running away, too. So if we're ever missing, just look for two boys working on one of the ships going to India."

Relieved, Mr. Laurence teased back, "How dare you talk that way, young lady? Now go and bring that boy down to dinner. Tell him everything's alright."

"He won't come, Sir. He's upset because you didn't believe him when he said he couldn't tell you. And you hurt his feelings when you shook him."

Mr. Laurence began to laugh. "Well, I suppose I should thank him for not shaking me back. So what's the boy want me to do?"

Jo suggested that Mr. Laurence write a formal apology—like one gentleman to another. Jo took it to Laury and advised him, "Turn over a new leaf, my boy, and begin again."

"I keep turning over new leaves. But then I spoil them," he said sadly.

Laury accepted the apology, and the little cloud blew over. Everyone thought the problem was settled, and soon forgot all about it. But Meg remembered how she'd felt about the "love letters." She kept thinking and dreaming about a certain young man. Once Jo happened to see a scrap of paper on which Meg had written the words, "Mrs. John Brooke." She groaned and threw it into the fire, feeling that Laury's prank had hastened the horrible day when Meg would leave her.

Chapter 22

$\mathcal{T}$he next few weeks were peaceful, like sunshine after a storm. Mr. March wrote that he might be well enough to come home early in January. Beth was soon able to lie on the sofa, play with her beloved cats, and mend her dolls' clothing. But since she was still too weak to walk on her own, Jo carried her beloved sister in her strong arms. Meg cheerfully burned her lovely hands cooking special treats for Beth. And Amy celebrated her return home by unselfishly giving away her treasures.

After several days of mild weather, Christmas morning was splendid. Mr. March had just written that he would soon be with them. Beth, wrapped up in the red wool shawl her mother had given her, felt unusually well. So Jo carried her to the window to see her special gift. Jo and Laury had created a beautiful lady out of snow. One hand held a basket of fruit and ice cream that Meg had made. The other hand held out piano music and a picture that Amy had drawn. The snow lady was covered with flowers, an afghan, and ribbons—all little gifts for Beth.

Then Jo started singing the carol she'd placed between the snow lady's lips:

May you be blessed, dear Princess Beth!
May nothing you dismay!
May health and peace and happiness
Be yours, this Christmas day!

After Jo had finished singing and Laury had presented all the gifts, Beth sighed, "I'm so full of happiness, I couldn't be one bit happier—unless, of course, Father was here."

And everyone agreed.

Then one more bit of happiness arrived. Laury opened the door, popped in his head, and said very quietly, "Here's another Christmas present for the March family."

He stepped aside, and in his place appeared a tall man, wrapped up to his eyes in coats and scarves, leaning on the arm of another tall man.

Suddenly, four pairs of loving arms embraced the first tall man. Beth, whose joy gave strength to her weak legs, ran straight into her father's arms. Mr. Brooke tried to get out of the way, but somehow ended up kissing Meg by accident. And Hannah sobbed tears of happiness onto the turkey, which she'd forgotten to put down when she rushed from the kitchen.

After Mrs. March thanked Mr. Brooke for his faithful care of her husband, he and Laury left quickly so that the family could be together.

Mr. March told how the mild weather allowed him to come home sooner than expected. Then he talked about how devoted Brooke had been, and how he was quite a fine and respectable young man. He paused, glanced at Meg, and then at his wife. But Meg turned away, blushing. Noticing, Jo thought how much she hated fine and respectable young men with brown eyes.

Later, Mr. Laurence, Laury, and Mr. Brooke joined the Marches for dinner. They told stories, sang songs, and had a very good time. They'd planned a sleigh ride after dinner. But the girls wouldn't leave their father's side. So the guests left early, and the happy family gathered together around the fire.

"Just a year ago we were complaining about the dreadful Christmas we were expecting. Remember?" asked Jo.

"I'd say it's been a rather pleasant year on the whole," said Meg, pleased with herself for treating Mr. Brooke in a dignified way.

"I think it's been a pretty hard one," observed Amy, thoughtfully, as she watched the light shine on her ring.

"I'm glad it's over, because we've got you back," whispered Beth to her father.

"It's been a rough road for you to travel, especially the last part of it," said Mr. March, nodding with approval at his four young daughters. "But you've been brave, and I think you'll find that, from now on, your journey will be easier."

"How do you know, Father?" asked Meg.

He took Meg's hand, and pointed to some calluses and a burned patch of skin. "I remember when you cared only about keeping this hand perfectly smooth. It was pretty then. But now I think it is much prettier. It shows that you've been giving to others, and that you've learned useful skills, like sewing and cooking. I'm proud to shake this good little hand. Though I hope it will still be a little while till I'm asked to give it away in marriage."

"What about Jo?" asked Beth. "Please say something nice. For she's tried so hard and been so very, very good to me."

"I'll admit that I miss the wild little 'son Jo' that I left a year ago. But now I'm pleased to have a strong, helpful, tenderhearted woman in her place. Her face is rather thin and pale from all her worry. But it's grown gentler, and her voice is calmer. And nothing is more beautiful than her short, curly hair. For the $25 was a wonderful gift from my good girl."

"Now tell about Beth," said Amy, unselfishly waiting for her turn.

"She's not as shy as she used to be," Mr. March began cheerfully. But remembering how he'd almost lost her, he held her close, saying tenderly, "I've got you safe, now, my Beth. And I'll try to keep you that way."

Then Father stroked Amy's shining hair and said, "I noticed that Amy ran errands for her mother all afternoon, and waited on everyone with patience and good humor. She hasn't stopped to look in a mirror, and hasn't even mentioned the very pretty ring she's wearing. I've always been proud of the graceful statues she has sculpted from clay. But I am even prouder that she has molded herself into a lovable daughter who can make life beautiful for herself and others."

Then, for the first time in weeks, Beth sat down at her little piano and softly touched the keys. In the sweet voice they feared they might never hear again, Beth sang:

Be happy with the things you have
For then you will feel satisfied.
You'll have no fear of loss or want
As long as gratitude's your guide.

Chapter 23

$\mathcal{W}$ith Father home and Beth improving, their happiness seemed complete. But something was still missing.

Mr. and Mrs. March glanced at each other anxiously as they watched Meg, for she seemed shy and distracted. She jumped when the door-bell rang, and blushed when people mentioned John's name. Jo shook her fist at Mr. Brooke's umbrella, which he'd forgotten and left in the hall. Amy observed, "Even though Father's safe at home, it seems as if everyone's waiting for something to happen." And Beth innocently wondered, "Why haven't our neighbors visited us recently?"

One day, Jo finally said to Meg, "You're not like your old self. You seem ever so far away from me. I do wish you'd talk to Brooke and get it over with."

"I can't say anything till he speaks. And he won't, because Father told him I'm too young." Meg smiled oddly, as if she might not agree with her father.

"If he did speak, you'd probably just cry or

blush or give in to him, instead of firmly saying 'no.'"

"I'm not as silly and weak as you think. I know just what I'd say. I've planned it all, so I won't be taken by surprise."

"Then would you mind telling me what you'd say?" asked Jo.

"Not at all. You may find it useful for your own romances."

"Not me. I'm never having any. I'd feel like a fool," gasped Jo, alarmed at the thought.

"Not if you liked someone very much, and that person liked you," Meg sighed.

"And the speech you'd tell that man?" demanded Jo.

"Oh, I'd say calmly, but firmly, 'Thank you, Mr. Brooke. You are very kind. But I agree with Father that I'm too young to make a commitment. So please, let's just keep being friends.'"

"It sounds pretty definite, but you'd never say it. You'd rather give in than hurt his feelings."

"No. I shall tell him I've made up my mind. And then I shall walk out of the room with dignity."

Meg was about to rehearse the dignified exit when the doorbell rang.

"Good afternoon," said Mr. Brooke. "I came to get my umbrella—that is, to see how your father's doing today."

Anxious to leave the room so that Meg could make her speech, Jo jumbled her words. "It's fine. He's in the hallway. I'll get him. And I'll go tell it you're here." And with that, Jo fled upstairs.

Meg started to leave the room, too, saying that she would go call her mother.

"Don't go. Are you afraid of me, Margaret?" asked Mr. Brooke, looking hurt. Meg blushed, surprised but pleased to hear him call her by her full name.

Wanting to look friendly and confident, Meg held out her hand and said, "How can I be afraid when you've been so kind to Father? I only wish I knew how to thank you for it."

"Shall I tell you how?" asked Mr. Brooke, taking the small hand in his own. He looked down at Meg with so much love in his brown eyes that her heart fluttered. She wanted both to run away and to stay and listen.

"Oh, no. Please don't."

"I won't hurt you. I only want to know if you care for me a little, Meg. I love you so much, dear," Mr. Brooke said tenderly, taking her other hand.

This was the moment for the calm, proper speech Meg had planned. But suddenly she forgot every word of it, and instead answered shyly, "I don't know."

"Will you try and find out?" he pleaded, pressing her hands warmly.

"I'm too young," Meg answered, wondering why she felt so fluttered, but also enjoying it.

"I'll wait. And in the meantime, would you be willing to try learning to like me? Would it be a very hard lesson, dear?"

"Not if I chose to learn it, but—"

"Please, Meg. I love to teach. And this would be easier to learn than German." John's eyes began to twinkle as he grew more confident that he was winning her over.

Meg saw the tenderness in his eyes, but his look of satisfaction annoyed her. She remembered Annie Moffat's foolish lessons about playing hard to get. Suddenly, she felt excited by the thought of having power over another person's feelings. So she suddenly pulled back her hands, tossed back her head, and said, "However, I don't choose to learn it. Please go away and let me be!"

Poor Mr. Brooke had never seen Meg in such a mood. He followed her as she walked away. "Can't I at least hope you might change your mind someday? I'll wait and say nothing until you've had more time. Don't play with my feelings, Meg. I thought you weren't like that."

"Then stop thinking about me. I'd rather you didn't," Meg said sharply, strangely enjoying her newfound power.

Pale and shaken, Mr. Brooke looked at her so sadly, so tenderly, that Meg felt herself changing her mind.

That's when Aunt March stepped into the room. She'd heard that Mr. March was home, and she hoped to surprise her nephew with a visit.

Instead, she surprised the young couple so much that Meg jumped as if she'd seen a ghost, and Mr. Brooke vanished into the next room.

"What is the meaning of this?" demanded the old lady, rapping her cane on the floor.

"It's Father's friend," Meg stammered. "I'm so surprised to see you!"

"Obviously." Aunt March sat down firmly. "And what did 'Father's friend' say that made you blush like a rose? I insist on knowing what's going on," she announced, with another rap of her cane.

"Mr. Brooke and I were only talking," Meg began.

"Brooke? That boy's tutor? Now I understand. Well, at least you haven't gone and agreed to marry him, have you, child?" cried Aunt March, looking horrified.

"Quiet. He'll hear you."

"Well, I've got something to say to you. And I won't leave until I've spoken my mind. Tell me, do you intend to marry this penniless peasant? If you do, I'll cut you out of my will. Not one cent of my money will ever go to you. Remember that, and be a sensible girl," Aunt March ordered.

"I shall marry whomever I please, Aunt March," Meg answered firmly. "And you can leave your money to anyone you like."

"Is that the way you take my advice, Miss Know-It-All? Well, you'll be sorry someday. You'll find it's hard to be in love when you're poor."

"Well, some people don't have much love even when they're rich." Even Meg was surprised by her bold answer. She wasn't used to feeling so brave, independent, and glad to defend John.

Aunt March then tried a different approach. "Now, Meg, my dear. Be reasonable and take my advice," she coaxed. "I just don't want you to spoil your whole life by making a big mistake. You know it's your duty to marry a rich man and help your family."

"Father and Mother don't think so. They like John, even though he is poor."

"Your parents don't understand the real world," Aunt March lectured. "They are as innocent as babies and still full of youthful ideals."

"I'm glad they are."

"Now, Meg," Aunt March demanded. "Does this worthless fellow at least have some rich relatives?"

"No, but he has many warm friends."

"Friends don't put food on the table. And they stop liking you if you're poor. Now, I don't suppose he owns a business, does he?"

"Not yet. But Mr. Laurence is going to help him."

"James Laurence is a cranky old fellow. You can't depend on him. If you marry a man without money, rich relatives, or a successful business, you'll end up working even harder than you do now. Why won't you listen to me and be comfortable forever? You could do so much better if you'd just wait a little longer. I thought you had more sense, Meg."

"I couldn't do better than John if I waited my whole life! He's good and wise. He's got heaps of talent. He's willing to work. He's so energetic and brave he's sure to be a success. Everyone likes and respects him. And I'm proud that he cares for me, even though I'm so young and poor and silly."

"Oh, no, child. The real reason he likes you is that you have a rich aunt."

"Aunt March, how dare you say such a thing? My John wouldn't marry for money, any more than I would. We are willing to work hard, and we intend to wait. I'm not afraid of being poor. So far I've been happy in my life—even without money. And I know I'll be happy with John because he loves me. And what's more—"

Something in the girl's happy young face made the lonely old woman feel angry and sad. "Well then, I wash my hands of the whole matter! Don't you expect anything from me when you're married. I'm done with you forever!"

Slamming the door in Meg's face, Aunt March stormed out of the house.

Meg wasn't sure whether to laugh or cry. But then Mr. Brooke rushed in and said, "I couldn't help hearing, Meg. I thank you for defending me. And I thank Aunt March for proving you do care for me—at least a little bit."

"I didn't know how much until she criticized you," Meg whispered, hiding her face in Mr. Brooke's jacket.

Fifteen minutes later, Jo crept downstairs. Having heard no sounds from the living room, she assumed that Meg had delivered her speech and sent Mr. Brooke away. But when she entered the room, Jo was shocked to find the couple sitting cozily on the sofa. Mr. Brooke jumped up, laughed, and kissed Jo on the cheek, saying, "Sister Jo, congratulate us!"

Jo ran upstairs and told her parents, "Oh, somebody go down quick! John Brooke is acting horribly. And Meg likes it!"

Mr. and Mrs. March ran into the living room, but were relieved to find that nothing "horrible" had happened. Meg and John explained their plans. They would wait three years to be married. Then Meg would be 21, and Mr. Brooke would have time to save some money.

Later that afternoon, Jo told Laury, "I don't approve of the marriage. But I've made up my mind to bear it, and I won't say a word against it. You can't know how hard it is for me to give up Meg," Jo added, her voice quivering.

"You're not giving her up. You'll just share her 50-50," Laury said, trying to console her.

"It can never be the same. I've lost my dearest friend," sighed Jo.

"You've still got me. Not that I'm good for much. But I'll be there for you, Jo, every day of my life."

"I know you will. You're always a great comfort to me, Laury," Jo said, shaking his hand.

"Well, now, cheer up, old fellow. Meg's happy, and Grandpa will give Brooke a helping hand. I'll finish college before long, and then we'll take a nice trip abroad."

"But there's no knowing what may happen in three years," Jo remarked, thoughtfully.

"That's true. But don't you wish you could look into the future and see where we'll all be then?"

"No. For I might see something sad. Everyone's so happy right now. I don't see how they could ever be any happier."

LITTLE WOMEN

Book Two

Chapter 24

$\mathcal{T}$hree years have passed, with few changes in the quiet family. The war has ended, though the hospitals are still filled with wounded soldiers. And many homes are now occupied by soldiers' widows.

Safe at home, Mr. March stays busy reading, learning, and serving others. As minister of a small church, he uses his book learning and wisdom of experience to guide and help others. Gentle, young at heart, sympathetic, and generous, he is a friend and role model to all. Even cynical and ambitious people admit that his ideals and beliefs are beautiful and true—even if they haven't made him rich.

John Brooke served dutifully as a soldier, but he was wounded and sent home after a year. As soon as he recovered, he took a job as a bookkeeper, deciding it was better to earn his own money than accept Mr. Laurence's generous offers of help.

Ned Moffat married Sallie Gardiner, and Meg couldn't help secretly envying her friend's fine house, splendid clothes, many servants, and extravagant lifestyle. But when she thought about how patiently and lovingly John worked to provide her with a little home of their own, Meg felt she was the richest, happiest girl in the world.

Aunt March was so charmed by Amy that she chose her, rather than Jo, to work at her house. She bribed Amy by offering her drawing lessons given by one of the best teachers in the area.

Beth grew even more pale and thin after her fever had gone. Though her eyes hinted at the pain she still suffered, she never complained, and always spoke hopefully about "being better soon." Peaceful and happy, Beth kept busy with her quiet duties.

Jo devoted herself to Beth's care, as well as to her writing. She was pleased that the local newspaper paid her to write, even though they were only trashy romance stories. Meanwhile, in her special corner of the attic, she worked hard at writing the novel that would one day make her famous.

In order to please his grandfather, Laury went away to college. But to please himself, he did as little work and had as much fun as possible. When he tried to help other people get out of trouble, he ended up getting into trouble himself. He played practical jokes on others, and was almost expelled for some of his pranks. But Laury's good intentions and generous spirit made everyone like him. And thinking about his grandfather's kindness, Mrs. March's motherly love, and the four innocent girl's faith in him kept him from doing anything truly bad.

Sometimes Laury brought his classmates home with him. But Beth was too shy and Meg too in love with John to spend time with them. Jo imitated the young men's gentlemanly words and manners. And, in return, they enjoyed her easy companionship, though none fell in love with her. But all were fascinated by Amy's beauty and charm. Many developed crushes on her, and they worshiped her as though she were a queen. And Amy learned to use and enjoy her power to order around the young men.

Mrs. March spent most of her time helping Meg prepare for her marriage. The day before the wedding, she and her daughters were putting the finishing touches on Meg's new home. It was a little brown house, with a tiny, bare yard. In it Meg had planted flowers, and hoped someday to add a fountain, too. The house was furnished with simple tables and chairs, plenty of books, a few pictures, and some flowering plants. What made it beautiful were the many gifts they'd received. Some were made by friendly hands, and all were offered by loving hearts.

Amy draped the plain curtains artistically. Hannah thoughtfully arranged every pot and pan. Beth set the table for the first meal. Jo scrubbed the floors and polished the doorknobs. Even Aunt March, who later regretted her threat, had secretly sent Meg a set of fine tablecloths and towels.

Finally Mrs. March asked Meg, as they inspected each room in the new house, "Are you satisfied? Does it seem like home? Do you think you'll be happy here?"

"Yes, Mother. Perfectly satisfied—thanks to all of you."

Just then, a tall young man with very short hair raced down the road and climbed over the fence without bothering to open the gate. He kissed Mrs. March on the cheek, patted Beth's head, grinned at Jo, and pretended to gaze in rapture at Amy.

"Now that I'm here, we can proceed with this wedding!" he grinned.

"And how is the lovely Miss Randal?" asked Amy, with a wink.

"More cruel than ever. I can hardly live without her!" he sighed, pretending to wipe a tear from his eye. "And you, Miss Amy, are becoming much too lovely for words."

Then Laury presented Meg with a small, wrapped box. "For Mrs. John Brooke, with many congratulations and compliments."

Meg unwrapped it, and smiled at Laury's latest joke present. Inside was a little whistle.

"You see, Mrs. Meg," Laury explained, "any

time John is away and you get frightened, just blow the whistle and the neighbors will come running."

The girls laughed, and then covered their ears when Laury showed how loud it was.

"Oh, and you can thank Hannah for protecting your wedding cake," Laury continued. "It looked so good I almost grabbed a piece. Now come along, Jo. I'm weak from hunger, and I can't get home without your help."

Jo let Laury lean on her arm as they walked away. "Now promise, Laury, that you'll behave well tomorrow. No pranks."

"Yes, ma'am."

"And don't look at me during the wedding ceremony. If you do, I'm sure to laugh."

"You'll be crying so hard you'll never see me through your tears."

"I never cry."

"Except when fellows go off to college?" Laury teased her.

"I only did that to keep the girls company."

"Like I said. Now tell me, Jo. Is Grandpa in a good mood this week?"

"Very. Why? You haven't gotten into trouble again, have you?"

"Me? Never!" Laury exclaimed, pretending to be shocked by the question. "I only want some money."

"You spend a lot of money, Laury."

"It's not that I spend it. It just spends itself. Before I even know it, it's gone."

"You're so generous and kind-hearted that you can't say 'no' to anyone who wants to borrow from you. We heard all about what you did for Henshaw."

"Oh, Grandpa made a big deal out of nothing. How could I let a fine fellow like Henshaw work himself to death, when he's worth more than a dozen lazy fellows like me?"

"I understand. But why do you waste your money spending it on seventeen jackets and endless ties and a new hat every time you come home?"

Laury laughed so hard that the hat he was wearing fell off, and Jo accidentally stepped on it. "Don't lecture me. I promise I'll dress nicely tomorrow and make all of you proud."

After a pause, Laury said quietly, "By the way, Jo. I think my buddy Parker is really falling for Amy. He talks about her all the time, and he's started writing her love poems. Should we try to nip this in the bud?"

"Of course. We don't want anyone else in this family to go off and get married for a long, long time."

"Yes, ma'am. You're still a child, Jo. But you'll be the next to go, and then we'll all be left broken-hearted."

"Don't worry. I'll never agree to get married.

Besides, nobody will ever want me."

"That's because you don't give anyone a chance," said Laury. "You won't show your tender side to anyone."

"That's because I'm too busy to bother with such nonsense. And I think it's awful to break up families. So let's just change the subject," said Jo, glaring at Laury.

"OK. But mark my words, Jo. You'll be the next one to go."

Chapter 25

$\mathcal{T}$he June roses over the Marches' front porch were red with excitement on the morning of the wedding. Meg herself looked like a rose, for her face bloomed with all that was best and sweetest in her heart and soul.

Meg decided to have a simple wedding. She gathered around her only those people she loved most dearly. She made her own wedding gown, sewing into it all her love and hopes. She wore no jewelry, and instead decorated her dress with John's favorite flowers, lilies of the valley that she'd planted herself.

"You look so sweet and lovely!" cried Amy. "I would hug you except that it might wrinkle your dress."

"Oh, please hug me everyone," said Meg, opening her arms to her sisters. "For I want lots of loving wrinkles pressed into my dress today."

Then Aunt March arrived, and was shocked that the bride herself ran over to welcome her. "My word, child! You shouldn't be seen until the last minute!"

"I'm not putting on a show, Aunty. No one's coming here to stare at me, or criticize my dress, or figure out how much the lunch costs. I'm too happy to care what anyone says or thinks. And I'm going to have my little wedding just the way I want it."

When Laury rushed in, Aunt March whispered to Amy, "Don't let that young giant come near me. He's more annoying than mosquitoes."

"He promised to be very good today," answered Amy. "And he can be perfectly elegant if he likes." Having said that, Amy slipped away to warn Laury not to annoy Aunt March by going near her—which, of course, made him decide to follow her like a shadow.

There was no bridal procession. But as Mr. March stood in front of the young couple to perform the ceremony, a sudden silence fell upon the room. The father's voice cracked with emotion, and the bridegroom's hand trembled. But Meg looked straight up into her husband's eyes and said "I will!" with such tender trust that her mother's heart rejoiced. Even Aunt March sniffed back her tears.

There was no display of wrapped gifts, for all the presents had already been put to use in the little house. The meal was simple—but with plenty of fruit and cake, beautifully decorated with more flowers from the Marches' garden.

Laury was surprised that there was only water, lemonade, and coffee to drink. "Has Jo smashed all the bottles by accident?" he whispered to Meg, winking at Jo.

"No. But Mother says that neither she nor her daughters will ever offer alcohol to any young man."

"Maybe that's not such a bad idea," Laury answered. "I've seen men take advantage of pretty women who've had too much to drink."

"You've never done that, have you?" asked Meg anxiously.

"Not yet. But I've never been offered a drink by a pretty girl."

"Promise me, then, Laury, that you'll never drink so much that you get drunk," Meg said, seriously. "That promise would give me one more reason to call this the happiest day of my life."

Laury hesitated. But Meg and Jo looked at him with such concern, that he couldn't refuse. "Then I promise, Mrs. Brooke!" he agreed heartily.

"I thank you very, very much," smiled Meg, happy that she could use the occasion to help her friend.

"And I drink to your resolution, Laury!" exclaimed Jo, raising her glass so energetically that she splashed him with her lemonade.

And in spite of many temptations, Laury kept his promise—and was grateful to his friends for doing him a service.

After lunch, seeing Meg and John standing together in the middle of the lawn, Laury shouted, "All the married people join hands! While you dance around the new husband and wife, the rest of us will prance around outside the ring."

Mr. and Mrs. March started the circle, and all the others joined in. Even Sallie Moffat whisked Ned into the ring. The crowning moment was when Mr. Laurence solemnly invited Aunt March to dance. Tucking her cane under her arm, the old lady joined the dance and hopped around the newlyweds.

When it was time to leave, Aunt March told Meg, "I think you'll be sorry you've married him. But I wish you well, my dear." Then she turned to Mr. Brooke and added, "You've got a treasure, young man. See that you deserve it."

Sallie turned to her husband and observed, "This is the prettiest wedding I've been to for ages, Ned. But I can't figure out why. There was nothing fancy or fashionable about it."

On their way home, Mr. Laurence said to Laury, "If you ever want to do this sort of wedding thing yourself, I'd be happy to see you do it with one of those little girls next door."

"I'll do my best to please you, Sir," Laury answered, sounding unusually obedient as he gently unpinned the flower Jo had placed in his buttonhole.

There was no honeymoon. The little house was so close that the newlyweds' only bridal journey was a quiet walk from the old house to the new. Finally Meg said to her family, with tears in her eyes, "Don't feel that I love you any less just because I love John so much."

Then, leaning on her husband's arm, Meg left the house. Flowers filled her hands, and sunshine brightened her happy face. The March family stood watching her walk away, their faces full of love and hope and tender pride. And so began Meg's married life.

Chapter 26

$\mathcal{L}$ike most people, it took Amy a long time to learn the difference between enthusiasm and dedication, between skill and inspiration. Amy quit sculpting her "mud pies" to devote herself to pen and ink drawings. Then, worn out by such detailed work, she shifted to bold charcoal sketches. Soon she'd covered all the walls with her artwork—and with charcoal dust. Next, Amy tried oil paints, followed by crayon sketches.

Then she made up her mind to go back to sculpture. Because it was hard to find models, Amy decided to make a plaster cast of her own pretty foot. But the plaster hardened sooner than she'd expected. Jo heard Amy screaming and hopping around wildly, with one foot anchored in a pan of solid plaster. Running to her sister's rescue, Jo tried to dig out Amy's foot with a knife. But she was laughing so hard that the knife went too far, and left a lasting reminder on Amy's foot of this particular artistic attempt.

Next, Amy devoted herself to sketching nature. She caught endless colds sitting on the damp ground, while trying to draw the perfect composition of stone, stump, mushroom, and blade of grass. As she studied the effects of light and shade, she burned her skin in the bright summer sun.

But true genius takes patience. So Amy kept up her efforts in spite of problems, failures, and frustrations. For she believed that someday she would create something worthy of the name "fine art."

In the meantime, Amy was developing into an attractive and pleasant young woman. She always seemed to say the right thing to the right person, and so made friends everywhere she went. But because she wanted to be accepted into high society, she put on fancy airs and pretended to be wealthy. Amy made the mistake of thinking that the "best" people were those who had the most money, status, and refined manners. She hadn't yet learned that being wealthy is different from being noble or good.

One day, Amy asked her mother if she could invite the girls from her drawing class to their house. "They'd love to see the river and the other things I've sketched. And they've been very nice to me, even though they're all rich and I'm so poor."

"Why shouldn't they be nice to you?" Mrs. March asked, angry that anyone might mistreat her daughter just because she wasn't rich.

"You know as well as I do that money makes a difference with nearly everyone," Amy answered without bitterness. "So can I ask the girls over for lunch next week?"

"Alright. What do you want for lunch? I suppose that sandwiches, fruit, cake, and coffee would be nice."

"Oh, dear, no! We must have lobster and French chocolate and ice cream. The girls are used to such things. Even though I have to work for a living, I want my lunch to be proper and elegant."

"How many young ladies are there?" her mother asked, looking worried.

"Fourteen, but I don't think they'll all come."

"This will be expensive, Amy."

"Not very. I've added up the cost, and I can pay for it myself."

"But since the girls are used to such things, don't you think something simpler might be a pleasant change for them? Then you wouldn't have to spend money on things you don't need, or pretend to be someone you're not."

"If I can't have it the way I want, then I won't have it at all," said Amy. "Besides, I know I can carry it off, if you and Hannah and the girls will help a little bit. I don't see why I can't do it as long as I'm willing to pay for it."

Although Mrs. March wished her children didn't have to learn life's lessons the hard way, she knew that experience was often the best teacher. So she gave Amy permission, as long as her sisters agreed to help.

Amy sent out the invitations, and nearly all the girls accepted. The lunch was scheduled for noon on Monday. But in case of bad weather, the party would be postponed until the next day.

On Monday morning, Amy was up at dawn, dragging everyone out of bed to help set up her lunch. The food was all prepared, the table set beautifully, and everything was in place. At 11 o'clock there was a sudden downpour, but just as quickly the sun came out again. But the rain must have dampened the young ladies' enthusiasm, because no one arrived for the feast. So at 2 p.m., the exhausted family sat down to eat all the food that wouldn't keep until the next day.

On Tuesday morning, the weather was perfect. "They'll surely come today, so we must fly around and get everything ready," announced Amy.

Though Amy didn't admit it, her enthusiasm, like her cake, was getting a little stale. Once again she prepared for the party, but now she found the work annoying and tiring. Still, she was determined to make her party a great success.

But only one girl, Miss Elizabeth Eliott, showed up. The Marches were so gracious and kind to their guest that she had a wonderful time.

When the party was over, Mrs. March commented, "Well, dear, you've had lovely weather for your party."

"Miss Eliott is very sweet, and she seemed to enjoy herself," added Beth.

"And your cake was so much better than mine. If you have any left over, could I take some home?" asked Meg, gently.

"Take it all," sighed Amy, thinking how she'd spent all her savings—and for nothing.

The next day, the Marches sat down to eat left-over salad for their fourth meal in a row. Trying to make Amy feel better, Mr. March said cheerfully, "You know, in ancient times, salad was one of the favorite dishes of kings and queens."

But as the scholarly father started lecturing on the history of salads, the women burst out laughing.

Then Mrs. March said gently, "I'm very sorry you were disappointed, dear, but we all did our best."

"I know," Amy sobbed. "And I'm satisfied. I did what I'd planned to do. It's not my fault that it failed. Let's give all of this food to the Hummels. I'm sick of looking at it. And you shouldn't have to die from an overdose of salads just because I've been a fool," she added, wiping away her tears. "Thank you all very much for helping me. And I'll thank you even more if you don't mention it again for at least a month."

And no one did. But for Amy's birthday, Laury gave her a coral pin in the shape of a tiny lobster.

Chapter 27

$\mathcal{E}$very few weeks, Jo would shut herself up in her attic room, put on her special "writing cap," and work on her novel with all her heart and soul. For the next week or two, she would write day and night—not even taking time to eat, sleep, or see anyone. Her family occasionally peeked in to see how she was doing. If the cap was pulled low across her forehead, it was a sign that hard work was going on. If it had been thrown on the floor, it was a sign of frustration or despair.

She was just recovering from one of these writing "whirlwinds" when she reluctantly agreed to escort old Miss Crocker to a lecture in town. Jo happened to sit next to a young man who was reading a newspaper story. When he finished, he noticed that Jo was reading over his shoulder. Grinning he offered her the paper.

Jo smiled as she read the trashy, but exciting tale of love, mystery, and murder.

"First-rate, isn't it?" he asked enthusiastically.

"I think even you and I could write as well as that," Jo answered.

"I'd sure be lucky if I could!" he exclaimed. "They say that Mrs. Northbury makes a lot of money writing stories like that."

"She does?"

"Sure. She knows just what people like, and gets paid well for writing it."

During the lecture, Jo copied down information about a contest the newspaper was running. If she wrote in that style, maybe she could win the $100 prize for the "best" short story.

Jo told no one about her plan. But the next day, she went right to work. She'd never tried to write a trashy "thriller" before. But she'd read so many books and experienced so many hardships that she was able to create an exciting story. When she finished, she secretly sent off the story.

For six weeks, Jo heard nothing. It was a long time to wait, and a long time to keep a secret. But just when she was beginning to give up all hope, a letter arrived from the newspaper. Jo opened it and started to cry. Inside was an encouraging letter and a check for $100.

All her years of hard work had finally paid off. So with great satisfaction and pride, Jo announced to her astonished family that she had won the prize. Everyone read the story and said it was wonderful. Her father praised the colorful language, original ideas, and thrilling ending. But then the thoughtful, gentle man shook his head and said very softly, "You can do better than this,

Jo. Aim high. Always do what's best—not what pays the most."

"Well, I think the money's the best part of it," said Amy, admiring the check. "What will you do with such a big fortune?"

"Send Beth and Mother to the shore, so Beth can grow stronger."

Jo was so pleased to be able to help her family that she happily spent her time writing more trashy, but profitable stories. Several were published. "The Duke's Daughter" paid the grocery bill. "A Ghostly Hand" put down new carpet. "The Curse of the Coventrys" provided new clothes for everyone. Finally, Jo stopped envying girls who were rich, for now she knew she could take care of herself.

Encouraged by the success of these stories, Jo decided to send her novel off to several publishers. One agreed to print it if she chopped it in half, cutting out those parts that Jo thought were especially well written.

Jo called a family meeting to ask their advice.

"Don't spoil your book, my girl," said her father. "Give it time to ripen, and publish it later."

"But if she publishes it now," argued Mrs. March, "she'll get useful criticism about her work. That will help her know what to do better the next time."

"Don't change a word," said Meg, who believed it was the best book ever written.

"Do as the publisher tells you. He knows what will sell, and we don't," said Amy. "Write a book that's popular, so you can get lots of money and become famous. Then later on you'll be able to write whatever you want."

Jo considered their advice, and then asked, "What do you think, Beth?"

"I'd so much like to see it printed *soon*," Beth said wistfully.

The look of sadness in Beth's eyes and her emphasis on the word "soon" froze Jo's heart with fear. So she decided to make the changes and publish her novel "soon"—before it was too late.

Jo set aside her own ideas and feelings, and bravely laid her beloved "first-born" novel on the table. She ruthlessly chopped and twisted her dear book to please the publisher. But by the time she'd followed everyone's suggestions, nothing special remained of her poor little book.

When the publisher printed it, Jo got $300—and plenty of praise and blame from the critics. Some wrote that it was "realistic, beautiful, and thoughtful." Others thought it "unbelievable, disgusting, and shallow." All seemed to think that the book had a hidden message. "But I only wrote it for fun and for money," sighed Jo. "Now I wish I'd either printed the entire book, or not printed it at all. I hate being misjudged."

It was a hard time for sensitive Jo. But after a while, she was able to figure out which criticism was useful, and which was silly. She could laugh at her poor little book, yet still take pride in the parts that were well written. And she felt wiser and stronger for the experience. "I guess a little criticism won't kill me," said Jo, finally. "And next time, I'll be ready to stand up and take another crack at it."

Chapter 28

$\mathscr{M}$eg began her married life determined to be the "perfect" wife. She wanted her husband to come home every night to a tidy house, a fancy dinner, and a smiling wife. She often told her husband, "Feel free to bring home a friend whenever you like. You don't have to ask me ahead of time. For you'll always find a neat house, a good dinner, and a cheerful wife."

With great love and energy, Meg carefully followed the recipes in *Mrs. Cornelius's Cookbook*. She treated them like complicated math problems, which she tried to solve patiently and dutifully. When she ended up making too much food, she invited her parents and sisters to dinner. When her dishes didn't taste very good, she gave them to the Hummel children. When John showed Meg how much money she was spending on food, she tried to save money by serving only bread and water for a few days. John tried not to complain, and Meg eventually learned how to cook good food without going over her budget.

They were very happy, even after they discovered that they couldn't live on love alone. John still found

Meg beautiful—even first thing in the morning. And Meg still found John romantic—even when he gave her only a quick kiss as he left for work. Soon the little house became a home. But before they worked out all the details, the young couple did what most young couples do. They got themselves into a jam.

John loved jellies. So when the grapes in their yard ripened, Meg decided to make her own jam, which he could have all winter. How hard could it be? She'd seen Hannah make jams, and there was a recipe for grape jelly in *Mrs. Cornelius' Cookbook.* She bought a dozen jam jars and several pounds of sugar. She paid one of the Hummel children to help her pick the grapes. Then she spent a long day picking, boiling, straining, stirring—and waiting for the jelly to thicken. When it stayed runny, she re-read the recipe, re-boiled the grapes, added more sugar, and strained everything again. But still the jelly wouldn't "jell."

Meg longed to run home and ask Mother to come help her. But she and John had agreed that they would never bother anyone with their private worries, mistakes, or quarrels. So Meg wrestled alone all that hot summer day, while the little Hummel child calmly ate bread and drank the liquid grape jam. At five o'clock, Meg finally sat down in the middle of the grape-stained kitchen floor and burst into tears.

At about the same time, John ran into his unmarried friend, Jack Scott. On the spur of the moment, he decided to invite him to dinner that night. He imagined how impressed his bachelor friend would be when John's pretty wife ran out to meet them, a cheerful smile on her lips and a delicious dinner waiting inside their tidy little "mansion."

But as they approached the house, no one ran out to greet them. There was still mud on the doorstep from yesterday's rain. Alarmed, John said, "I'm afraid something has happened. Why don't you wait in the garden, Jack, while I see what's happened to Mrs. Brooke."

Opening the door, John was greeted by the sharp smell of burned sugar. In the kitchen, one pot of jelly was boiling over, another was burning on the stove, and a third had spilled all over the floor. With her apron over her head, the charming Mrs. Brooke was sobbing mournfully.

"My dearest, what's wrong?" cried John, expecting to hear about horrible burns or a family tragedy.

"Oh, John! I'm so tired and hot and frustrated! Help me or I'll die!" Meg threw herself into his arms, getting sticky jam all over his clothing. It was a "sweet" welcome, but not the kind that John had in mind.

"Don't cry, dear," John said, tenderly kissing the top of her head. "Tell me what terrible thing has happened."

"The—the jelly won't jell, and I don't know what to do!"

"Is that all?" John laughed merrily. It was the last time he ever laughed at one of his wife's "tragedies."

"Throw it out the window!" he continued. "I'll buy you tons of jelly if you like. But for heaven's sake, stop crying. For I've brought Jack Scott home to dinner and—"

"John Brooke, how could you do such a thing?" Meg exclaimed, pushing him away.

"But you keep telling me to bring home anyone anytime. I've never done it before. And I'll be damned if I ever do it again!"

"I should hope not! Take him away immediately. I can't see him. And I haven't had time to cook dinner. I thought we could eat at Mother's." And Meg's tears began again.

"It's a problem, I know. But we can pull through, and even have a good time. We're both starving, so we don't care what we eat. A little bread and cheese would be fine." Then, grinning, John teased, "We won't even ask for jelly." That was his second mistake.

Meg found his "joke" cruel, not funny. She retorted, "Take that Mr. Scott up to Mother's. Tell him I'm away, sick, dead—anything. I won't see him. And you two can laugh at me and my jelly as much as you like!" With that, Meg threw her apron on the floor and ran into her room to cry alone.

When Meg finally went down to the kitchen, the Hummel child reported that the two men had eaten bread and cheese. They'd laughed a lot, and Mr. Brooke told her to throw away all the sweet stuff and hide the jars.

Meg longed to go tell Mother. But she was ashamed of her own failure, and didn't want other people to know how "cruel" John had been to her. So she cleaned the kitchen, put on a pretty dress, and waited for John to come home and apologize.

But John saw things differently. He didn't show that he was angry, but he felt that Meg had deserted him in his time of need. It wasn't fair to tell him to bring friends home anytime, and then get angry, blame him, and abandon him when he took her at her word.

By the time he got home, John had calmed down. *Poor little thing!* he thought. *She was trying so hard to please me. She was wrong, of course. But she's young. I must be patient, calm, and kind—but firm, quite firm. I must teach her where she failed in her duty as a wife.*

Meg longed to run and meet John, ask his forgiveness, and let him kiss and comfort her. But she, too, decided to be quite firm and teach him his duty as a husband. So when John walked in the door, Meg calmly rocked in her chair and worked on her sewing—and completely ignored him.

John was disappointed that his wife didn't offer an apology. So he sat down, picked up a paper, and pretended to be more interested in reading it than in talking.

Neither spoke. Both looked quite "calm" and quite "firm." And both felt terribly uncomfortable.

Oh, dear, thought Meg. *Married life is so difficult. As Mother says, you need endless patience, as well as love.* Then Meg remembered other advice her mother had given her—advice she'd thought was silly at the time.

"John is a good man," Mother had said. "But neither of you is perfect. You must remember that, and learn to accept and live with his faults, just as you must with your own. You call him 'fussy.' But that's because he is very precise and values the truth. Never lie or deceive him, Meg. And be very careful not to make him angry with you. John rarely loses his temper. But if he does, it will be hard to make peace with him. So be the first to apologize if you both make mistakes. And try to avoid little arguments, misunderstandings, and hasty words. For they often lead to bitter sorrow and regret."

This was their first serious disagreement. Thinking back on it, Meg realized that her words had been silly and unkind. Her anger seemed childish now. Her eyes filled with tears as she thought of how poor John must have felt when he came home to such a mess. She wasn't sure she could swallow her pride and ask his forgiveness. But then she realized, "This is our first serious disagreement. If I do my part to work it out, then at least I won't feel guilty."

Meg walked slowly across the room, and stood beside her husband. When he didn't turn his head, she bent over and kissed him gently on the forehead.

Of course, that one kiss of apology was better than a thousand words. John held her in his arms and said tenderly, "I was wrong to laugh at those poor little jelly jars. Forgive me, dear. I'll never do it again."

But he did—hundreds of times. And so did Meg. Laughing together, they both agreed that it was the sweetest jelly they'd ever made. For out of that "jam" they learned how to keep the family peace.

A few days later, Meg invited Mr. Scott to dinner. She served a special meal—without a "cooked wife" for the first course. Meg was so charming that Mr. Scott told John he was a "lucky fellow." And all the way home, he pitied himself for not having a wife.

That fall, Meg faced new challenges. Sallie Moffat often invited "that poor" Meg to spend the day at her big house or go shopping with her. Meg started to envy Sallie's pretty things, and pity herself because she didn't have them. Sallie was very kind, and offered to buy things for Meg, or give her some of her own things. But Meg never accepted them, knowing that John wouldn't approve.

Meg knew where John kept his money. He trusted her to take whatever she wanted. He asked only that she pay the bills on time, write down how she'd spent the money, and remember that she was a poor man's wife. Until now, Meg had spent the money wisely, and never worried about showing John the accounting book once a month.

But Meg didn't like having Sallie pity her and treat her as if she were poor. So she started buying a few pretty things that didn't cost very much. Gradually the little things added up. When Meg saw the total at the end of the first month, she felt guilty and scared. But John was so busy for the next two months that he left the accounting up to her.

At the end of the third month, Meg did something she later regretted. Sallie bought a fancy silk dress, and Meg longed for one, too. She was tempted to buy a lovely purple gown on sale for only $50. It was expensive, but she could take $25 from the household fund—if only she dared. And it was only a month until New Year's Day, when Aunt March usually gave Meg and her sisters $25 apiece.

Sallie urged her to buy the dress, and offered to lend her the money. Then the salesman held it up to her, saying, "It's a real bargain, ma'am."

"I'll take it," Meg answered, giving in to the temptation. As they left the store, Sallie laughed, as if it were nothing. But Meg felt as if she'd stolen something, and was waiting for the police to track her down.

Once home, Meg thought the dress seemed less shiny, and it really didn't look very good on her. Instead of giving her delight, it haunted her like the ghost of a terrible mistake.

When they sat down that night to go over the records, Meg started to panic. "John, dear, I'm ashamed to show you my book. I bought something really expensive, though my New Year's money will partly pay for it. But I was sorry as soon as I bought it, for I knew you'd think it was wrong of me."

John glanced at the first few items on the list, and noticed she'd spent $9 on a pair of shoes. Laughing, he said, "I'm not going to beat you for buying a pair of fancy shoes. I'm rather proud of my wife's ankles. And I don't mind if she spends $8 or $9 on a pair of shoes—especially if they're going to last a long time."

"It's worse than shoes. It's a silk dress."

John looked Meg in the eye, and asked in a strangely stiff voice, "Well, dear, what's the total for the last three months?"

Meg turned the page and pointed to the number. It was bad enough without the silk dress. But the extra $50 made it a shocking sum.

For a minute, the room was very still. Trying to control his anger, John said sharply, "I'm sure that the dress will make my wife look as fine as Ned Moffat's wife."

"I know you're angry, John. But it's hard to watch Sallie buy all she wants, and then see her pity me because I can't. I try to be satisfied, but I'm tired of being poor."

The moment she said that, Meg could have bitten out her tongue. Those words deeply wounded John, for he worked hard to support her. Instead of buying things he wanted, he made sacrifices so that Meg could spend money on herself.

John's voice shook as he said quietly, "I was afraid of this. I do my best, Meg."

Those few words broke Meg's heart more than any scolding. "Oh, John, my dear, kind, hard-working husband. I didn't mean it! I don't know how I could say something so untrue and ungrateful!"

John was very kind and forgave her right away. But Meg knew she'd broken her promise to love him for better or for worse, for richer and for poorer. Not only had she spent his hard-earned money foolishly, but then she blamed him for being poor.

For the next week, John worked so late that he didn't come home until long after Meg had cried herself to sleep. Then Meg found out he'd cancelled the order for a new overcoat to replace his old, worn-out one. When she asked why, John said simply, "I can't afford it, dear."

Meg said no more. But John found her a few minutes later, with her face buried in the old overcoat, crying as if her heart would break.

That night, they had a long talk. Meg realized

that being poor had given John the strength and courage to make his own way in the world. And it had taught him to accept his loved ones' shortcomings with tender patience. Now, instead of resenting his poverty, Meg loved her husband even more for it.

The next day, Meg put her pride in her pocket, went to Sallie, and told her the truth. She asked her friend to buy the silk dress from her as a favor. Then Meg took the money and bought the overcoat John wanted and needed.

When John came home, Meg put on the new overcoat and asked, "How do you like my new silk gown?"

After that, John was eager to come home early, and Meg spent less time shopping with Sallie. Every morning, a very happy husband put on the overcoat. And every evening a devoted wife took it off.

The first year of marriage continued happily until midsummer. Then Meg experienced a new, tender, and deeply touching moment in her life.

When Laury came home from college, he first stopped at Meg's house. To his surprise, Hannah greeted him at the door, and explained that everybody else was upstairs.

Soon Jo appeared in the living room, proudly carrying a bundle wrapped in a blanket. "Close your eyes and hold out your arms," she told Laury, her eyes twinkling.

When Laury opened his eyes, he stared in shock. "Twins, for goodness sake! Quick! Somebody take 'em before I drop them both!"

Jo rescued the babies, while Laury smiled lovingly at the newborn twins. "Are they both boys? What are you going to name them?"

John answered proudly, "A boy and a girl. Aren't they wonderful?"

"The most amazing children I've ever seen," Laury agreed.

"The boy's name will be John Laurence, and the girl will be Margaret," explained Amy. "We'll call her Daisy, so as not to confuse her with Meg. And I guess we'll call the boy Jack or something."

"Since 'demi' means 'half,' and a 'demijohn' is a kind of jug," Laury began, "let's call him Demijohn—Demi for short!"

"Daisy and Demi—just the thing! I knew Laury would do it!" exclaimed Jo, clapping her hands.

And Laury really did "do it." From that time on, the babies were always called "Daisy" and "Demi."

Chapter 29

"Come, Jo. It's time."

"For what?"

Amy reminded Jo that she'd promised to spend the afternoon visiting some of their neighbors. But Jo hated getting all dressed up on a pleasant Saturday afternoon. Even worse, she hated having to act like a "proper young lady" and make foolish small talk with people she thought rich and snobby.

But a promise was a promise. So Jo put down her pen and put on her hat.

"Jo March! You don't plan on leaving the house looking like that, do you?" Amy exclaimed in horror.

"Why not? I'm cool and comfortable. If people care more about my clothes than about me, then I don't want to see them."

"But, Jo, you look so noble when you wear your best clothes. And I'm afraid to go alone. Do, please, come and take care of me."

"I don't know which is more absurd—my being noble or your being afraid to socialize. Tell me exactly what to do, and I'll try to obey your commands."

"You're a perfect angel, Jo," said Amy.

Then she picked out clothes for Jo to wear, ordered her to keep her shoulders back, inspected her one more time, and scolded, "You forgot to button one of your cuffs. You must be careful about all the little details, Jo, for it's the details make up the pleasing whole."

Jo sighed and said, "I'm perfectly miserable. But if you think I'm presentable, then I shall die happy."

As they approached the first house, Amy said, "Now Jo, dear, the Chesters consider themselves very elegant people. So I want you to be on your best behavior. Just be calm, cool, and quiet. That's safe and ladylike, and you can easily do it for fifteen minutes."

"So you want me to act 'calm, cool, and quiet'? Yes, I think I can play the part of a snobby young lady for fifteen minutes."

Amy looked relieved—until she realized that Jo took her at her word. For there sat Jo, calm as a dead fish, cold as an iceberg, and silent as a potato. Each time the Chesters tried to draw her out, she answered with a simple "yes" or "no." As Amy and Jo left the house, they heard Mrs. Chester comment, "That Miss Josephine March is such a dull creature—and a snob!"

Jo laughed, but Amy frowned. "Do try to be sociable at the Lambs' house. Gossip like the other girls, and flirt with the boys. The Lambs are wealthy, and valuable people for us to know. Please try to make a good impression on them."

"OK, then. Now I'll play the role of a charming girl—and imitate Miss May Chester."

As soon as they arrived, Mrs. Lamb pulled Amy aside to tell her a long story about her daughter's illness. That left Jo alone to mix with the young ladies and young gentlemen. Amy saw them gather around Jo, and soon heard gales of laughter coming from them. Amy gasped and blushed when she finally heard bits of what Jo was saying. For Jo was entertaining them with stories of Amy's adventures as a young child. Her explanation of how Amy painted old clothing to make it look new completely humiliated her.

Unable to get away from Mrs. Lamb, Amy was relieved when she finally heard Mrs. Lamb's daughter change the subject. "We read one of your stories the other day and enjoyed it very much," the young lady said politely.

"Sorry you couldn't find anything better to read," Jo answered stiffly. "I write that rubbish because common people pay to read it, and I need the money."

Then Jo abruptly turned away and whisked Amy out of the house.

"Didn't I do well?" Jo asked, pleased with her performance.

"Nothing could have been worse," Amy answered. "Why did you say those things?"

"Why, to amuse them. They know we're poor, so it's no use pretending we can have things as easy and fine as they do."

"But you don't need to keep reminding them how poor we are. You don't have enough pride. And you never know when to speak and when to keep quiet."

Poor Jo looked upset. "Then how shall I behave here?" she asked, as they reached the Browns' house.

"Just as you please. I wash my hands of you," was Amy's short answer.

"Then I'll enjoy myself with the boys."

Amy spent time amusing Miss Brown and Mr. Tudor, a young gentleman whose uncle had married a distant relative of an English lord. Amy was impressed by his family background, and hated to tear herself away from his company.

When she finally found Jo, Amy was horrified by what she saw. Jo was sitting cross-legged on the grass, with a muddy dog lying on her white holiday dress. A small child was catching turtles with the pretty handkerchief Amy had lent her. And another child was using Jo's best hat to catch gingerbread crumbs. But everyone was having a good time.

As they left the Browns' house, Amy asked, "Why do you always avoid Mr. Tudor?"

"Don't like him. He puts on airs, snubs his sisters, and disrespects his parents."

"You could at least treat him politely. You greeted him with only a cool nod. But you smiled and shook Tommy Chamberlain's hand. And Tommy's father only works in a grocery store. If you'd treated each boy the opposite way, that would have been right."

"No, it wouldn't," answered Jo. "I neither like, respect, nor admire Tudor—even if he is related to a lord. Tommy's poor and shy and smart and good. Even though his father handles brown paper bags instead of gold and silver, he's a true gentleman."

"Women should learn to be pleasant—especially poor women. For they have no other way to repay the kindness they receive. If you'd remember that, people would like you more than me."

"I wish it were easy for me to do little things to please people, the way it is for you," Jo sighed. "For me, it's easier to risk my life for a person than be pleasant to him when I don't feel like it. It's awful to have such strong likes and dislikes."

"It's even worse that you can't hide them. I don't approve of Tudor any more than you do. But I don't feel I have to tell him so. You don't have to be disagreeable just because he is."

"But I think girls ought to let boys know

when they're wrong. I know that from trying to make Laury a better person."

"Laury's special. He's not like other boys," insisted Amy.

"So we're supposed to accept people and things we hate, just because we're poor?"

"I can't argue that it's right. I only know that it's the way things work. And people who try to change the world for the better only get laughed at for their efforts."

"Well, I'd be glad to reform things. You'll do better in the world. But I'll have a great time trying to improve it. I rather enjoy stirring people up."

"Well, calm down, now," Amy warned, as they approached Aunt March's house. "Don't upset Aunt with your revolutionary ideas."

"I'll try not to. But when I'm with her, revolutionary speeches just pop out of my mouth. I can't help it."

Amy and Jo were surprised to find their Aunt Carrol involved in a very serious discussion with Aunt March. The two women stopped talking as soon as the girls entered. It was clear that they'd been talking about their nieces.

"Are you going to help with the charity fair, dear?" Mrs. Carrol asked Amy.

"Yes, Aunt. Mrs. Chester asked me if I could work at one of the tables, since I have no money, but only time, to give."

"I'm not," announced Jo. "The Chesters think they're doing us a great favor to allow us to work at their high society fair."

"But the fair is to help the freed slaves. It's not just an excuse for a party," Amy explained. "I think the Chesters are very kind to let me share in the work and the fun."

"Quite right and proper. I like your grateful spirit, my dear. It's a pleasure to help people who appreciate our efforts. Some people do not, and that is annoying," said Aunt March, looking fiercely at Jo.

"I don't like favors. They make me feel like a slave. I'd rather do everything for myself and be perfectly independent," answered Jo, not knowing that these angry words would cost her several years of pleasure.

"I told you so," said Aunt March, nodding at Aunt Carrol.

"Do you speak French, dear?" asked Mrs. Carrol, touching Amy's hand.

"Pretty well, thanks to Aunt March. She lets Esther talk to me as often as I like," answered Amy, with a grateful look, which made the old lady smile.

"And you?" Mrs. Carrol asked Jo.

"Don't know a word. Can't stand French; it's such a slippery, silly sort of language."

The ladies exchanged another look. Then Aunt March asked Amy, "And your eyes aren't bothering you any more?"

"Not at all, thank you ma'am. I'm very well. And I'm planning to work hard so that I'll be ready to go to Rome, if ever that joyful opportunity comes my way."

"Good girl! You deserve to go. And I'm sure you will someday," said Aunt March, patting Amy's hand.

"Good girl! Bless your buttons!" squawked Polly.

"What an observant bird," remarked the old lady.

"Time to rise, my dear?" cried Polly, hopping toward the dish of sugar cubes.

"Yes, thank you. Let's go, Amy," said Jo abruptly. She shook her aunts' hands in a gentlemanly way, but Amy kissed them both on the cheek. The two ladies were left with the impression of shadow and sunshine.

"You'd better do it, Mary," said Aunt March, after the nieces had left. "I'll supply the money."

Aunt Carrol replied, "I certainly will, if her mother and father agree."

Chapter 30

$\mathcal{M}$rs. Chester's fair was so very elegant that the young ladies of the neighborhood thought it a great honor to be asked to work at a table. Amy was delighted to be put in charge of the art table. It was placed near the entrance and always drew a crowd.

For weeks, Amy worked hard to get people to donate art for her table. Everything was going smoothly, except for one thing. Mrs. Chester's daughter May was jealous because Amy was a better artist and more popular with the boys. So when May heard a rumor that "one of the March girls" had been making fun of her at the Lambs' house, she complained to her mother. Assuming it was Amy, not Jo, who had ridiculed her daughter, Mrs. Chester decided to seek revenge.

So the evening before the fair opened, Mrs. Chester and May approached Amy, who was putting the finishing touches on her pretty table. "I'm sorry, dear," Mrs. Chester said coldly, "but I think my own daughter should take over the art table. It's the most popular table—and some would say the most attractive one. Since we are the sponsors of the fair, it makes sense for one of my girls to be here. Wouldn't you like the flower table instead? The younger girls tried to tend it, but it's been hard for them."

"And the flower table," May sneered sarcastically, "is always a favorite with the gentlemen."

"As you wish, Mrs. Chester," Amy said calmly, trying hard to control her anger.

"I suppose you can put your own artwork on the flower table, if you like," added May.

"Oh, certainly, if it's in your way," Amy answered, sweeping her artwork into her apron and walking away.

The little girls at the flower table welcomed Amy's help and her wonderful artwork. But it was late, and Amy was tired. The little girls were no help, and it was too late to ask people to contribute more flowers.

When Amy told her story at home, everyone was indignant. Her mother said it was a shame, but she'd done the right thing. Jo said she should tell those mean people she wouldn't work at the fair, after all.

"Just because they're mean is no reason I should be mean. I think I have a right to feel angry and hurt, but I don't intend to show it. That will affect them more than if I act angry or offended, won't it, Marmee?"

"That's right, my dear. It's best to answer meanness with kindness—though it's hard to do sometimes."

The next morning, Amy saw a group of girls, standing around May's table and gossiping. At one point she overheard May say sadly, "It's too late to fill up the table with other artwork. It was perfect before Amy took away the things she'd donated. Now it's spoiled."

"She'd probably put them back if you asked her," someone suggested.

"How could I after all the fuss?" May sighed.

Amy called across the room, "You're welcome to have them if you want them, May. You don't even have to ask. I was just thinking I'd offer to put them back because they belong on your table, not mine. Please take them, and forgive me if I was hasty in taking them away last night."

With a nod and a smile, Amy delivered her artwork and hurried back to her own table.

"Now, I'd call that lovely of her, wouldn't you?" exclaimed one girl.

But another young lady answered, "Oh, sure. Very lovely, since she knew she couldn't sell them at her own table."

For a minute, Amy was sorry that she'd made the sacrifice. But then she realized it was better to do the right thing, and clear the air.

It was a very long, hard day for Amy. The little girls ran off to play, leaving Amy alone at her table. Not many people wanted to buy flowers because they could grow them in their own gardens. Before long, even the pretty bouquets she'd arranged began to droop. She dreaded going back the next day.

Amy looked sadly across at the art table. It was the most attractive table in the room. People crowded around the table, and May collected money all day long.

The next morning, Amy was surprised to see Jo all dressed up. She hinted that "the tables were about to be turned."

"Don't do anything rude, Jo," begged Amy.

"I merely intend to make myself so charming that people will spend the entire day at your table. Laury and his boys will help, and we'll have a good time."

When Jo told Laury how badly Amy had been treated, he promised to make his friends buy every flower at her table. And he had the Laurences' gardener send over their finest flowers, all arranged perfectly.

Soon Amy's corner became the liveliest spot in the room. Laury and his friends bought up all the flowers, and everyone admired Amy's taste.

Wondering what had happened to Amy's own artwork, Jo then walked over to May's table. She didn't see any of Amy's things, but all the vases that May had painted were still on the table.

"How is Amy doing?" asked May, by now feeling bad about the way she'd acted.

"She's sold everything on her table, and now she's enjoying herself. You know, 'the flower table is always a favorite with the gentlemen.'"

"Well, all of Amy's work sold out long ago, and it made a lot of money for our charity," May answered.

Jo rushed back to tell the good news. Then Amy ordered Laury's friends to buy things from the other tables. "Gentlemen, I want you to be as generous with them as you've been with me—especially the art table."

"To hear is to obey, though 'March' is fairer far than 'May'!" said young Mr. Parker, taking a bow.

"Buy the vases," Amy whispered to Laury.

The fair turned out to be a great success. As they were leaving, May gave Amy a hug and a look that said "forgive and forget." Amy did, and was satisfied.

When Amy got home, she found May's vases lined up on the mantelpiece, each overflowing with flowers. "A reward for Miss March's generous spirit!" Laury announced.

"You've got more principle and generosity and nobleness of spirit than I thought, Amy. And I respect you for it with all my heart," said Jo.

"Yes, we all do," added Beth. "And we love you for being so ready to forgive."

"Why, you needn't praise me so much. I only did as I'd want others to do to me. You laugh at me when I say I want to be a lady. But by that I mean a true gentlewoman in both thought and action. I want to be above the meanness and foolishness that spoil so many women. I have a long way to go, but someday I'd like to be the kind of woman that Mother is."

Jo hugged her and said, "Now I understand what you mean, and I'll never laugh at you again. I think you've learned the secret to true politeness, and I'd like to take lessons from you."

A week later, Mrs. March received a letter from Aunt Carrol. Beth and Jo watched her read it with delight, and asked what she'd said.

"Aunt Carrol is going abroad next month, and she wants—"

"—me to go with her!" Jo interrupted, flying out of her chair in joy.

"No, dear. Not you. Amy."

"Oh, Mother! She's too young. I'm the oldest, and I've wanted it for so long. It would do me so much good. I must go! Amy has all the fun, and I have all the work. It isn't fair!"

"I'm afraid it's partly your own fault, dear," explained Mrs. March gently. "Aunt spoke to me at the fair, and said she regretted your rudeness. In her letter she writes, 'I'd planned at first to ask Jo.

But she said that doesn't like favors and she hates French. Amy will make a pleasant companion for her cousin Flo. And she will accept the opportunity with gratitude.'"

"Oh, my big mouth! My horrible mouth! Why can't I learn to keep it quiet?" groaned Jo.

"I wish you could have gone," Mrs. March said. "But since you can't, try not to spoil Amy's pleasure."

"I'll try," said Jo, unable to hold back the tears. "And I'll try to learn from Amy's example. But it won't be easy. I'm so bitterly disappointed."

Then Beth whispered to Jo, "I don't mean to be selfish, but I'm glad you're not going yet. I still need you right now."

As soon as Amy heard the wonderful news, she began sorting her paints and packing her pencils. She let her family take care of such "unimportant details" as clothes, passports, and money.

"This isn't just a pleasure trip," Amy explained. "It will determine my career. If I have a future as an artist, I'll find out in Rome."

"And if you don't?" asked Jo.

"Then I'll come home and teach drawing for my living."

"No, you won't. You hate hard work. You'll end up marrying some rich man and live in luxury all your life," said Jo.

"I doubt it," answered Amy. "But that would make me happy, too. If I can't be an artist myself,

I'd like to be able to give money to help those who are."

Jo sighed. "Your wishes always come true, and mine never do."

"Would you like to go to Europe?" asked Amy.

"You bet!"

"Well, I'd be happy to send for you in a year or two, if I can. Then we could see all the great works of art."

"Thank you. And I'll be happy to remind you of your promise."

At last, Mr. March and Laury took Amy's bags and drove her to the port. Jo tried to look cheerful. But as the carriage disappeared from view, Jo ran up to the attic and cried and cried.

Amy didn't break down until the ship was just about to leave. Then she suddenly realized that a whole ocean was about to separate her from the people she loved best. She held onto Laury one last time and sobbed, "Oh, take care of them for me. And if anything happens—"

"I will, dear. I will. And if anything happens, I'll come and comfort you," whispered Laury, little dreaming that someday he would be called upon to keep his word.

So the happy-hearted girl sailed away, while her father and friend watched from shore, hoping that nothing but good fortune would come her way.

Chapter 31

London, England

Dearest People,

At last we've arrived in England!

Aunt Carrol and cousin Flo were seasick the whole way over. So after I took care of them, I went on-deck and enjoyed myself. Such beautiful sunsets! Such splendid air and rolling waves! Everyone was very kind to me, especially the officers. Don't laugh, Jo. Gentlemen can come in very handy on a ship. And if I didn't let them help me, they'd have nothing to do and would probably smoke themselves to death.

It was heavenly, but I was glad to see the Irish coast. It was so green and sunny, with ruins on the hills and deer feeding in the parks.

One of my new acquaintances, Mr. Lennox, got off the ship in Ireland. But guess what that silly Lennox did! He had a bouquet of flowers sent to my room, with a card saying, "Compliments of Robert Lennox." Wasn't that fun, girls? I really like traveling.

Then we took a train from the coast to London. It was like riding through a long picture gallery, full of lovely landscapes. I'd never seen such perfect colors—the grass was so green, the sky so blue, the grains so yellow, the woods so dark. At one point, Flo jumped up and pointed to a gray building in the trees. "Oh, what a lovely castle!" she shouted. "Can't we visit it sometime? Please, Papa!"

Without looking up from his boots, Uncle calmly answered, "No, my dear. Not unless you want to drink beer. That's not a castle; it's a brewery."

Of course, it was raining when we got to London. We couldn't see anything except fog and umbrellas. But we still shopped a little between the showers. Aunt Mary bought me some lovely new things—a white hat with a blue feather, and a matching dress.

Everyone rides horses around here—old men, fat ladies, little children. But they look so stiff. I'd love to show them how to ride like an American—fast and free. The young people do a lot of flirting. I saw one couple exchange rosebuds, which British lovers wear in buttonholes. I thought that was a rather nice little idea.

Who do you think we ran into yesterday afternoon? Laury's English friends, Fred and Frank Vaughn! They've both gotten so tall, and Frank is walking better now. Laury told them we'd be here, and they invited us to the theater. Frank devoted himself to Flo. And Fred and I talked about the past, present, and future as if we'd known each other all our lives. Tell Beth that Frank asked how she was doing, and said he was sorry to hear she'd been ill. Fred still remembers Jo's big hat, and the fun we had at "Camp Laurence." It seems like ages ago, doesn't it?

I can hardly sleep, my room's so full of pretty things. And my head's a jumble of theaters, gowns, and gentlemen who twirl their blond mustaches like true English noblemen.

I miss you all, and can't wait to see you again.

> With all my love,
> Amy

Paris, France

Dear girls,

In my last letter, I told you about how kind the Vaughns were. What I liked best were our visits together to the art museums—all those rooms filled with pictures by the great English painters! London was wonderful, thanks to Fred and Frank. We were very sorry to leave them. Grace and I have become great friends, and the boys have been very nice fellows—especially Fred. We were so glad they promised to meet us in Rome next winter.

Well, we'd just arrived here in Paris when Fred unexpectedly showed up. He said he'd come here for a little vacation on his way to Switzerland. Aunt looked worried at first. But Fred's so polite and speaks French so well that we're all very glad he came. Uncle doesn't know more than ten words in French. He tries to make up for it by speaking English very loudly—as if that would help people understand him!

Such delightful times we're having! Sightseeing from morning till night, and stopping for nice lunches in the cafés. I spend every rainy day at the Louvre, awed by the wonderful paintings. And the shops! The jewelry almost drives me crazy because I can't afford to buy anything. Fred wanted to give me something, but of course I wouldn't let him.

In the evenings, we sometimes just sit on our balcony, talking and looking up at the sparkling lights of the city. Fred is very entertaining. In fact, he's the most pleasant young man I've ever known—except for Laury, whose manners are even more charming. I only wish that Fred had brown hair, for I think dark-haired men are much more handsome than blonds. But the Vaughns are very rich and come from a fine family, so I shouldn't complain.

I'll keep writing in my diary, as Father advised. That and my sketchbook will give you a better idea of my trip than these scribbled letters.

> Hugs and kisses,
> Amy

Heidelberg, Germany

My dear Marmee,

Some important things have been happening, and I wish you were here.

One moonlit night, we were sailing up the Rhine River. About one o'clock, Flo and I woke up to beautiful music. Fred and some German students he'd met were singing a serenade beneath our window. It was the most romantic thing I've ever seen—the river, the boats, the castles! There was moonlight everywhere, and music that would melt a heart of stone.

When they were done, we threw down some flowers. They picked them up, kissed their hands to us, and went off laughing. The next morning, Fred showed me one of the crumpled flowers he'd saved, and he looked at me very sweetly. I laughed and said Flo had tossed it at him. He looked disappointed and threw it away.

At Baden-Baden, Fred lost some money gambling, and I scolded him. He needs someone to look after him. Kate once said she hoped he'd marry soon, and I agree that it would be a good thing for him.

Fred has been so kind and jolly that we've all become fond of him. Now I'm wondering if the moonlight walks, balcony talks, and daily adventures have meant more to him than just having fun with a traveling companion. I haven't flirted with him—truly, Mother!— and have tried to act the way you taught me. I can't help it, though, if people like me.

Now I know you'll shake your head and the girls will say it's wrong. But I've made up my mind. If Fred asks me to marry him, I will say "yes." I'm not madly in love with him, but I do like him. We get along well, and I could learn to love him if he loves me and lets me do what I want. He's handsome, young, smart, and very rich—much, much richer than the Laurences. His family are kind, well-bred, generous people, and they like me. Maybe it seems wrong to marry someone for his money, but I hate being poor. One of us MUST marry someone rich. Meg didn't, Jo won't, and Beth can't right now. So I shall, and that will help the whole family.

Last night at sunset, I was sitting alone outside the castle, trying to sketch the beautiful gardens. I felt like I was in a romantic storybook—the rolling river below and the sound of a band in the distance. I had a feeling something was going to happen, and I was ready for it.

After a while, I heard Fred's voice. He looked so upset that I asked what was wrong. He'd just gotten a letter, begging him to come home, for Frank was very ill. Fred had only enough time to say goodbye to me. I felt sorry for him, and disappointed for myself. But then he looked at me tenderly and said, "I'll come back as soon as I can. You won't forget me, will you, Amy?"

I didn't promise, but I shook his hand. I know he wanted to say more, but there wasn't time. We'll see each other again in Rome. And then, if I don't change my mind, when he says, "Will you, please?" I'll say, "Yes, thank you."

Of course, this is all very private. But I wanted you to know what's going on. Don't worry about me. You know I'm always careful, and I won't do anything rash. But send me as much advice as you want. I'll use it if I can. I really wish I could see you for a good long talk, Marmee.

Love,
Amy

Chapter 32

"*J*o, I'm worried about Beth."

"Why, Mother? She seems a bit stronger than before."

"It's not her health; it's her spirits," Mrs. March explained. "She sits alone and doesn't talk to Father as much as before. When she sings, the songs are always sad ones. I found her crying over Meg's babies the other day. Something's on her mind. I've tried to ask her about it, but I don't want to force her to tell me. Would you try finding out what it is?"

"I think she's growing up, and has a woman's hopes and fears and dreams. Why, Mother, Beth's eighteen, though we still treat her like a child."

"How fast you do grow up," sighed Mrs. March, with a tender smile.

"Can't be helped, Marmee. So you'll just have to let your little birds leave the nest. But I promise never to hop very far away."

"Now that Meg's gone, I know I can count on you, Jo. The only thing I wish for is to have Beth grow strong and cheerful again."

"Just one wish? Aren't you the lucky woman! I've got loads of things I wish for."

"What are they, my dear?"

"After I take care of Beth's problem, I'll tell you mine."

For the next few days, Jo watched Beth closely. One Saturday afternoon, she saw Beth looking out the window sadly. When Beth heard Laury call up to them, she leaned forward, smiled, and nodded. Then she whispered, as if to herself, "How strong and healthy and happy that dear boy looks."

Then Beth's smile disappeared as quickly as it had come. A tear fell onto the windowsill, and she looked wistfully off into the distance.

Instead of talking with Beth, Jo relied on her own observations, lively imagination, and experience in writing romance stories. In Jo's mind, there was only one explanation. Beth must have fallen in love with Laury!

But what if Laury didn't love her back? "Why, he'll just have to," Jo said to herself. "I'll make him!"

Everyone seemed to think that Laury was growing fonder than ever of Jo. Of course, Jo enjoyed playing and joking with the fellow. But she had no interest in having a romantic relationship with him. So every time he made a move, she stopped it right away.

When Laury first went to college, he fell in

love with a different woman every month. Jo was amused by his changing feelings—first hope, then despair, and finally sorrowful acceptance. But one day, Laury hinted that he'd found his one true love. He announced that he was going to become a serious student so that he might win her over.

That night, as usual, Beth lay on the sofa, and Laury sat near her. He was very gentle and kind to her, and entertained her with gossip about college life. Jo watched, and thought she saw a special tenderness in the way Laury tucked in the blanket over Beth's feet.

She would be so good for him, Jo thought. *And he could make her life so easy and pleasant. If only he loved her. And I do believe he would if only the rest of us were out of the way.*

Now that Meg was gone and Amy in Europe, that left only Jo to get out of the way. But where could she go?

Just then, Laury got up from his chair, and sat down next to Jo on the sofa. He spread out his arms on the back of the sofa, and stretched his feet out in front.

Jo glared at him and asked sharply, "So how many bouquets of flowers have you sent Miss Randal this week?"

"Not a single one. I swear. Besides, she's engaged."

"Well, I'm glad. It's a foolish waste of your

money to send flowers and things to silly girls you don't really care about."

"That's because the sensible girls I do care about won't let me send them 'flowers and things.'"

"You know that Mother doesn't approve of flirting. And you do flirt a lot, Laury."

"Wish I could say the same for you."

"Well, it does look like fun. But I just can't seem to learn how to do it."

"Take lessons from Amy. She's got a real talent for it."

"Yes, she does. And she never seems to go too far. I guess some people can please without trying. And others of us always say and do the wrong thing at the wrong time."

"Well, I'm glad you can't flirt. It's refreshing to see a sensible girl who can be jolly and kind without making a fool of herself. Some of the girls I know go too far. If they only knew how we fellows talk about them afterward, they'd change their ways."

"Girls say even worse things about the fellows. For you're as silly as they are. If you acted properly, then they would, too. But since you seem to like their nonsense, they keep it up, and then you blame them."

"We may sometimes act as if we liked flirts. But gentlemen never talk about the modest girls behind their backs—except with respect."

"If you really mean that, Laury, then go and devote yourself to one of those 'modest girls' you say you respect."

"You really advise that?" asked Laury, looking both pleased and anxious.

"Yes, I do. But first wait till you finish college. In the meantime make yourself worthy of—" Jo caught herself just in time. "You know, whoever she may be."

That night, Jo heard Beth sobbing quietly. Anxiously she asked, "What is it, dear?"

"I thought you were asleep," Beth answered, trying to choke back the tears.

"Is it the old pain, Bethy?"

"No. It's a new one. But I can bear it."

"Tell me all about it, and let me cure it as I did the other one."

"You can't. There is no cure." Beth clung to her sister, and cried so despairingly that Jo was frightened.

"Where's the pain? Shall I get Mother?"

"No, no. Don't tell her. I'll be better soon. I'll be quiet now and go to sleep. I promise."

Jo sat silently with her for a few minutes. Finally she asked tenderly, "Is something bothering you, dear?"

Silence. Then finally Beth answered, "Yes, Jo."

"Wouldn't you feel better if you told me about it?"

"Not now. Not yet."

"Then I won't insist. But remember, Bethy, that Mother and I are always glad to listen and help you."

"I know. I'll tell you when it's time."

The next day, Beth seemed happier again. But Jo made up her mind to "get out of the way" so Laury would forget about her, and instead fall in love with Beth.

A few days later, Jo decided to share her plans with her mother. "You asked me the other day what I wished for, Marmee. One thing is to go away somewhere this winter."

"Why, Jo?"

"I feel restless. I want to see and do and learn more than I can here. If you don't need me this winter, I'd like to hop to New York and try my wings. You mentioned that your friend, Mrs. Kirke, was looking for someone to sew for her and teach her children."

"You wouldn't mind working at the large boarding house they own?"

"It's honest work, and I'm willing to work hard."

"But what about your writing?"

"I may not have time to write in New York. But I'll see and hear new things that will give me fresh ideas for my stories."

"Are those your only reasons for going away?"

"No, Mother." Jo paused, and then explained. "It may be vain and wrong for me to think this, but I'm afraid that Laury is becoming too fond of me."

"Then you don't feel the same way about him?"

"Goodness, no! I love the dear boy like a friend. But that's all."

"Well, I must admit that I don't think the two of you are right for each other. You're too much alike—hot-tempered, strong-willed, and fond of your freedom."

"But Laury's such a catch. Mrs. Moffat would think you were crazy not to have me marry him."

"Ah, Jo, all mothers hope for the same thing—to see their children happy. Meg is happy, and I'm pleased with her success. You should enjoy your liberty until you get tired of it. For only then will you find that there's something sweeter than freedom. I'm concerned about Amy, but her good sense will help her. As for Beth, I hope only that she may be healthy. By the way, she's seemed happier the past day or two. Have you spoken with her?"

"Yes. She admitted that something was bothering her, and she promised to tell me about it when the time was right. But I think I've figured out what it is."

Jo explained. Mrs. March looked doubtful,

but she agreed that Jo should go away for a while so that Laury could get over his feelings for her. Jo hoped that Laury would get over her as easily as he'd gotten over his other crushes.

That evening, the Marches had a family meeting, and agreed to Jo's plan. Mrs. Kirke was glad to offer Jo her home and enough work to support herself independently.

When everything was arranged, Jo anxiously told Laury the plan. To her surprise and relief, he took it very quietly. He did indeed seem to be keeping his promise to turn over a new leaf.

The night before she left, Jo said to Beth, "I want you to take special care of something while I'm gone."

"You mean your papers?"

"No. I mean Laury. Be very good to him, won't you?"

"Of course. But I can't take your place, and he'll miss you very much."

"Oh, he'll survive. So remember. I'm counting on you to make sure he's happy and doesn't get into too much trouble."

"I'll do my best, for your sake," Beth promised, wondering why Jo looked at her so strangely.

When Laury said goodbye, he whispered earnestly, "It won't do a bit of good to go away, Jo. I'm keeping my eye on you. So watch what you do, or I'll come get you and bring you home."

Chapter 33

New York
November

Dear Marmee and Beth,

I've got heaps to tell, even though I'm not a fine young lady traveling in Europe, like Amy.

As the train pulled out of the station and I lost sight of Father's dear old face, I almost shed a tear. But next to me was a lady with four small children, all crying. So every time they opened their mouths to scream, I popped in a piece of Hannah's gingerbread. The sun came out, and we all ended up enjoying the trip.

Mrs. Kirke welcomed me so kindly that I felt right at home—even in that big boarding house full of strangers. My room is in the attic, but there's a nice table by a sunny window where I can write whenever I like. The two little Kirke girls are pretty, though rather spoiled. But I won them over when I told them the story of "The Seven Bad Pigs." So I think I'll do well as their governess.

"Now, my dear, make yourself at home," said Mrs. K in her motherly way. "I'm on the go from morning to night, taking care of my boarding house and all the people who rent rooms in it. But it's a relief to know the children are safe with you. There are some pleasant people in the house, and your evenings are always free if you'd like to socialize."

But I'm really shy, though no one believes it. So at first I was worried about eating at the big table with all the boarders.

My first day here, I spent time settling into my new "nest." Then I started down the many stairs to the first floor. That's when I saw something I liked. The little servant girl was trying to carry a large bucket of coal up the stairs. A gentleman came along behind her, took the heavy load out of her hand, and carried it all the way up the stairs. He nodded to her and said with a thick foreign accent, "The little back is too young for such heaviness."

Wasn't that good of him? As Father says, little things show one's true character. When I mentioned this to Mrs. K, she laughed and said, "That must have been Professor Behr. He's always doing things like that."

Now don't laugh at his awful name. It isn't pronounced "Bear" or "Beer"—but something in between. Mrs. K told me he was from Berlin, Germany. She said he's very well educated and kind, but very poor. His sister married an American man, but then they both died. So he helps support his two little orphan nephews, Franz and Emil. He earns money by giving lessons in the room that's next to the nursery, where I sew and look after Mrs. K's children. There's a glass door in between, so I'm going to peep in on him. Then I'll tell you how he looks. He's almost forty, Marmee, so you don't have to worry.

Tuesday Evening

What a morning! The children kept running around wildly instead of learning their lessons. At one point I really thought I'd have to tie them down. But then I had an idea. Why not try gymnastics? So I kept them moving until they were glad to sit down and rest.

That gave me a chance to spy on Professor Behr. He's rather large, with a bushy beard, the kindest eyes I've ever seen, and a wonderful big voice. His clothes are worn out, but he looks like a gentleman, even though his jacket is missing two buttons.

This morning, he arranged his books on the shelf, turned the plant on the windowsill toward the sun, and stroked the cat, who welcomed him like an old friend.

Then there was a light knock at the door. "Come in!" he called out in a loud, clear voice.

A tiny morsel of a child entered the room, carrying a big book. Slamming it on the table, she ran to meet him. "Me wants my Behr!"

"Then you shall have your Behr, my little Tina," said the Professor. Laughing, he picked her up and held her high in the air, while she bent down to kiss him.

"Now me muss study my lesson," she said.

So he gave her a pencil and paper, opened up the dictionary she'd brought, and watched in a fatherly way as the little girl scribbled words.

I later found out that Tina is the child of the French woman who does the ironing in the house. The little thing loves Mr. Behr, and follows him around the house like a puppy. This delights him, for he is very fond of children, even though he's a bachelor.

Then two snobby young ladies arrived for their German lessons. They didn't pay attention to their teacher, and kept making the same mistakes over and over. I pitied the poor man, for it must have been hard for him not to lose his patience.

That night Mrs. Kirke encouraged me to have dinner with the boarders, and invited me to sit next to her. The long table was full. The gentlemen shoveled in their food and disappeared as soon as they were done. The young couples had private conversations, the married ladies were busy with their babies, and the old gentlemen discussed politics. The only one who might be interesting to get to know is an unmarried lady with a sweet face.

At the far end of the table was the Professor. He shouted answers to the deaf old gentleman on one side, and talked philosophy with a Frenchman on the other. In between, he ate his food with a hearty appetite. Amy would have been horrified, but I like to see people enjoy their food.

Then I overheard one young man say to another, "She's a governess or something."

"Why would they let an ordinary governess sit at our table?"

"Friend of the old lady's," he answered, as they strutted off to smoke their cigars.

At first I was angry. But then I thought that being a governess was as good a job as theirs. At least I have the good sense not to smoke myself to death, like those two "fine" young "gentlemen."

Thursday

The single woman is Miss Norton. She seems rich, well mannered, and kind. She has fine books and pictures, knows interesting people, and seems friendly.

Yesterday little Minnie Kirke introduced me to Mr. Behr. "This is Mamma's friend, Miss March."

"Yes," added her little sister, Kitty. "She's jolly, and we like her lots!"

"Ah, yes. I hear these naughty girls make trouble for you, Miss March. If so again, you call me and I come," he said, pretending to frown, but with such a twinkle in his eye that the little girls laughed in delight.

Saturday

Not much news, except that Miss Norton asked me if I would be willing sometimes to go with her to lectures and concerts. She pretended that I'd be doing her a favor, because she'd feel safer having someone go with her. But I'm sure she knows I can't afford to go on my own. Still, she made the offer out of kindness, so I accepted it gratefully.

Later this afternoon I heard such loud noises coming from the room next to the nursery that I ran in to see what had happened. There was Mr. Behr, down on his hands and knees. Tina was on his back, Kitty was leading him with a jump rope, and Minnie was feeding two small boys through "cages" built of chairs.

"Welcome to our zoo!" shouted Kitty.

"I'm riding the effalunt!" announced

Tina, holding on by the Professor's hair.

"Franz and Emil are the wild tigers," explained Minnie. "They come every Saturday afternoon. That's when Mamma lets us do what we like, doesn't she, Mr. Behr?"

The "effalunt" sat up and said with a straight face, "I give you my word it is so, Miss March. But if we make too big a noise, you shall say 'Hush!' and we will go more softly."

I promised to do so, but I left the door open and enjoyed the fun as much as they did. They played tag and danced and sang. And when it got dark, they all piled onto the sofa around the Professor and listened to him tell charming fairy tales about the little "koblods" that ride snowflakes as they fall.

Send me Amy's letters as soon as you can. I haven't heard anything from Laury. Is he studying so hard that he can't find time to write to his friends? Take good care of him for me, Beth. And tell me all about the twins. And give heaps of love to everyone.

Jo

P.S. On rereading this letter, it does seem rather "Behr-y." But I'm always interested in odd people, and I really don't have anything else to write about.

J

December

My Dearest Bethy and Marmee,

At last the little Kirke girls have settled down, and I'm able to teach them a few things. They're not as interesting as Tina, Franz, and Emil, who are quiet, jolly little children. The Professor and I have such fun with them on Saturday afternoons!

We've become very good friends, and I've begun taking German lessons from him. Here's how it happened. One day, Mrs. K mentioned that she offered to do his laundry, but his clothes are really a mess. "He's so good-natured and gentle with the children. But they tug at his sleeves and pull off his buttons. Or he uses his handkerchiefs to bandage their fingers, or his socks to make puppets. He's so kind, but absent-minded—and absolutely terrible with a sewing needle!"

"Then let me mend his clothes," I said. "He doesn't need to know. He's so nice about lending me his books."

I hoped he wouldn't notice that the holes in his socks had been mended properly. But one day he caught me sewing a button on his shirt.

"So!" he said. "You spy on me, and I spy on you. And this is not bad. Only I want to know if you have a wish to learn German."

"Yes. But you are too busy. And I'm too

stupid to learn," I answered, blushing.

"Then we will make the time, and we will find a way for you to learn. At evening, I will give a little lesson with much gladness. For I have a debt to pay you, Miss March," he said, pointing to my sewing. "You two kind ladies think I am a stupid old fellow, and won't notice that the socks don't have holes anymore. Maybe I think that buttons grow back after they fall off? But I have an eye, and I see much. And I have a heart, and feel thanks for this. So, a little lesson now and then—or no more good fairy gifts for me."

Of course, I had to agree. But after four lessons, I still couldn't learn the grammar. The Professor was very patient with me, but he looked at me with such despair that I didn't know whether to laugh or cry. So I tried both. That only made him throw the grammar book on the floor in disgust, and march out of the room. I couldn't blame him, but I felt ashamed and abandoned. I was just about to go off and cry by myself, when he returned. He smiled at me as if I'd just accomplished the most wonderful thing in the world.

"Now we shall try a new way. No more of that dull book. It must go in the corner for making us trouble. You and I will read this nice little storybook together."

He spoke so kindly that I lost my shyness. I read the German fairy tales with all my might. After the first page, he clapped his hands and said, "Now we go well! My turn!" And away he went, rumbling out the German words with his strong voice. I didn't understand half of what he read, but he was so serious and I was so excited that I couldn't help laughing.

By now, I can read my lessons pretty well. The Professor sneaks grammar lessons into stories the way parents hide pills inside candy. I like it very much, and he hasn't given up yet. Isn't that good of him, Marmee? I want to give him something nice for Christmas, for I don't dare offer him money.

I'm glad Laury seems so happy and busy, and that he's given up smoking. See how you manage him better than I ever did? I'm not jealous, Bethy dear. Read him bits of my letters, please. I'm so glad you're doing well.

January

Happy New Year to you all, my dearest family! And that includes, of course, Mr. L and a young man by the name of Laury.

I loved your bundle of presents: Beth's "bib" to keep ink off my shirt, Hannah's box of gingerbread, Marmee's flannel nightgown, and Father's books, with his notes in them. Thank you all heaps and heaps!

On New Year's Day, Mr. Behr gave me a fine book of Shakespeare's plays. He's kept it with the other books he values most, and I've often admired it. "You often say you wish a library of your own," he began, as he presented it to me. "Here I give you a whole library. For between these lids (he meant 'covers') are many books in one. Shakespeare can help you understand people better. Read the book well. It will help you 'read' people in the real world, and then recreate them with your pen."

Inside the cover he'd written, "For Miss Josephine March, from her friend, Friedrich Behr."

I thanked him as well as I could. I never knew how much I could learn from Shakespeare. But then again I never had a "Behr" to explain it to me. I'm glad you like what I've told you about him, and I hope you will meet him someday. Mother would admire his warm heart, and Father his wise head. I admire both, and feel rich in my new "friend, Friedrich Behr."

Not having much money, or knowing what he'd like, I gave him a few little things— some useful, some pretty, and some funny. And poor as he is, he gave something to every single person in the house—from the servant girl to the children to Miss Norton. I was glad to see that everyone gave him something, too.

As I think it over, I feel as if I'm making some progress, in spite of my many failures. For now I'm cheerful all the time, I'm glad to work hard, and I'm more interested in other people than I used to be.

And I love you all!

Jo

Chapter 34

For years, Jo had dreamed of having enough money to fill the March home with comforts, to give Beth everything she wanted, to travel to Europe herself, and to donate large sums of money to charity. So she decided to write trashy stories—just to make money. But she almost lost more than she gained.

One day Jo put on her best clothes and bravely walked up two flights of dark and dirty stairs. She walked into a cloud of cigar smoke. Inside a filthy room, three "gentlemen" slouched in the chairs, with their feet on their desks.

"Excuse me," she murmured. "I'm looking for the *Weekly Volcano* office. I wish to see Mr. Dashwood, the editor."

One pair of shoes went down to the floor, and a gentleman in a rumpled shirt walked over to her.

Blushing, Jo held out her manuscript and stammered, "A friend of mine wanted—that is—her story—your opinion—could write more if—"

Mr. Dashwood grabbed the manuscript. He frowned as he turned the neat pages with his dirty fingertips.

Then he looked Jo over, from the ribbon on her hat to the bows on her shoes. "Well, you can leave it if you want. We've already got more of this stuff than we need. But I'll glance at it, and give you an answer next week."

When Jo returned the next week, Mr. Dashwood was alone. "We'll take this if you don't object to a few changes. It's too long. So I've marked the passages that need to be left out."

Jo hardly recognized the crumpled manuscript he handed her. He'd crossed out everything that was of value—that is, everything that showed the difference between right and wrong. Jo felt as if she were being asked to cut off her baby's legs so it would fit into a new cradle.

"But, sir, I thought that every story should have some sort of a moral. So I had some of the villains learn from their mistakes and change their ways."

Mr. Dashwood smiled, for now Jo was defending the story as her own—not her friend's. "People want to be entertained, not preached at," he claimed. "Morals don't sell, you know."

"So with these changes, how much—?"

"$25. After it's published."

"Well then, you can have it," said Jo, handing back the story. "And if my friend has another story—?"

"We'll look at it. Can't promise we'll take it. Tell her to make it short and spicy. Leave out the moral stuff. And your friend's name is—?"

"She doesn't wish her name to be printed," Jo said, blushing. Mr. Dashwood must have realized there was no "friend." But she still didn't want anyone to find out that she was the author of such trashy stories.

After Jo left the room, Mr. Dashwood put his feet back up on his desk, took a puff on his cigar, and muttered, "Poor and proud. But now that Sam's quit, she'll have to do. At least I won't have to pay her as much."

So Jo wrote lots of stories, and her starving wallet grew fat with cash. But she was afraid to tell her family about the stories. She had a feeling that Father and Mother would not approve.

To find material to write about, Jo had to learn about the darker side of life. She searched police records and read about murders, rapes, and kidnappings. She frightened one librarian when she asked for books about poison. In her imaginary world, she lived with villains, criminals, and evil people of all kinds.

At the same time, Jo was discovering a real-life hero—Mr. Behr. She became interested in him even though he wasn't as perfect as her imaginary heroes. At first, Jo couldn't understand why everybody liked him. He was neither rich nor famous, young nor handsome, brilliant nor powerful. Yet people were attracted to him, the way they are drawn to a warm, cozy fire. He was poor, yet always giving away things; a stranger, yet everyone's friend; not young in years, but young at heart.

Finally, Jo decided it was his good will toward others that gave Mr. Behr both dignity and beauty. For he turned only his sunny side to the world. His eyes were never cold or hard. And the lines by his mouth were souvenirs of friendly words and cheery laughs.

Then Jo discovered that Mr. Behr was not only good. He was also very intelligent and well educated. Of course, he was too modest to talk about his accomplishments. But a visitor from Germany told Jo that Mr. Behr had been an honored Professor at a university in Berlin before he came to the United States.

One evening Miss Norton invited Jo and the Professor to a special lecture and dinner with famous authors. Jo was ready to bow down before the writers she'd worshiped from afar. But then she discovered that the poet whose delicate style she'd admired ate like a pig. The great novelist she'd respected held a bottle in each hand, and poured wine down his throat. The fine, well-bred lady who wrote such exciting short stories fell asleep at dinner and snored loudly.

After dinner, several people joined them to discuss philosophy. They threw words and ideas back and forth. Jo couldn't follow the arguments. But she felt as if they were shredding all the beliefs and values she'd held since childhood.

Mr. Behr shook his head and frowned. When he saw Jo's dismay, he finally spoke up and defended all the old, important truths. When he argued that people were, in fact, responsible for their actions, Jo felt like clapping her hands. She began to see that having a good character is better than having money, fame, intelligence, or beauty. And her friend Friedrich Behr had not only a good character, but truly a great one.

A few days later, Mr. Behr was picking up a paper airplane that one of the children had made. Unfolding it, he saw it was a page from the *Weekly Volcano*. "I wish these newspapers did not come in the house. They are not for children to see or read. It is shameful that people write such harmful things."

Noticing that Jo blushed, Mr. Behr wondered whether she might be one of those writers. He might have told himself it was none of his business. But instead, he reached out to save his friend, the same way he'd stop a child from falling down the stairs. "Some people may find these stories pleasant. But they corrupt innocent minds. I'd rather give my children explosives to play with than such bad trash to read."

"Not all of it's bad—just silly," Jo answered, without looking at her friend. "Many respectable people earn an honest living by writing such stories. And if people want to buy the stories, I don't see any harm in supplying them."

"If respectable people knew the harm they did, they would not feel it was an honest living. No one has the right to put poison in candy, and then let little children eat it. People should think about what they do. Better to shovel dirt than to write such things."

That night, Jo carefully reread all the stories she'd written. Now she saw them the way the Professor saw them—as dangerous trash. *I've been hurting myself and others, just to make money,* Jo thought.

So she took the whole bundle and stuffed it into the fireplace. When three months of hard work was nothing but ashes, Jo looked at the money she'd earned. What should she do with that?

She tried writing stories that preached morals. But they sounded more like sermons or essays. No one would publish them. Maybe Mr. Dashwood was right; morals didn't sell.

Then she tried writing a children's story. Only one person was interested in paying her for it, and only if she rewrote the ending. But Jo refused to have the little boys and girls in the story be eaten by bears for not joining the publisher's religion.

So Jo decided to stop writing for a while. In the meantime, she spent more of her time patiently studying German. That winter, she learned other lessons besides German. For the Professor helped her in many ways, proving himself a true friend.

And Jo was happy.

When it was time for her to go back home in June, everyone was sorry she had to leave. The children cried, and even Mr. Behr looked upset. When it was her turn to say goodbye to the Professor, Jo invited him to visit her family if he was ever in the area. "I want them all to know my friend."

"Do you? Shall I come?" he asked, with an eager look she didn't see.

"Yes. Come next month. Then you could come to Laury's graduation."

"Is this your best friend—the one you talk about?" he asked, suddenly sounding worried.

"Yes. I'm very proud of my boy Laury, and I'd like you to meet him."

Jo looked up, and realized that Mr. Behr might think that Laury was more than a "best friend." The thought made her so uncomfortable that she blushed.

Misinterpreting this, the Professor said politely, "I fear I won't have time to visit. But I wish the friend much success, and you all happiness." With that, he shook hands warmly and went back to his room.

That night, Mr. Behr kept thinking about Jo. He put his head on his hands for a minute. Then he started pacing around the room, as if looking for something he couldn't find. "It is not for me," he sighed at last. "I must not hope it now."

Even though it was early, Mr. Behr went to the station with Jo the next morning to see her off. He handed her a bunch of violets to keep her company on the train. As his smiling face faded in the distance, Jo thought happily, *Well, I've written no books and earned almost nothing. But I've made a friend worth having. And I'll try to keep him all my life.*

Chapter 35

$\mathcal{L}$aury did in fact turn over a new leaf that year. He earned high honors, and he gave a wonderful graduation speech. They were all there—his proud grandfather, Mr. and Mrs. March, John and Meg, Jo and Beth. Afterward, Laury asked Jo if she would be at their usual meeting spot the next morning to welcome him home from college.

Jo agreed, but afterward had second thoughts. *What if he says something? What will I do?*

By the next morning, Jo realized she was silly to imagine that Laury might propose to her—especially when she'd always made it clear they'd never be more than friends. She was relieved that he greeted her with an unromantic, "Hey, Jo!" and then chattered away as they walked up the road.

But when they turned onto the little path near the river, Laury slowed down. He seemed to be searching for the right words to say. During one long pause, Jo noticed he was looking down at her with a serious expression. Fearing that the dreaded moment had come, Jo begged, "No, Laury. Please don't say it."

"I will. And you must hear me out, Jo," he answered in an excited, urgent tone of voice.

"All right, then. I'll listen," sighed Jo.

"I've loved you ever since I met you, Jo. I couldn't help it. I've tried to show you how I feel, but you wouldn't let me."

"I tried to spare you from this. I thought you'd understand—"

"Yes, but sometimes girls say 'no' when they mean 'yes.'"

"Not me. I never wanted you to fall in love with me. That's why I went away."

"I thought so. But it only made me love you more. I've worked so hard to please you. I stopped drinking and smoking and gambling. I studied hard and waited and never complained. I hoped if I changed, you'd love me, even though I'm not good enough for you." Laury's voice broke, as he tried to hold back the tears.

"But you are—in fact, you're much too good for me. I'm so grateful to you, and proud and fond of you. I don't know why I can't fall in love with you. I've tried. But I can't change how I feel. And it would be a lie to say I love you that way when I don't."

Laury took both her hands and looked straight into her eyes. "Really, truly, Jo?"

"Really, truly, Laury dear," Jo answered reluctantly.

Laury dropped her hands, threw himself on

the ground, and put his head in his hands. He was so still that Jo was frightened.

"Oh, Laury! I'm sorry—so very sorry. I wish you wouldn't take it so hard." Jo patted his shoulder and said sorrowfully, "You know people can't just make themselves love other people."

"Sometimes they can."

"But that's not the right kind of love." Jo paused, and then added, "Laury, there's something I want to tell you."

He jumped as if he'd been shot, and cried out fiercely, "Don't tell me that, Jo! I can't bear to hear it now!"

"Tell you what?"

"That you love that old man."

"What old man?" Jo asked, thinking he must mean his grandfather.

"That devil of a professor—the one you were always writing about. If you say you love him, I swear I'll do something desperate."

Jo wanted to laugh, but she controlled herself. "Don't swear, Laury! My Professor isn't old or bad, but good and kind. And he's the best friend I've got, next to you. Besides, I have no intention of loving him—or anybody else."

"But you will someday. And then what will I do?"

"You'll love someone else, too, like a sensible boy. And then you'll forget all about me."

"I can't love anyone else. And I'll never

forget you, Jo! Never! Never!" Laury cried, stamping his foot.

"Now Laury, you still haven't heard what I've been trying to say. I really do want to do the right thing and make you happy."

Seeing a ray of hope, Laury looked at her with eyes full of love and longing, his lashes still wet with bitter tears.

Jo tried once again to reason with him. "I agree with Mother that you and I would be miserable together. We both have quick tempers and strong wills. And we never agree with each other. So let's be sensible, and just stay good friends."

"I won't be sensible. Besides, everyone expects us to get married. Don't disappoint them, dear! Grandpa has set his heart on it, your family likes the idea, and I can't live without you. Say you will, and let's be happy. Please, please do!"

"I can't say it honestly, so I won't say it at all. Someday you'll see that I'm right, and you'll thank me for it."

"I'll be damned if I do!" Laury shouted, jumping up and looking ready to bolt away.

"Yes, you will," insisted Jo. "You'll get over this, and you'll find some lovely girl who adores you. Like you, she'll enjoy living in a fine house and being part of high society. I wouldn't. And you'd hate my spending so much time writing, but I couldn't live without it. We'd be so unhappy! I don't think I'll every get married.

For I love my freedom, and I don't want to give it up for any human being."

"You think so now. But there will come a time when you'll love someone enough to live and die for him. And I'll have to stand by and watch!" Laury threw his hat on the ground in tragic despair.

Starting to lose patience, Jo cried out, "Then you'll just have to do the best you can! I don't know what else to say. I'll always be fond of you as a friend. But I'll never marry you. And the sooner you accept that, the better off we'll both be!"

Stunned, Laury looked at her a moment. Then he turned sharply away, saying in a desperate tone of voice, "One day you'll be sorry, Jo."

Frightened, Jo asked, "Where are you going?"

"To the devil!"

Jo's heart stood still, as she watched Laury run down the hill toward the river. But instead of plunging himself into the water, Laury jumped into his boat and rowed away with all his might. She watched him desperately trying to run away from a grief he carried in his heart.

Jo felt as if she'd murdered some innocent creature. "I wish he'd love Beth," she thought. "But I'm beginning to think maybe I was wrong about what was bothering her. Oh, dear! I can't understand how people enjoy attracting lovers and then rejecting them. It's so dreadful!"

When Jo told Mr. Laurence what had happened, the old gentleman was disappointed. But he knew even better than Jo that love can't be forced. Still, he was very worried that Laury might do something dangerous if he stayed home and kept running into Jo. So he decided to take Laury to Europe.

That evening, the old man placed his hands on Laury's shoulders and said very quietly and gently, "I know all about it, my boy. I'm disappointed, but the girl can't help it. So what will you do now?"

"Nothing. Anything! I don't care what becomes of me!" Laury shouted bitterly.

"Now, don't do anything rash. Why not go abroad and forget all this? I promised you could go after you finished college."

"But what's the point of going alone?"

"I'm not suggesting you go alone. I have business in London that I need to look after. You'd be free to go wherever you want—Italy, Germany, Switzerland. You could enjoy the art, music, scenery—and have all kinds of adventures."

The idea of new adventures was like a small green oasis in the middle of a desert of despair. In spite of himself, Laury's broken heart jumped at the offer. "Whatever you want, sir. It doesn't matter to me where I go or what I do."

"It matters to me, though. You are free to do whatever you want, as long as you use your freedom to good purpose. Promise me that, Laury."

"Anything you like, sir."

The old gentleman gave a sigh of relief. He knew that Laury didn't care now. But he hoped that promise might someday keep Laury from getting into trouble.

Mr. Laurence made all the arrangements quickly, before Laury changed his mind or did anything desperate. When it was time to say goodbye, Laury pretended to be cheerful. But when Mrs. March kissed him and whispered some motherly advice in his ear, Laury's brave front started to dissolve. He hurried to give each person a hug, and then ran out the door, as if running for his life.

Jo followed so she could wave her hand to him if he looked back. He did. And, seeing her, he came back, put his arms around her, and looked at her with one last, pathetic appeal. "Oh, Jo, can't you, please?"

"Laury, dear, I only wish I could!"

At that, Laury let go of Jo, muttering, "That's all right. Never mind." He turned quickly and went away without another word.

But it wasn't all right. And Jo did mind. For she felt as if she'd stabbed her dearest friend. When he left her without another glance, she knew the boy Laury would never come again.

Chapter 36

$\mathcal{W}$hen Jo came home that spring, she was struck by the change in Beth. Her face had become almost transparent, as if life were slowly being drained from it. No one spoke of the change, or seemed aware of it. For it had come about so gradually that those who saw her every day didn't notice it.

Jo confessed to her parents that she'd written trashy stories. They agreed to let her use the money to take Beth to the seashore. There she could spend time in the open air, and let the fresh sea breezes blow a little color into her pale cheeks.

One day Beth was lying very still on the beach, with her head on Jo's lap. Thinking Beth was asleep, Jo put down her book. Her eyes filled with tears, as she thought bitterly about how Beth was slowly drifting away from her. When her eyes finally cleared, she saw that Beth was looking tenderly up at her. "Jo, dear," Beth said quietly, "I'm glad you know. I've wanted to tell you, but I couldn't."

Then Beth became the stronger one, and tried

to comfort Jo. "I've known it for a long time, dear. Now that I'm used to it, it isn't so hard to bear."

"Is this why you were so unhappy last fall, Beth?"

"Yes. That's when I stopped hoping to get better. But I didn't want to admit it. When I saw you all so well and strong and full of happy plans, I realized I could never be like you. And that made me miserable, Jo."

Jo imagined how hard it must have been for Beth to learn to say goodbye to health, love, and life. "Oh, Beth! If only you'd told me! Then I could have comforted and helped you!"

"But it seemed selfish to frighten you when Marmee was already worried about Meg, and Amy was away, and you were so happy with Laury."

"And I thought you loved Laury, Beth. I went away because I couldn't love him."

Beth looked amazed at the idea. "Why, Jo! How could I, when he was so fond of you? I do love him dearly—but like a brother. And I do hope someday he will be my brother."

"Not through me," said Jo, decidedly. "Amy's the only one left. In fact, they'd be perfect for each other. But right now, the only one I care about is you, Beth. You must get well."

"I want to, Jo. But every day I lose a little, and I don't think I'll ever get it back. It's like the tide, Jo. When it turns, it goes slowly. But it can't be stopped."

"But it must be stopped. Nineteen is too young, Beth. I can't let you go!"

Beth held Jo close, sobbing. "I don't want to go. But I am willing."

The first bitter wave of this great sorrow broke over them together. Then Beth said, calm once more, "You'll tell them when we go home?"

"I think they'll see it," sighed Jo.

"Perhaps not. I've heard that the people who love you the most are often the blindest to such things. I don't want any secrets. And it's kinder to prepare them. John and the babies will comfort Meg. But you must be there for Father and Mother. Will you, Jo?"

"I'll try. But don't give up yet, Beth," urged Jo, trying to sound cheerful.

Beth answered quietly, "I don't know how to explain it. I just have a feeling I was never meant to live long. I'm not like the rest of you. I never made plans about what I'd do when I grew up. I never wanted to go away. The hard part now is simply that I have to leave all of you. I'm not afraid. But I'll miss you so much!"

For several minutes there was no sound but the sigh of the wind and the lapping of the tide. A seagull flashed by, sunshine on its silvery breast. Beth watched it disappear, her eyes full of sadness. Then a little gray sand bird hopped right up to her. Beth smiled and felt comforted by the trust and friendship it seemed to offer.

"Look how tame it is, Jo! Mother said they reminded her of me. They're neither wild nor beautiful. But they're busy, trusting, contented little things. You are like the seagull, Jo—strong and wild, fond of the storm and the wind, flying far out to sea, happy to be all alone. Meg is like the turtledove, for she is loyal and loving. Amy is like the lark—trying to get up high in the clouds, but always coming back down to her nest. She's ambitious, but her heart is good and tender. No matter how high she flies, she'll never forget home. I do hope I'll see her again, but she seems so far away."

Jo thought that the greatest change in Beth was that she could talk so openly, unlike the shy old Beth. "I intend to make you all better by the time she comes home next spring, and—"

"Jo, dear, don't hope for that any more. It won't do any good. Let's just enjoy being together while we wait. We'll have happy times, for I don't suffer much. And I think, if you help me, the tide will go out easily."

When they got home, Father and Mother could see clearly what they had hoped not to see. Tired from her short trip, Beth said how glad she was to be home and went straight to bed. Her father, leaning against the mantelpiece, hid his head in his hands. Her mother stretched out her arms as if reaching out for help. And Jo went to comfort her without a word.

Chapter 37

*O*n Christmas Day, all the tourists in Nice, France, were strolling along the great avenue that borders the Mediterranean Sea. A tall young man was walking slowly, his hands behind him, a rather sad expression on his face. He looked like an Italian, dressed like an Englishman, and had the free spirit of an American. Young ladies looked at him and smiled their approval. But he showed no interest in any of them.

Suddenly a young lady in a carriage caught his attention. She had blonde hair and was wearing a pretty blue dress. He stared a minute. Then his whole face woke up. Waving his hat wildly, he hurried to meet her.

"Oh, Laury! Is it really you? I thought you'd never come!" Amy exclaimed.

"I was delayed, but I promised to spend Christmas with you, and here I am."

"I have so much to say, I don't know where to begin! Get in and let's go for a ride. Tonight there's a Christmas party at our hotel for all the Americans staying there. You'll come, of course? Aunt will be charmed."

"Thank you," answered Laury, leaning back in his seat.

As he sat next to Amy, she felt a new sort of shyness with him. She tried to make cheerful conversation, but Laury didn't seem interested in the sights and sounds of the city. Amy thought him more handsome than ever. But he looked so moody—not exactly unhappy, but tired, and no longer the merry-faced boy she used to know.

"What are you thinking?" she asked finally.

"That 'mademoiselle' has become quite charming," he answered, bowing formally, with his hand on his heart and an admiring look on his face.

Amy blushed with pleasure at the compliment. But she also missed the honest, open, easygoing relationship they used to have.

After picking up the mail from home, Amy read the precious letters while Laury drove the carriage.

"Mother says that Beth is very ill. I often think I should go home. But they all tell me to stay, saying that I'll never have another opportunity like this."

"I think you're right to stay. There's nothing you could do there, and everyone is pleased to know you're well and happy, my dear."

Amy felt reassured by the brotherly "my dear." She felt that if anything bad did happen at home, at least she wouldn't be alone in a strange land.

Then Amy showed him a sketch of Jo writing her stories. Laury smiled, took it, and put it in his pocket, saying he wanted to make sure it didn't blow away.

That night, Amy took special care to make herself attractive. She was starting to see her old friend Laury in a new light—not as "our boy," but as a handsome and pleasant man. She put on Flo's old white silk gown. Since she couldn't afford jewelry, she decorated her outfit with fresh flowers and delicate vines.

When Laury arrived, he found Amy standing by a window. He looked pleased as his eyes rested on her slender figure, dressed in white against a background of red curtains. He offered her a small bouquet of flowers, bowing deeply. "Yet they're no match for your beauty," he added stiffly.

"Oh, please don't."

"I thought you liked that sort of thing."

"Not from you. It doesn't sound natural. I liked your old, down-to-earth ways better."

"I'm glad," Laury answered, looking relieved. Then he asked Amy if his tie was on straight, just as he used to when they went to parties at home.

That evening, the ballroom was crowded with rich and royal guests from all over the world. There was a Russian prince, a Polish count, a French friend of the Emperor, and a Lord Something-or-Other from London. They all asked Amy to dance. And since she loved to dance, she graciously accepted—hoping that Laury would see her and wish he were dancing with her instead.

As Amy waltzed away with the Count, Laury was relieved to sit down with her Aunt Carrol. His look of contentment annoyed Amy, so she ignored him until dinner.

But Laury was watching her—and with pleasure. She danced with such spirit and grace! Soon Laury decided that "little Amy" would someday make a very charming woman.

When it was finally time for dinner, Laury stood to give Amy his seat. He looked refreshed and excited as he gazed down at Amy.

"What do you call these flowers?" he asked, touching one of the buds on her shoulder. "I've never seen them before."

"Why, they grow wild. You've seen them all over the place, silly!"

"But they were never worth noticing until I saw them on you."

"None of that foolish talk. It's forbidden. I'd rather have coffee than compliments. And don't slump."

Laury stood straight up, and accepted the empty cup she handed him. He felt an odd sort of pleasure in having "little Amy" tell him what to do. She'd lost her childlike shyness, and become a strong woman.

"But where did you learn to—you know—to make yourself look so—" Laury didn't know how to explain the change he saw.

"I've been studying, not just playing. And the wildflowers cost nothing. I'm used to making the most of my poor little things."

Amy immediately was sorry she'd said this, fearing it wasn't in good taste. But Laury liked her better for it. He respected her strength in making the most of every opportunity. And he admired the cheerful spirit that brightened poverty with flowers. Amy didn't know why he looked at her so kindly, or why he devoted himself to her for the rest of the evening. But suddenly Amy and Laury were seeing each other in a delightful new way.

Chapter 38

*B*ack in America, Meg devoted herself entirely to her two little babies. She hovered over them day and night, leaving herself no time to take care of the house—or her husband.

After work, if John called out a cheerful "Hello!" to his wife, Meg would hiss back, "Hush! You'll wake the babies!" If he suggested they go to a lecture or concert, she would scold him, "Leave our children for my own entertainment? Never!"

But John adored the babies. So he was willing to give up his wife's attention and his own comfort for the sake of his children.

By the time the children were a year old, Meg had become anxious and worn out—a slave to her babies. John felt like an intruder every time he dared enter his home, which was now ruled by two demanding babies. Meg spent the evenings singing endless lullabies to the children and bribing them to go to sleep. Abandoned by his wife, John eventually started visiting his friend Jack, who had recently married a pretty young woman. There he would play chess or discuss politics with

Jack. It never occurred to him that Meg might miss him.

At first, Meg was relieved to know that John was having a good time with his friends. It was better than his making noise in the house and waking the children. But once the babies started going to sleep at more regular times, Meg began to miss her husband's company. She wanted him to stay home, but she wouldn't tell him so. For she was hurt that he couldn't figure out what she wanted without being told. She began looking in the mirror and saying, "I'm getting old and ugly. John would rather visit his friend's pretty wife."

Meg tried to comfort herself with the babies' love. But her spirits drooped, and she grew thin and pale. One day her mother found her in tears, and insisted on knowing what was wrong.

"Oh, Mother, I feel like a widow!" Meg sobbed. "John's away at work all day. And at night, when I want to see him, he's always over at the Scotts'. It isn't fair! I have to work so hard and never have any fun. Men are so selfish!"

"So are women. Don't blame John till you see what you're doing wrong."

"But it's not right for him to neglect me."

"Don't you neglect him, too?"

"Why, Mother! I thought you'd be on my side."

"I am. I sympathize with you. But I think you're the one who's wrong, Meg."

"I don't see how."

"Has John ever 'neglected' you when you've made a point of spending time with him? You see, Meg, in loving your children, you've forgotten to love your husband, as well. Children should draw you nearer to each other. Instead, you've treated them as if they belonged only to you. You've haven't let John do anything for the children except earn money to support them. He misses spending time at home. But it isn't home without you. And you're always in the nursery."

"Shouldn't I be there?"

"Not all the time. Don't neglect your husband because of the children. And don't shut him out of their lives. Teach him how to help you with the children. For they need him, too."

"You think he'd do that?"

"I know he will. When you and Jo were little, I made the same mistake. Poor Father offered to help, but I refused. So he spent all his time with his books. But Jo was too much for me to handle alone, and you were so sick that I became ill myself. So Father came to the rescue. That's the secret of our home happiness. He doesn't let his work tear him away from our home life. And I try not to let my household cares interfere with my interest in his activities. We each have our interests, but at home we always work together."

"Tell me how to be as good a wife and mother as you, Marmee."

"Well, dear, you could let John help manage Demi. And Hannah could come help you. Go out more, get some exercise, and do things that will make you cheerful. Take an interest in whatever John likes. Talk with him, share ideas, and educate yourself about what's going on in the world. For it all affects you and your family."

Meg decided to follow her mother's advice. She tidied the house, dressed up, and prepared a special dinner for John. Then she put the children to bed early. But strong-willed Demi made up his mind that he would not stay in bed. Poor Meg sang and rocked and told bedtime stories. Good-natured Daisy soon fell asleep. But naughty Demi would not shut his eyes.

When Meg heard John tiptoe into the house after work, she pleaded with her young son, "Will Demi lie still like a good boy, while Mamma gives poor Papa his tea?"

"Me wants tea!" announced Demi.

"If you go to sleep like Daisy," Meg promised, "I'll save you a sugar cube for breakfast."

At that, Demi shut his eyes tight, hoping to make breakfast come faster.

Meg slipped away and ran down to greet her husband. She smiled cheerfully and poured him a cup of tea.

"Why, this is quite delightful, little mother! Just like old times," John grinned, picking up his cup.

But his first sip was interrupted by Demi's voice, as he ran into the room. "It mornin'! Me wants soogar!"

"No, Demi," said Meg. "It isn't morning yet. You must go to bed and not trouble poor Mama. Then you can have some sugar."

Not getting what he wanted from his mother, Demi climbed onto his father's lap. There he could easily help himself to one of the sugar cubes. Smiling up at his father, Demi said, "Me loves Parpar."

But John shook his head and said to Meg, "You told him to stay in his room. If you don't make him do it, he'll never learn to obey you."

So Meg led Demi back to his bed, and told him to stay there till morning. But then she gave him a sugar cube. As Meg went back to the table, Demi happily sucked on his sugar and planned how to get more.

Soon the meal was interrupted again. Demi walked into the room and demanded loudly, "More soogar, Marmar!"

"I'm afraid you've let the child make you his slave," John said to Meg. "Put him in his bed and leave him. It's the only way he'll learn."

"But he never stays there unless I sit with him."

"I'll manage him. Demi, go upstairs and get in bed, as Mama told you."

"No!" the child shouted, helping himself to a sugar cube.

"You must never say that to Papa. I'll carry you to bed if you don't go yourself."

"Go away! Me no love Parpar!" shouted Demi, hiding behind his mother.

But Meg handed over the little rebel, saying, "Be gentle with him, John."

All the way upstairs, Demi kicked and screamed at his father. The minute he was placed in his bed, he rolled off it and headed for the door. Each time his father caught him by his pajamas and put him back in bed. After repeating this a few times, Demi was too worn out to get up. So he roared at the top of his voice. Usually Meg gave in at this point. But John sat patiently. No sugar. No lullaby. No story.

Disgusted and frustrated, Demi now started wailing for "Marmar."

His cries went straight to Meg's heart. Running up to the room, Meg begged, "Let me stay with him, John. He'll be good now."

"No, my dear. I told him he must do as you said and go to sleep. And so he must—even if I have to stay here all night."

"But he'll cry himself sick," pleaded Meg, feeling guilty about having deserted her baby.

"No, he won't. He's so tired he'll soon drop off to sleep. Then he'll understand that he has to mind you. Don't interfere. I'll manage him."

"He's my child. And I can't have his spirit broken by harshness," Meg protested.

"He's my child, too. And I won't have his character spoiled by your giving into him all the time. Go downstairs, my dear, and leave the boy to me."

John took charge of the situation so calmly that Meg agreed—as long as she could give her baby a goodnight kiss.

After that, Demi's sobs quieted down, and he curled up under the covers. When John peeked under them to see if his son was asleep, the little boy held out his arms and said, "Me be good now."

Although John was firm, he was also merciful. He held his son in his arms, and patiently waited for the child to fall asleep. But their little struggle was more tiring to the father than a whole day at work. Soon both father and son were fast asleep.

Having heard nothing for quite some time, Meg starting imagining that something horrible had happened. Finally she slipped into the room, fearing the worst. But when she saw the two faces on the pillow, she smiled, thinking, "John does know how to manage children without being too harsh. He'll be a great help, for Demi is getting to be too much for me to handle by myself."

When John came downstairs at last, he was afraid his wife would be annoyed with him for

delaying their dinner. Instead, she was contentedly doing her sewing. Then John was even more
surprised and pleased when Meg asked him to
talk about the upcoming election. For Meg hated
politics, believing that the only thing politicians
cared about was calling each other names. But
she kept her thoughts to herself, and tried to look
interested.

She's trying to like politics for my sake, thought
John. *So I'll take an interest in her sewing. That's
only fair.*

After watching Meg for a minute, John said,
"That hat's very pretty. How do you keep it on?"

Meg showed him where she'd sewn on bits
of lace. Then she put on the hat and tied it under
her chin. "It's my very best hat, to wear to concerts or the theater."

"The bonnet is lovely, but I prefer the face
inside. For it looks young and happy again."
Then John kissed Meg's smiling face.

"I'm glad you like it. For I'd like you to take
me to a concert some night. I really need some
music to help me feel back 'in tune.' Would you,
please?"

"Of course, I will—with all my heart. I'll take
you anywhere you'd like to go. You've been shut
up for so long, it will do you good to get out.
And I'll enjoy seeing you happy again."

"Oh, John. I'm sorry I've been so worried
and stressed lately. I've neglected you terribly.

But I'm going to try to make our home what it used to be. You don't mind, do you?"

Not only did John not mind. He was so relieved and pleased that he threw his arms around Meg, and almost crushed the lovely little hat.

Of course, things weren't perfect after that. But their house became a home once again. John brought order to a house once ruled by the babies. Meg became calmer and more cheerful once she and her husband started sharing more duties, interests, and time alone together.

John never wanted to leave his home—except when he went out with Meg. Now the Scotts came to visit the Brookes. Everyone found the little house full of happiness and family love. Even Sallie Moffat liked to spend time there. "It's always so quiet and pleasant," Sallie used to say to Meg. "It does me good." But Sallie never figured out what was missing from her own house—which was filled with splendid things, but seemed empty and lonely.

With each year of married life, John and Meg learned more about helping one another. They learned to walk side by side, through both sunny and stormy weather. Even when they had to face sorrow, poverty, and old age, they faced it together. And together they created a real home—one filled with riches that money can never buy.

Chapter 39

$\mathcal{L}$aury planned to spend only a week in Nice, France. But he stayed a month. He was tired of wandering alone, and was relieved to be with someone familiar.

Amy had never pampered Laury the way her sisters did. But she was glad to see him now. He reminded her of the dear family she missed more than she would say.

They took comfort in each other's company, and spent much time together riding, walking, and dancing. Laury became more and more impressed by Amy's artistic skills and her pleasant charm. Amy, however, became more and more disappointed in Laury because the talented young man was just drifting along, doing nothing—trying to forget about Jo, and nursing his wounded pride.

One lovely day, Amy invited Laury to go for a ride to the nearby Italian village of Valrosa, in the hills above the Mediterranean Sea. Twisted old olive trees covered the hills with their silvery gray leaves. Ripe, golden apricots hung from the trees. Beyond the green slopes and gray cliffs, the sharp, white peaks of the Alps stood out against the clear Italian sky.

The village was named Valrosa because it was in a valley filled with roses. Bright blossoms covered the walls of houses, climbed up pillars, pushed between the bars of gates, and everywhere welcomed visitors with their sweet perfume.

"What a honeymoon paradise!" said Amy, enjoying the view onto the sunny Mediterranean. "Have you ever seen such roses?"

"No. And I've never felt such thorns!" complained Laury, who had just pricked his thumb trying to pick a big red rose. The flower reminded him of Jo, who always looked beautiful in that color.

"Try to pick lower down, where there aren't so many thorns," said Amy. She picked three tiny white roses, and put them into Laury's buttonhole.

But the pale roses reminded him of the flowers that Italians placed in coffins. For a moment, Laury wondered if it was a sign that something inside him had died.

Quickly shaking the thought from his head, Laury teased, "Thank you, ma'am. I promise to take your advice." He was joking now, but a few months later he would do just that.

"Laury, when are you going to see your grandfather?"

"Very soon."

"You've said that a dozen times within the last three weeks."

"I like to be consistent."

"Oh, Laury. You really ought to go."

"Are you trying to get rid of me?"

"Now, Laury. You know your grandfather is waiting for you. Why don't you go?"

"Just being wicked."

"You mean, just being lazy."

Amy shook her head and opened her sketchbook. She was tired of seeing her friend just throw his life away. Not knowing about Jo, Amy assumed Laury had run off to Europe because he'd been rejected by some stuck-up college woman. She thought he'd already wasted enough time just moping around. And she made up her mind to try to tell him so.

"So what are you going to do now?" Amy challenged him.

"Smoke a cigarette—if you'll let me."

"You know I don't approve of smoking. But I do need a figure to sketch."

"Shall I pose for you standing on my feet—or standing on my head?"

"Just stay where you are. You can even go to sleep if you like," Amy answered forcefully. "I intend to spend *my* time productively—working hard on my drawing."

Laury stretched out on the grass and closed his eyes.

Amy began to sketch him, taking artistic pleasure in studying his profile. Then, hoping to shake her friend out of his gloom, Amy asked, "What would Jo say if she saw you now?"

"What she always says. 'Go away. I'm busy!'" Laury gave a strained laugh, and his face hardened with pain, frustration, and bitterness. Hearing Jo's name touched a wound that had not yet healed.

Amy noticed the expression, and wondered whether instead some charming French woman had broken his heart. "You've changed so much, I worry that—" Amy began anxiously.

Laury looked straight into her eyes. Just as he used to tell her mother, he said, "It's all right, ma'am."

"I'm glad of that! So tell me. What's really going on?"

Laury shook his head. "Nothing to tell. I thought maybe you'd gotten some news from home."

"Not lately. But I thought your friend Jo might be sending you tons of letters."

"You know, it's hard to keep in touch when I'm wandering all over Europe."

Laury paused. He wondered whether Amy knew why he was so depressed and wanted to talk about Jo. But when she didn't say anything, he changed the subject. "So when do you start working on your masterpiece?"

"Never," Amy answered sadly. "After seeing all the fine works of art in Rome, I know I'll never be a great artist."

"But why give up, when you have so much talent and energy?"

"Talent isn't genius, and energy won't make a masterpiece. I want to be a great artist—or no artist at all."

"So now what will you do with your life?"

"I'll polish my other talents and become a great wife."

Laury admired Amy's determination to pursue a new goal instead of mourning the loss of an old one. "So now I'm going to play 'big brother.' I heard rumors about Fred Vaughn. You're not engaged yet, I hope?" Laury asked, suddenly looking very serious.

"No."

"But you will be, if he properly goes down on one knee and asks?"

"Probably."

"Then you're in love with old Fred?"

"I could be if I tried."

"How innocent you are! He's a good fellow, Amy. But he's not the kind of man I thought you'd like."

"He's rich, well-mannered, and a gentleman," Amy began. She felt a little ashamed of herself for wanting to marry a man for security, rather than for love.

"I see. Social queens need money. So you plan to marry a wealthy man. I know that's what many women do. But I wouldn't have expected it from one of the March women."

"Nevertheless, it's true."

Laury turned away. He didn't know why, but somehow he felt disappointed by her firm decision to marry Fred Vaughn.

Laury's silence and her own shame made Amy decide to try once more to shake her friend out of his despair. "I wish you'd do me the favor of doing something productive."

"I'd wish you'd make me," he answered, gently teasing her. "Treat me like an egg or a drum. Beat me until you're tired, if that would give you pleasure."

"Flo and I have a new name for you. It's 'Lazy Laurence,'" Amy said sharply.

"Not bad. Thank you for the nickname," Laury answered calmly.

"So do you want to know what I honestly think of you?" Amy asked, frustrated that Laury wasn't taking her seriously.

"Dying to be told."

"Well," said Amy sadly, "you disgust me."

The concern in her voice made Laury ask quickly, "Why?"

"Because you've had every chance to be good, useful, and happy. And yet, you insist on being selfish, lazy, and miserable."

"Yes, ma'am. Do go on, please. This is quite interesting."

"I thought you'd find it so. Selfish people always like to talk about themselves."

"You think I'm selfish?" Laury asked with alarm. He'd always thought of himself as generous.

"Yes, very selfish," Amy said calmly. "You've been in Europe for six months and done nothing but waste your time and money. And you've disappointed your friends."

"Don't I deserve a vacation after spending four years working hard in college?"

"You don't look as if your vacation has been much fun. And it certainly hasn't made you a better person. I don't think you're nearly as nice as you were back home. You've grown disgustingly lazy, you gossip, and you waste your time. You'd rather be flattered by silly people instead of being loved and respected by wise ones. You've got money, talent, health, social connections, and good looks. It's the truth. I can't help saying it. But with all these splendid things, you do nothing but waste your life. Instead of being the man you ought to be, you're just—"

"—A knight in shining armor who's fallen off his horse," Laury teased.

But Amy's words struck him hard. Feelings of anger and hurt gave him new energy.

Laury put his hand on Amy's sketchpad, so

that she couldn't draw. Imitating a little child, Laury teased, "Oh, I promise I'll be good!"

But Amy didn't laugh. Instead, she tapped his hand with her pencil and said seriously, "Aren't you ashamed to have a hand that does nothing but wear fancy gloves and pick flowers for fine ladies? At least you're not wearing expensive jewelry—only the little ring that Jo gave you so long ago. Oh, how I wish she were here to help me!"

"So do I!" Laury groaned, hiding his face under his hat and digging his hand into the grass.

Hearing him sigh, Amy's eyes filled with tears. With a voice that was beautifully soft and gentle, she continued, "I'm sorry. They should have told me. If they had, I would have been more patient and kind with you. But now that I realize how much Miss Randal hurt you, I hate her more than ever!"

"Miss Randal!" Laury said angrily, throwing his hat on the ground. "You know perfectly well that I've never cared for anyone but Jo!"

Surprised and upset, Amy asked, "You mean Jo was unkind to you? I always thought she loved you dearly."

"She was kind—but not in the way I wanted. Besides, if I'm such a good-for-nothing fellow, it's lucky for her she didn't love me back. Still, it's her fault I'm this way. And you may tell her so," Laury said bitterly.

"I'm sorry, Laury. I didn't know. But I can't help wishing you'd handle it better. Even if you can't win her love, at least you could earn her respect."

Suddenly Laury felt shaken out of a gloomy dream, and he could not go back to sleep. "Do you think Jo would be as disgusted with me as you are?"

"Yes, if she saw you now. She hates lazy people. Now, why don't you do something really splendid and make her love you?"

"I tried, but it was no use."

"You think it was enough just to study while you were in college? But you owed at least that much to your grandfather. It would have been shameful if you'd failed."

"But I did fail, for Jo wouldn't love me."

"No, you didn't fail. You proved you could do something if you tried. If you'd only make up your mind to do something else, you'd soon be happy and forget about your trouble."

"That's impossible."

"Try it and see. I may not be wise, but I've learned to observe others. Go ahead and love Jo forever. But don't let your love ruin you. For it's wrong to throw away so many other good gifts just because you can't have the one you want."

Laury sat turning the little ring on his finger.

Amy finished up her sketch and put it in front of him.

"How well you draw!" Laury said with surprise and pleasure. "That's me, all right."

"That's how you are now. And this is how you used to be," said Amy, placing another sketch in front of him. It was an old drawing that Amy had brought from home. Although it was not as well drawn as the newer sketch, it showed Laury taming a horse. Laury's strength, courage, and energy as a horseman contrasted with his lazy grace as a vacationer.

Laury looked from one picture to the other. Then he blushed and pressed together his lips. Finally he saw what Amy had been trying to tell him.

Laury stood up and looked at his watch. "Thank you, ma'am," he said, with a touch of coldness in his voice. "Your drawing has much improved over the past few months."

Now I've offended him, thought Amy. *Well, if it does him good, then I'll be happy. And if it makes him hate me, then I'm sorry. But it's the truth, and I can't take it back now.*

All the way home they chatted and laughed. But both felt uncomfortable. As Laury dropped Amy off at her aunt's house, she asked, "Will we see you this evening, my 'big brother'?"

"Unfortunately, I have another commitment. Au revoir, mademoiselle." Laury shook her hand and said gently, "Goodbye, dear."

The next morning, Laury did not visit as usual. Instead, he sent Amy a letter, which at first made her smile.

My Dear Teacher,

You'll be delighted to know that "Lazy Laurence" has gone to his grandpa, like a good little boy. Enjoy your winter in Italy. Valrosa will be a wonderful place for your honeymoon. Fred will do well with a teacher like you. Tell him so, with my congratulations.

Gratefully,

Your Struggling Student

Amy was pleased that her lecture had pushed Laury to get on with his life. But then, as she glanced around the empty room, she sighed, "But oh, how I'll miss him!"

Chapter 40

At first the March family felt bitter about their dear one's illness. But soon they accepted what they couldn't change, put away their grief, and tried to make Beth's last year a happy one.

They gathered around Beth's bed, and surrounded her with all the things she loved most—flowers, pictures, piano, cats, Father's best books, Mother's easy chair, Amy's finest sketches, Meg's babies. After Beth admitted, "I feel stronger when you are here," Jo never again left her sister's side. John saved money to buy Beth fresh fruit all winter, and Old Hannah cooked her favorite foods. From across the Atlantic Ocean came little gifts and cheerful letters.

For the first few months, Beth kept busy knitting mittens for poor children. But soon she said her needles were too heavy to lift, and she put them down forever. Talking tired her out, and pain conquered her weak body. At night she would cry out, "Help me! Help me!" Her family, unable to ease her pain, ached with grief.

Finally, Beth's weary young body stopped rebelling against death. The old peace returned.

And Beth started weaning herself from her dear old life.

With eyes made clear by many tears, Jo recognized the beauty of her sister's life. Although Beth had achieved neither fame nor fortune, her life was full of simple, unselfish goodness. Such humble virtue made her life a true success—one that is possible for everyone.

One night, after Jo had fallen lightly asleep, Beth lay awake, wondering if she'd accomplished anything of value in her short life. She'd created no fine drawings. She'd published no stories. She'd had no children. Had her life been useless?

Unable to sleep, Beth looked for something to read. Next to the bed, she happened to find a little poem Jo had scribbled on a scrap of paper. Though the words were blurred with Jo's tears, Beth could read the poem she'd written.

MY BETH
My dearest sister, now you leave
This life with all its pain.
Although I cannot help but grieve,
My loss becomes my gain.
A hero you have been to me.
You're gentle, wise, and strong.
Your grace and your humility
Will help me when you're gone.
You've set aside your own harsh fears

And shown us how to cope.
In life and death, in joy and tears,
You've taught us love and hope.
Much more than works of hand or mind,
Your spirit I admire.
And when you leave this earth behind,
Your life will still inspire.

Jo was startled awake when she heard Beth sigh. "What's wrong, Beth?" Jo asked anxiously.

"Nothing, dear. It's just that I found your poem. I'm so happy I read this. I'm not as good as you make it seem, but I've tried to do right. And now that it's too late to do any better, it's a comfort to think I haven't wasted my life. I've been loved, and maybe I've helped someone."

"Oh, Beth, you've helped me so much—more than anyone else in the world! I used to think I couldn't live without you because I love you so much. But now I know that even death can't take away all that you've given me."

"I, too, no longer fear death. Remember, Jo, that love is the only thing we can carry with us when we go. Love doesn't die. And it makes the end so much easier."

That year, spring came early. The sky grew clearer, and the earth greener. Buds appeared on the tree outside Beth's window. One morning, just before dawn, Beth laid her head on her mother's arm and drew her last breath.

Through their tears, parents and sisters watched the bright spring sunshine stream across the beloved face. The pain was replaced by a quiet peace. A bird sang joyfully from the budding tree, and flowers blossomed at the window. And the family felt thankful that Beth was well at last.

Chapter 41

*A*my's "lecture" helped Laury—though he did not admit it until long afterward.

For the next several weeks, Laury devoted himself to his grandfather. The old gentleman was so pleased that he told Laury to return to Nice. Something there had improved his outlook.

Laury would have loved to go back, but his wounded pride wouldn't allow it. He kept thinking about Amy's cutting words: "She hates lazy people," and "Do something really splendid and make her love you."

Finally Laury decided that he was ready to bury his love for Jo. He'd prove that one girl's rejection couldn't ruin his life. Besides, if he produced something wonderful, maybe Jo would end up at least respecting and admiring him.

His grandfather suggested that Laury spend time with some friends in Vienna, Austria. There Laury decided to express his feelings by composing music. He tried to write a sorrowful piece. Instead, he found himself humming a merry waltz he'd heard at the Christmas ball in Nice.

Next Laury tried writing an opera. The romantic lead was supposed to be like Jo. But all he could remember were Jo's unromantic qualities.

So instead of writing operas about dark-haired Jo, he imagined a charming character with golden hair, dressed in a white silk gown decorated with fresh wildflowers and delicate vines. He saw her dancing—almost floating—with princes and counts and lords. The young woman's face was a blur, and Laury never decided what her name would be. But she overcame all obstacles with beauty, intelligence, courage, and grace.

The more music Laury wrote for the character, the more he fell in love with her.

But the more he wrote, the more he also came to realize that Amy was right. Talent wasn't genius. And not everyone who loved music could become a great composer. So Laury tore up his music sheets, one by one.

"Now, what shall I do?" he asked himself.

Hoping for inspiration, he studied a picture of the great composer Mozart. *Now, he was a great man,* Laury thought. *When he couldn't have the woman he wanted, he married her younger sister, and was happy.*

Laury was surprised to find that his feelings for Jo were slowly shifting from passionate love to brotherly affection. But when he saw the little ring Jo had given him so long ago, Laury made up his mind. "I can't give up without one more try."

He seized pen and paper, and wrote Jo. He told her he couldn't settle down as long as there was any hope that she might change her mind. Couldn't she—wouldn't she—reconsider?

Finally Jo's answer arrived. No, she definitely couldn't and wouldn't. She was busy caring for Beth, and wanted never again to hear the word "love." She begged him to treat her as a loving sister, and to find happiness with someone else. Then she added, "Please don't tell Amy that Beth is worse. There's no need to ruin the rest of her stay in Europe. Perhaps Beth will hold on until Amy comes home in the spring. But please write often to Amy, so she won't worry, or feel lonely or homesick."

Poor Amy, thought Laury. *I'm afraid it will be a sad return home for her.*

Slowly he took off the little ring, placed it with a stack of letters from Jo, and locked them all away in a drawer.

Then he opened another drawer, where he'd put several of Amy's notes. They still smelled sweetly of the little dried roses she'd placed inside one of them. With a sad smile, he wrote a warm and cheerful letter to Amy, just as Jo had asked.

Amy wrote him back right away, confiding how much she missed her family. Soon letters began flying back and forth between them.

Early that spring, Laury sold his picture of Mozart and burned his opera. He went back to Paris, hoping a certain person might show up there. Even though he really wanted to go to Nice, Laury was too proud to go without first being invited.

But Amy would not invite him. For just then she had her own problem to work out.

Fred Vaughn had returned to Nice. He had an important question to ask Amy. Not long ago, she'd decided she would answer, "Yes, I will."

But instead, Amy said, "No, thank you."

She now knew that money and status alone couldn't satisfy the new desire that filled her heart with hopes and fears. Laury's words about Fred Vaughn haunted her: "He's a good fellow, Amy. But he's not the kind of man I thought you'd like." And she was ashamed of having told Laury she'd marry for money, not love.

What Amy really wanted was to be a lovable woman—not a social queen. She couldn't understand why Jo wasn't willing to try to love Laury. How hard could it be? Amy thought many people would be glad to have such a dear boy care for them.

That spring, Amy spent less time socializing with other people, and more time on her art. She sketched mostly from her imagination—young men lying on the grass with their hats over their eyes, a curly-haired young woman dancing with a tall gentleman, both their faces a blur.

Twice a week she sent Laury letters filled with personal stories, lively gossip, and lovely sketches. In one, she wrote that Fred Vaughn had gone off to Egypt. Laury read it and understood. *Poor fellow,* he thought. *I can sympathize with what he's going through.* He sighed with relief, and re-read Amy's letter with delight.

In May, Amy and the Carrols traveled to Vevay, Switzerland, a resort town on the shores of Lake Geneva. There Amy received a letter from home, telling her that Beth's health was failing. Since there wasn't enough time to return home to say her goodbye, her family insisted that she stay in Europe.

But Amy's heart was very heavy. She longed to be home. And every day she looked across the lake, hoping that Laury would come and comfort her.

The moment he heard that Beth had died, Laury left for Vevay, keeping his promise to comfort Amy. His heart was full of sorrow and joy, suspense and hope.

When he arrived, Laury found Amy all alone in a pleasant old garden on the shores of lovely Lake Geneva. Amy often sat on this quiet bench to read or work, or to console herself with the beauty all around her. That day, Laury first saw Amy's gentle, tender side—a side no one had ever seen before. Everything about her suggested love and sorrow—the black ribbon in her hair, the tear-stained letters in her lap, the look of pain and patience in her face.

The moment Amy saw him, she exclaimed in a voice full of love and longing, "Oh, Laury! Laury! I knew you'd come to me!"

Amy jumped up and ran into Laury's arms. As he bent down protectively, Laury felt that Amy was the only woman in the world who could fill Jo's place and make him happy. And Amy felt that no one could comfort and support her as well as Laury. Though neither of them spoke for a moment, both of them felt the truth and were satisfied.

Then Amy went back to her garden seat, blushing as she thought about how she'd thrown herself at Laury. "I'm sorry. I couldn't help it. I felt so lonely and sad. And I was so very glad to see you."

"I came the minute I heard. I wish I could say something to comfort you for the loss of dear little Beth. I feel so—and I—"

Suddenly shy, Laury didn't know what to say. He wanted to lay Amy's head on his shoulder, and tell her to have a good cry. But he didn't dare. So instead, he took her hand and squeezed it sympathetically.

"You don't need to say anything," Amy said softly. "Your being here is such a comfort to me. You don't need to go back right away, do you?"

"Not if you want me here, my dear."

"I do, very much. Aunt and Flo are kind. But you're like one of the family."

Amy looked like a homesick child, her heart full of sorrow. Suddenly, Laury forgot his shyness, and said, "Poor little soul! You look as if you've grieved yourself sick! I'm going to take care of you. Now come walk around with me. It's too cold for you to sit still on this bench."

Laury gently helped Amy to her feet, and strolled with her up and down the sunny walk. Amy was relieved to have a strong arm to lean on, a familiar face to smile at her, and a kind voice to talk cheerfully to her alone.

The charming old garden had sheltered many lovers over the years. The ivy-covered walls gave them privacy, and the rippling lake carried away the echo of their words. For an hour, this new couple walked and talked, enjoying this special moment together. When they finally left the garden, Amy felt as if she'd left behind her heavy load of loneliness and sorrow.

That evening, Mrs. Carrol saw a much happier Amy. "Now I understand," the good woman smiled to herself. "She's been longing for young Laurence."

So Mrs. Carrol warmly invited Laury to stay. Because she had already made plans with her daughter, she asked Amy to entertain their young guest.

Amy, of course, did not refuse. In fact, she seemed very much to enjoy being left alone to entertain her friend.

When they were in Nice, Laury had dozed and Amy had scolded. In Vevay, Laury never sat still. He was always walking, riding, boating, or studying hard. He said it was the mountain air that made him feel more energetic. Amy used the same excuse to explain why she suddenly felt happier and healthier.

The fresh winds blew away their sorrows, doubts, and fears. The warm spring sunshine brought out new ideas, tender hopes, and happy thoughts. The lake seemed to wash away the troubles of the past. And from high up on the grand old mountains, Amy and Laury seemed to get clearer views of life and love.

Soon Laury's deep and growing love for Amy cured him of his quick and foolish passion for Jo. It all came about so naturally. Laury knew that everyone—even Jo—would be pleased. But this time around, he made up his mind to take things more slowly and calmly.

Of course, he hardly needed to declare his love for Amy. She knew it without words and had given him his answer long ago.

Laury had imagined that he'd ask Amy in the moonlit garden, kneeling gracefully before her and looking romantically into her eyes. Instead, the matter was quickly settled one day on the lake, and under the bright noontime sun.

Laury and Amy were in a little rowboat, gliding past a romantic castle. They were talking about a love story set in the nearby mountains, when suddenly a silence fell between them. Amy looked up, and saw that Laury was leaning on his oars, gazing at her intently. Not knowing how to answer his gaze, Amy hastily said, "You must be tired. Let me row for a while."

"I'm not tired. But you can take an oar if you like," Laury answered, making a little room for her on the tiny seat.

Amy squeezed into the space beside Laury, a little embarrassed to be sitting so close to him. But she rowed well. Their two oars worked together in perfect harmony, and the boat floated smoothly through the water.

"Don't we pull our oars well together?" asked Amy, not daring to look into Laury's eyes.

"Yes, we do. So well that I wish we might always pull together in the same boat," Laury said tenderly. "Will you, Amy?"

Very softly she answered, "Yes, Laury."

Chapter 42

$\mathcal{I}$t was easy for Jo to give up her own dreams when she was caring for Beth. But when her beloved sister was gone, nothing remained but loneliness and grief. Jo thought it wasn't fair that some people seemed to get all sunshine, and some all shadow. She tried more than Amy to be good. But unlike Amy, she never got anything except disappointment, trouble, and hard work.

Jo despaired at the thought of spending the rest of her life doing dull chores in that quiet house. "I can't do it. I wasn't meant for a life like this. I know I'll do something desperate if no one comes to help me."

At night Jo would wake up, thinking she heard Beth calling her. Then she would look at the empty bed and cry, "Oh, Beth! Come back!"

Her mother, hearing her sobs, would come and comfort her, holding her in her arms. As one heart spoke to the other, the two women grew closer. They shared their grief as well as their hopeful acceptance.

Once her aching heart started to heal, Jo turned to her father for help. "Talk to me as you did to Beth. Help me become a wiser and better person."

"My dear," her father answered, "that would be such a comfort to me." He hugged her close, as if he, too, needed help and wasn't afraid to ask for it.

For the first time, father and daughter spoke as two adults—with mutual sympathy and mutual love. Jo spoke honestly about her sadness, resentment, and fears. And her father gave her the help she needed.

The parents who had taught one daughter to meet death without fear now tried to teach another daughter to accept life without distrust or despair—and to pursue her dreams with gratitude and power.

Jo had often said she wanted to do something splendid, no matter how challenging the work. Now she had her wish, for what could be more beautiful than devoting her life to her parents, and making their home happy and tidy?

But Jo was restless. She felt guilty about not doing what she thought was her duty. And yet, she couldn't seem to find a way to do it cheerfully.

One day, noticing Jo's dark mood, her mother suggested, "Why don't you write? That always used to make you happy."

"I don't have the heart to write. And even if I did, no one likes what I write."

"We do. Write something for us. And never mind the rest of the world. Try it, dear. I'm sure it would do you good. And it would please us very much."

"Don't think I can," Jo mumbled.

But an hour later, she was sitting at her desk with her "writing cap" on, scribbling hard.

Jo never knew how it got there, but something in that story went straight to people's hearts. Her family laughed and cried over it. Then, against her will, Jo's father sent it to a magazine. To her utter surprise, the magazine not only paid for the story, but also requested more. Newspapers reprinted it. Friends, strangers, and critics admired it. Jo was astonished by its success.

"I don't understand. What can there be in such a simple little story to earn so much praise?"

"There's truth in it, Jo. That's the secret," her father explained. "You've found your style at last. You wrote it without thinking about fame or money. And you put your heart into it. You've tasted the bitter part of life. Now comes the sweet part. Do your best. And enjoy your success as much as we do."

"If there's anything good or true in what I write, I owe it all to you and Mother and Beth," said Jo, more touched by her father's words than by any amount of praise from other people.

Love and sorrow had taught Jo how to write from the heart. Now her stories earned her both money and a good reputation.

When the news arrived that Amy and Laury were engaged, the March family was delighted. Mrs. March was pleased that Amy had decided to marry for love, not money. And she was relieved that Jo did not seem jealous.

"Now, Mother," Jo began. "Did you really think I would be so silly and selfish?"

"I only thought you might have changed your mind," Mrs. March answered. "Forgive me, dear. But I can't help noticing that you seem very lonely. That look of longing in your eyes goes to my heart."

"No, Mother. I'm glad Amy has learned to love Laury. I am lonely. But I hope I'd never marry someone just because I wanted to be loved."

"I'm glad of that, Jo. Remember that there are many different people who love you. Try to be satisfied with the love of your family and friends until the best lover of all comes along."

"I had no idea that my heart could hold so much love. I don't understand why it never seems full anymore."

"I do," Mrs. March said with a wise smile.

One afternoon, restless and sad, longing to

be loved, Jo wandered up to the attic. In the corner were four little wooden chests, each marked with a different name. They were filled with special things each sister had saved from childhood. Inside hers, Jo noticed a bundle of old exercise books. Looking at them, she smiled, remembering that pleasant winter at kind Mrs. Kirke's. As she opened one of them, she noticed a little message written by the Professor. The friendly words took on a new meaning and touched a tender spot in her heart.

"Wait for me, my friend. I may be a little late, but I shall surely come."

Oh, if only he would! Jo thought, her lips trembling. *My dear old Fritz—always so good, so patient with me. I didn't value him enough when I was with him. But how I would love to see him now! Everyone seems to be leaving me, and I feel all alone.*

Holding the message close, as if it were a promise not yet fulfilled, Jo started to cry.

Chapter 43

𝒜lone in the house late one afternoon, Jo
stretched out on the old sofa, looking at the fire.
Jo loved lying there on Beth's little red pillow,
planning stories, dreaming dreams, or thinking
tenderly about the sister who never seemed far
away. Jo's face looked tired, and rather sad, for
tomorrow was her birthday. She thought about
how fast the years went by, how old she was getting, and how little she seemed to have accomplished. She was almost 25 years old, and had
nothing to show for it. But Jo was wrong. Soon
she would see how much she had already done—
and be grateful for the chance.

"I'm going to end up an old maid—with a pen
for a husband and a family of stories for children,"
Jo sighed. She didn't realize yet that kindness and
respect can be as sweet as romance and passion.

Jo must have fallen asleep. Suddenly she imagined that Laury's ghost was leaning over her. But
when she felt him bend over and kiss her on the
cheek, she jumped up, shouting, "Laury! Oh, my
Laury!"

"You're glad to see me?"

"Glad! I'm overjoyed! But where's Amy?"

"We stopped at Meg's on the way here. But then they wouldn't let go of my wife."

"Your what?"

"Oh, dear! Now I've said the wrong thing."

"You've gone and gotten married!"

"Yes. But I'll never do it again," Laury promised, looking pleased and proud.

"Heaven help us. What awful thing will you do next?" Jo gasped.

"An interesting way to congratulate us," Laury teased.

"What do you expect, when you sneak up on me with such surprising news? Now sit down here and tell me all about it, you ridiculous boy."

"Boy? Don't I look like a married man and head of a family?"

"Not a bit. And you never will. The idea of you married and settled is so funny that I can't help laughing."

Jo was delighted to see Laury's eyes sparkle as he told her about their quiet wedding in Paris and their honeymoon in Valrosa. "It was love among the roses!" he beamed.

Then Laury grew serious. "Jo, dear, I want to say one thing, and then we can set it all aside. I shall never stop loving you. But now I love you as my sister, and I love Amy as my wife. I think this is how it was meant to be. If I had been patient and listened to you, I would have learned this without making a fool of myself. So now can we go back to the happy times when we first became friends?"

"No, Laury. We can never go back to those happy times when we were young. But though I'll miss my boy, I shall love the man. And I'll admire him even more, for now he has become the man I hoped he would. We can't be little playmates any longer. But we can love and help one another all our lives, can't we, Laury?"

He did not say a word, but took her hand. Out of the grave of his boyish passion rose a beautiful, strong friendship that would sustain them both.

"Poor Jo!" Laury said quietly. "While we were off having fun, you've had to bear your sorrows alone. What a selfish beast I've been!"

"But I had Father and Mother to help me, and the dear babies to comfort me. Knowing that you and Amy were safe and happy made it easier to bear the troubles at home. Sometimes I'm lonely, but that's probably good for me, and—"

"Well, you'll never be lonely again," Laury interrupted, putting his arm around her protectively. "Amy and I want you to be part of our lives, and be happy and friendly together, just as we used to be."

"If I'm not in the way, that would be very pleasant. You always were a comfort to me, Laury." Jo leaned her head on his shoulder, just as she did years ago, when Beth was ill and Laury had stood by her, gently stroking her hair.

Suddenly, the whole family trooped in, and everyone hugged and kissed all over again. Mr. Laurence's crustiness had softened. He smiled warmly at the newlyweds, whom he called "my children." Amy had completely won his old heart. And Laury enjoyed watching the two of them enjoy each other's company.

Meg noticed that Amy had become an elegant and graceful woman. Meg felt self-conscious about her own plain dress, and thought that the dazzling young Mrs. Laurence would entirely overshadow the young Mrs. Moffat.

Watching the young couple, Jo thought, *How well they look together! I was right to tell Laury to look for a beautiful, charming girl instead of clumsy, annoying old Jo.*

Mr. and Mrs. March smiled and nodded at each other, happy that their youngest child had become rich in better things than money. For now she had a wealth of love, confidence, and happiness.

"Love has done much for our little girl," her mother said softly.

"She's had a good example to follow, my dear," her husband whispered back, looking lovingly at his wife's worn face.

Soon Hannah announced that it was time for tea. Everyone walked into the dining room. They talked and talked—trying to catch up on everything that had happened during the last three years.

Suddenly, a sense of loneliness and longing came over Jo. Hearing a knock at the door, Jo jumped up from the table. Wiping away the tears, she opened the door.

Another "ghost" had come to surprise her— yet another unexpected birthday gift. For there stood a tall bearded gentleman, his smile beaming at her from the darkness.

"Oh, Mr. Behr! I'm so glad to see you!" Jo cried out, as if afraid the night would swallow him up before she could get him inside.

"And I to see Miss March. But maybe not today? I see you have company."

"Oh, no. It's just the family. Come in and join us," Jo said, unable to hide her joy. Showing the visitor inside, Jo quickly shut the door behind him.

"If I shall not be one guest too many, then I will so gladly see them. But you have been ill, my friend?" he asked with sudden concern, as the light fell on her face.

"Not ill, but tired and sad. We've had trouble since I saw you last."

"Ah, yes. I know. My heart was sore for you when I heard," he said gently, taking her hand.

Jo felt then that nothing could ever comfort her as much as the look in his kind eyes, or the grasp of his big, warm hand.

With overflowing pride and pleasure, Jo

introduced Professor Behr to her family. At first, everyone greeted him kindly for Jo's sake. But very soon his noble spirit opened their hearts. The little children flew to him like bees to honey. The women silently flashed their approval to one another. Mr. March was delighted to find someone who shared his values. Mr. Laurence, though weary from the voyage, became too interested in the conversation to fall asleep. Quiet John listened and enjoyed the talk.

And Mr. Behr felt like a traveler who knocks at a strange door, and when it opens, finds himself at home.

Only Laury watched the guest with a kind of brotherly suspicion. But soon Mr. Behr's warmth and simple goodness won him over.

Mr. Behr rarely spoke directly to Laury. But when he looked at this handsome young man, a shadow passed across his face. Then he'd glance sadly at Jo, as if regretting his own lost youth.

Jo kept her face turned toward the little sock she was knitting, hoping no one would notice her excitement. But occasional glances at Mr. Behr refreshed her like sips of water after a dry, dusty walk. Jo was thrilled when Mr. Behr won an intellectual argument with Laury, and thought how much her father would enjoy having someone like "her Professor" to talk with every day. She also noticed how noble and dignified Mr. Behr looked in his very best suit. And his face—animated by the lively conversation—actually looked young and handsome.

Suddenly it was time to end the delightful evening. "Let's have our good old sing, the way we used to," suggested Jo. "For we are all together once more."

And in a way, they really were all there. For Beth's peaceful presence was with them. Even death could not break the bonds of love that held together this family. Above her beloved piano, Beth's picture smiled upon them, as if saying, "Be happy. I am here."

"Play something, Amy. Show how much you've improved," Laury suggested with husbandly pride.

"I can't show off tonight, dear," Amy whispered, her eyes filled with tears.

Instead, she sang Beth's favorite songs with a heartfelt tenderness that touched the listeners' hearts. The room was very still when, singing about sorrow and hope, Amy's voice suddenly broke.

Before the silence became too painful, Jo suggested that they finish with a song that Mr. Behr knew.

Clearing his throat, Mr. Behr walked over to Jo and asked, "You will sing with me, then? We go excellently well together."

At that moment, Jo would have joyfully agreed to do anything he proposed. Though she sang no better than a cricket, she happily hummed along, and listened to the mellow voice that seemed to sing for her alone.

Everyone applauded and showered the singer with praise.

Mr. Behr smiled and thanked them graciously. But he almost forgot his manners when, as Amy put on her coat to leave, Laury shook his hand and said, "My wife, Amy, and I are very glad to meet you, sir. Please remember that there is always a warm welcome waiting for you at our home."

Hearing for the first time that Laury was happily married to Jo's sister—and not to Jo—the Professor's face lit up, and he shook Laury's hand so heartily that Laury thought him the friendliest old fellow he'd ever met.

Then the Professor said to Mrs. March, "I, too, shall go now. But I shall gladly come again if you will permit me, dear madam. For I have some business that will keep me in the city for a little while."

A glance at Jo's eyes told him that both mother and daughter would happily welcome him in their home.

After the last guest had gone, Mr. March observed, "Mr. Behr seems like a wise man."

"And a good one, too," added Mrs. March, approvingly.

"I thought you'd like him," was all Jo said, wondering what unexpected "business" might have brought him to their city.

Chapter 44

$\mathcal{T}$he next day, Laury asked Mrs. March, "Please, Madam Mother, could you lend me my wife for half an hour?" For Amy had spent the entire morning sitting with her family in her childhood home.

"Go, dear," Mrs. March told Amy, pressing the hand that now wore a wedding ring. "I forgot that you have another home now."

"I'm afraid I can't get along any more without my little woman," Laury explained. "She's like a compass that keeps me pointed in the right direction."

"And it's been easy sailing so far," added Amy. "I don't know how long it will last, but I'm not afraid of storms, for I'm learning how to sail my ship."

"What are you going to do with yourselves after you get settled?" asked Jo.

"We have our plans. I'm going to work hard and prove to Grandfather that I'm not spoiled. And Amy's going to reach out to help other people."

After the young couple had left, Mr. March

observed, "How happy those two seem together!"

"Yes, and I think it will last," added Mrs. March, with the satisfaction of a pilot who has brought her ship safely into port.

"Happy Amy!" Jo sighed. Then she smiled brightly, seeing Professor Behr eagerly open the gate.

Later that evening, Laury suddenly exclaimed to his wife, "Why, Mrs. Laurence, I think that Professor intends to marry our Jo!"

"I hope so. Don't you, dear?"

"Well, my love. I think he's quite a catch— though I wish he was a little younger and a lot richer."

"Now, Laury. If they love one another, it doesn't matter one bit how old they are or how poor. Women should never marry for money."

As soon as the words were out of her mouth, Amy looked anxiously at her husband. "Oh, my dearest, you know I would have married you even if you didn't have a penny. In fact, I sometimes wish you were poor so that I might show how much I love you. Don't you know I'd gladly row in the same boat with you, even if you had to earn your living by rowing on the lake?"

"I do indeed. And yesterday I even told Marmee that her daughter had learned to follow her mother's fine example. She looked as glad and grateful as if I'd given her a check for a million dollars to spend on her favorite charity."

Gently touching his face, Amy answered, "And I'm prouder of my good husband than of all his money."

After a moment, Amy asked quietly, "Will you care if Jo does marry Mr. Behr?"

"My dear, right now I'm the happiest fellow alive. Can you doubt that I would gladly dance at Jo's wedding, knowing that you're my wife?"

Amy looked up at Laury and was satisfied. Her little jealous fear vanished forever.

"I only wish we could do something to help out that fine old Professor," Laury said. "Couldn't we invent a rich uncle who conveniently died in Germany and left him a small fortune?"

"Jo would find out. She's very proud of him, just as he is."

"Well, we won't interfere now. But let's watch for our chance. I owe Jo a lot for my education, and she believes that people should pay back their debts. Maybe that's how I'll get around her pride."

"It's so delightful to help others!" Amy observed. "That was always one of my dreams. And thanks to you, the dream has come true."

"I've seen so many talented young fellows enduring real hardships, just to make their dreams come true. They worked like heroes—so full of courage, patience, and determination. I'd like very much to help them out."

"And I'd like to help young women who suffer in silence," Amy said. "People have been very kind to me. And whenever I see girls struggling as we used to do, I want to put out my hand and help them—just as I was helped."

"And so you shall!" Laury exclaimed. "Let's create and fund a program to help young women with artistic talent. Sharing our wealth with others will add pleasure to our own lives."

The young couple shook hands upon it. And their hearts were more closely knit together by a love that remembered those people less fortunate than they.

Chapter 45

*N*o one ever found out what "business" was keeping Professor Behr in town so long. But every evening he came to the house and asked to visit with Mr. March. For a while, the good father believed that the Professor came mainly to have long philosophical discussions with him.

But young Demi soon became jealous of the visitor. He noticed that his favorite Aunt Jo liked playing with the "bear man" more than with him. He consoled himself by helping himself to the chocolate drops that the Professor kept in his jacket pocket.

One evening, Mr. Behr interrupted a lesson in which Mr. March was teaching Demi the letters of the alphabet. Both were lying on the floor, their legs in the air forming the letter "V." When Jo looked up to see Mr. Behr grinning at them, she said in horror, "Oh, Father! Father! The Professor's here!"

Mr. Behr laughed his rich laugh, greeted Mr. March, and put Demi on his knee. "So what have you been up to today, little fellow?"

"Me went to see little Mary."

"And what did you do there?"

"I kissed her!" Demi answered, reaching into the jacket pocket.

"Goodness! You seem a bit young for that. And what did little Mary say to that?"

"Oh, she liked it. And she kissed me. And I liked it," Demi answered proudly, with his mouth full of chocolate. "Don't little boys like little girls?"

"Now, who put that into your head?" asked Jo.

"Isn't in my head. It's in my mouth!" Demi answered, sticking out his tongue to show the chocolate drop on it.

"You should save some chocolate for your friend, my little man," Mr. Behr said, offering some to Jo with a look that was sweeter than the candy.

Noticing the look, Demi asked the Professor, "Do big boys like big girls, too?"

Unable to lie, Mr. Behr mumbled an answer that made Mr. March suddenly notice a special glow in Jo's face. That made the kind father sink back into his chair, feeling at once both very happy and very sad.

Chapter 46

$\mathscr{L}$ate every afternoon, Jo visited Meg and the children. There were two paths she could take. But no matter which one she took, she always seemed to run into Mr. Behr. He would be walking rapidly, and seemed surprised to see her. If Jo was on her way to Meg's, he always seemed to have something to take the children. And if she was coming back home, he said he was just strolling out to the river, and would be happy to walk with her as far as her home—unless her family was tired of his visits.

Of course, Jo had to invite him in. It would be rude not to. And she always asked Hannah to make fresh coffee, since "Friedrich—I mean, Mr. Behr—doesn't like tea."

By the second week, everyone knew perfectly well what was going on. But everyone acted as if they were blind to the changes in Jo. No one asked her why she sang all the time, or fixed up her hair three times a day, or had rosy cheeks when she returned from seeing Meg. And everyone pretended that Professor Behr was only discussing philosophy with

Mr. March—when, in fact, he was giving Jo lessons in love.

For two weeks, the Professor came every evening without fail. But then, without a word, he did not show up for three whole days. Everyone looked concerned.

At first, Jo was just worried. But by the third afternoon she said with annoyance, "Probably went home as suddenly as he came. It doesn't matter to me, of course. But at least he could have come and said goodbye like a gentleman."

Putting on her pretty new hat, Jo announced that she was going in town to buy some writing paper.

"You'd better take the little umbrella, dear. It looks like rain," her mother suggested, pretending not to notice that Jo was rather dressed up just for running errands.

"Yes, Marmee. And do you want anything in town?"

"If you're going by the fabric store, I need some light cotton material and narrow purple ribbon. And if you happen to meet Mr. Behr, bring him home to tea. I'd really like to see the dear man," Mrs. March added.

Somehow, Jo found herself wandering far from the fabric and paper goods stores. Instead, she looked in the windows of hardware stores and plumbing supplies shops—places men shopped—

as though waiting for someone. As busy men pushed past her, her hopes sank.

A drop of rain reminded her to save her new hat—even if it was too late to save her heart. But she'd forgotten to take the little umbrella, and soon she was soaked.

Ashamed of herself for putting on her best clothes to run errands, Jo hurried down the muddy street. After a while, she noticed that a rather ragged blue umbrella seemed to stay constantly over her head. Looking up, she saw Mr. Behr looking down at her.

"I feel I know the lady who braves the rain without an umbrella. What are you doing here, my friend?"

"Shopping."

Mr. Behr smiled. "May I go with you, and help you with packages?"

"Yes, thank you," Jo answered, blushing. Taking his arm, Jo felt as if the sun had suddenly burst out.

"We thought you had gone," Jo said, trying to hide her joyful face under her hat.

"You thought I might go with no goodbye to those who have been so wonderfully kind to me?"

"No. But we missed you—especially Mother and Father."

"And you?"

Jo was so worried about keeping her voice

calm that it came out sounding cold. "I'm always glad to see you, sir."

The word "sir" chilled the Professor, and his smile disappeared. Quietly he said, "I thank you, and come one more time before I go."

"You're going, then?"

"I have no longer any business here. It is done."

Jo was surprised to hear the disappointment in his voice. She asked, "Things worked out the way you wanted, I hope?"

"I guess so. For I have found a college where I can teach. And I will earn enough to help my little Franz and Emil. I should be grateful for this, no?"

"Oh, yes!" Jo exclaimed. "How splendid! You'll be doing what you like, and we'll see you often—and the boys, of course!"

"Ah, but we shall not meet often, I fear. For this college is in the West."

"So far away!" Jo sighed, stepping carelessly into a puddle of water, as though it no longer mattered what happened to her clothes—or herself.

Mr. Behr had mastered several languages. But he had not yet learned about Jo's rapidly changing moods. So his hopes were crushed when she said briskly, "Here's the store. I'll be quick."

But Jo was so upset that she bought wool fabric instead of cotton, and orange ribbon instead of purple. As he watched Jo blush and stumble, Mr. Behr began to wonder whether Jo cared more about him than she admitted.

Back on the street, Mr. Behr cheerfully took the packages. He splashed through the puddles as if he suddenly enjoyed walking in the rain.

Stopping in front of a window full of fruit and flowers, Mr. Behr suggested that they buy a few things for the babies. "Let's have a farewell feast if this must be my last visit to your so pleasant home."

Jo was shocked to see Mr. Behr buy boxes of expensive fruits, large bags of nuts, and a huge bunch of roses.

As they left the store, the Professor gave Jo the flowers to hold and once more opened the old umbrella.

"Miss March, I have a very big favor to ask of you," the Professor began.

"Yes, sir?" Jo asked, her heart beating wildly, and heat rising to her face.

"I am bold to ask you this question. But I have so little time left before I leave."

"Yes, sir?" Jo gasped, clutching the flowers so tightly that she crushed them.

"Would you—?"

Jo held her breath.

"That is—I mean—would you kindly help me choose a dress for my little Tina?"

"Yes, sir," Jo answered flatly, suddenly as calm and cool as if she'd stepped into a refrigerator.

"Perhaps also a shawl for Tina's mother, for she is so poor and sick. Yes, yes. A thick, warm shawl would be a friendly thing to take her poor mother."

Jo quickly recovered from her surprise that the Professor wanted only her advice about clothing. *I'm letting my imagination run wild,* Jo thought. *But he's getting dearer every minute.'*

Inside the shop, the clerk suggested that Jo try on a pretty, but comfortable gray shawl. "Does this look OK to you, Mr. Behr?" Jo asked, modeling it for him.

"Excellent!" answered the Professor, paying for the shawl and the little girl's dress that Jo had selected.

"Now shall we go home?" he asked Jo, enjoying the sound of the word "home."

"Yes. It's late," Jo said sorrowfully. She was sad that this was her last evening with Mr. Behr, and that he seemed to care for her only as a friend. She stumbled and dropped the roses in the mud.

When the Professor stopped to pick up the poor little flowers, he noticed a few drops on Jo's cheeks. Bending down, he asked in a wonderfully sweet, tender voice, "Heart's dearest, why do you cry?"

Unable to hide her feelings anymore, Jo sobbed, "Because you're going away."

"That is so good!" exclaimed Mr. Behr. "My dearest Jo, I have nothing to give you but much love. I came to see if you could care for me as more than a friend. Can you make a little place in your heart for old Friedrich?" he added, all in one breath.

"Oh, yes!" said Jo. She grasped his arm with both hands, and looked up at him with an expression that showed how happy she'd be to walk through life beside him. It wouldn't even matter if he had nothing more than an old umbrella to protect her—as long as he was the person carrying it.

This was not an easy place for Mr. Behr to propose to Jo. It was too muddy for him to go down on his knees. His hands were too full to take her in his arms. He would have gladly kissed her—but they were standing on a busy public street. But his face expressed so much love and joy that there actually seemed to be little rainbows in the drops that sparkled on his beard.

Mr. Behr's hair was wet and matted, and his fingers poked through the holes in his gloves. Yet Jo thought he looked as handsome as a Greek god.

And Mr. Behr thought Jo the most beautiful woman alive—even though her boots were covered with mud, her hat a soggy rag, and her face wet with tears.

They slowly strolled home. In spite of the rain, mud, and cold, they felt as though they were in paradise. It seemed to Jo that her place had always been by the Professor's side. How could she have ever chosen any other path in life?

Finally, Jo asked shyly, "Friedrich, why didn't you tell me all this sooner?"

"Now I shall have to show you all my heart. But I so gladly will, for you must take care of it from now on. You see, Jo, I had a wish to tell you when you left New York. But I thought you were engaged to the handsome young friend."

"Oh, no. Laury was only a boy, and soon got over his silly little crush. And I never loved anyone before you."

"Then I am happy. For I have waited so long for you, my dear Jo."

"But how did you know to come here—just when I wanted you?"

"This," Mr. Behr said, taking from his pocket a worn page from a magazine.

When she saw it, Jo was embarrassed. It was a poem she'd written long ago, when she was more concerned about earning money than writing well.

Jo re-read the poem, entitled "In the Attic." It was signed only with the initials "J.M." Each stanza described a chest filled with childhood treasures. One verse described the chest marked "Jo."

Headless dolls and stories wild.
Journals of a stubborn child.
Memories still sweet, but few.
Dreams that haven't yet come true.
Now the woman, early old,
Listens as the days grow cold.
Still she hears the sad refrain
In the falling summer rain.
Still she hears, with heart now numb,
"Merit love, and love will come."

"It's very bad poetry," Jo frowned, tearing up the sheet that the Professor had treasured for so long. "But I wrote it one day when I was very lonely. I never thought you'd read it."

Watching the pieces float away, Mr. Behr smiled. "Let it go. It has done its duty. For when I read that, I thought she must be sad and lonely. She would find comfort in true love. And my heart is so full—full of love for her. I must go and ask her, 'If this heart is not too poor a thing to give for what I hope to receive, will you take it, my love?'"

"And now you know that it is not too poor, but the one precious thing I need," whispered Jo.

"At first I could not dare to think that, even though you welcomed me so kindly. But soon I began to hope. And I said to myself, 'I will have her—even if it kills me!'"

Jo thought that was splendid, and decided to try always to be worthy of his love.

It was so wonderful confiding in each other that now she asked, "What made you stay away so long?"

"It was not easy. But I had not the heart to take you from your so happy home until I could offer you one of my own. How could I ask you to give up so much for a poor old fellow, whose only wealth is a little learning?"

"Don't be afraid of being poor. I've been poor long enough to stop fearing it. Besides, I'm happy working for those I love. And don't call yourself old. Forty is the prime of life. And I'd love you even if you were seventy!"

The Professor was so touched that his eyes brimmed with tears. But his hands were too full of packages and umbrella to wipe them. So Jo gently smoothed them away. Then, taking a few packages, she laughed, "You know, Friedrich, that I must carry my own share and help earn money, too. Agree to that, or I'll refuse to go with you," she said firmly, as he tried to take back the packages.

"We shall see. But have you patience to wait a long time, Jo? I must go away and first earn some money for my little nephews. Even for you, I may not break my word to my sister. Can you forgive that, and be happy while we hope and wait?"

"I know I can," Jo answered. "For we love one another, and that makes all the rest easy to bear. I, too, have my duty and my work. And I couldn't be happy if I neglected them, even for you. So you do your part out West, and I will do mine here. And we'll both be happy, hoping for the best."

"Ah! You give me such hope and courage. And I have nothing to give back but a full heart and these empty hands," the Professor said, putting down the packages when they arrived at the Marches' front door.

Putting both her hands into his, Jo whispered tenderly, "Not empty now." And she gently kissed her Friedrich under the umbrella.

Then, turning from the night and storm and loneliness, Jo opened the door to a home filled with light and warmth and peace. With a glad "Welcome home!" Jo led her true love inside, and shut the door.

Chapter 47

*F*or a year, Jo and her Professor worked and waited, hoped and loved. They couldn't afford to meet more than a few times. Between visits, they wrote so many long letters that Laury said he wished he owned a paper company.

The second year began sadly. Mr. Behr couldn't find a job that paid enough for him to marry Jo and buy a house.

Then Aunt March died suddenly. They mourned the loss of the cranky old lady, for they loved her in spite of her sharp tongue.

But soon their sorrow turned to joy. For in her will, Aunt March left Plumfield, her large country home, to Jo.

Laury told Jo that Plumfield would bring her lots of money.

"But I don't intend to sell it," Jo announced firmly.

"My dear girl, it's a huge house and will cost a fortune to care for. The garden, orchard, and grounds need constant work. I don't imagine your Professor is much of a farmer?"

"He'll try if I ask him."

"So you plan to live off what you can grow? Sounds heavenly, but you'll find that farming is terribly hard work."

"The crop we're planning to raise will make quite a profit," Jo laughed.

"And just what, ma'am, is this profitable crop?"

"Boys."

Everyone stared at Jo in surprise.

"I want to open a school for little boys," Jo explained. "It will be a good, happy, homelike school. I'll take care of them, and my Friedrich will teach them."

Laury appealed to the family for help. "That's just like Jo—running after an impossible dream! What kind of a plan is that?"

"I like it," Mrs. March said firmly.

"So do I," Mr. March agreed, thinking he'd enjoy helping teach the young boys.

Meg looked at her one, very demanding son and sighed. "Jo will have so much work."

"Jo can do it—and be happy doing it, too!" exclaimed old Mr. Laurence. He'd been looking for a way to help Jo and the Professor, but knew they'd never accept cash from him. "Tell us all about it."

"Well, my dear people," Jo continued, "I've been planning this for a long time—long before my Friedrich came. I've seen so many poor, lonely, deprived little boys go to ruin only because no one helped them when they needed it. I seem to understand their problems and feel their needs. Oh, I'd so much like to be a mother to them!"

Mrs. March gave Jo's hand an encouraging squeeze.

Smiling, with tears in her eyes and an enthusiasm she hadn't shown for a while, Jo continued. "I told my plan to Friedrich once. He said it was just what he'd like, too, and agreed to try it if we ever got rich. He's been doing it all his life—helping poor boys, I mean, not getting rich. Now, thanks to my good old aunt, who loved me better than I deserved, we have a place to start our school. Plumfield is big enough, with lots of rooms, strong and simple furniture, and plenty of space outside for playgrounds. The boys could help in the garden and orchard. Friedrich could teach his own special way, and Father could help him. I can cook and manage and pamper and scold the boys, and Mother can help me out sometimes. I've always wanted lots of boys. Now I can pack Plumfield full of them!"

Laury couldn't believe that everyone else seemed to be taking Jo's plan seriously. "If I may ask, Lady Behr, how do you intend to pay for your school? If all your students are poor, how will you make a profit?"

"Oh, I'll have rich students, too. Sometimes they're neglected because their parents are too busy or because they don't learn quickly enough. Some cause problems, and some lose their mothers. Some just have to get through a few difficult years. I know what it's like. And I'd like to show those children I see the honesty and love in their hearts, even when their bodies are unruly or their heads get them in trouble. Once the rich boys bring in some money, then I can take in the poor children for free."

Jo paused a moment, and then grinned at Laury. "And I know I can do it. Haven't I already helped one troublesome boy become a responsible young man?"

"And I thank you for doing everything that could possibly be done," Laury answered with a grateful look.

"Well, I've succeeded beyond my hopes. For you've learned to help not only yourself, but other people, too. And when I have the school, I'll just point to you and say, 'There's your model, my boys.'"

"Well, any progress I've made has been thanks to you, and to these two, as well," Laury said, gently placing one hand on his grandfather's gray head, and the other on Amy's golden one.

"I do think that families are the most beautiful things in the whole world!" Jo burst out joyously. "When I have one of my own, I hope it will be as happy as the three I know and love the best."

It was an astonishing year. Things happened in an usually quick and delightful way. Almost before she knew it, Jo was married and living at Plumfield. It was hard work, of course. But Jo's first "crop" of boys soon sprang up like wildflowers in the sunshine. Even the wildest ones were eventually tamed.

Mr. Laurence kept finding very poor boys and begging the Behrs to take them into the school. That way, he got around Jo's pride by offering to pay for their support—and then a little more. There were shy boys and daredevils. There were boys who stuttered and boys who had trouble reading. Some boys ran all over the place, and other boys needed crutches. They welcomed a biracial child, who'd been turned away by other schools—even though some people threatened to take their own children out of the school.

Soon every room in the big house was full. The garden was filled with young "farmers." Pets ran all over the grounds. And three times a day, Jo smiled at her Friedrich from the head of a very long table. From both sides of the table, the boys turned their loving eyes and grateful hearts to the woman they called "Mother Behr."

They were not angels, by any means. Some caused Jo and the Professor much trouble and worry. But Jo's faith in the goodness in each little heart gave her patience, skill, and, ultimately, success. No boy could hold out for long against

Father Behr's sunny goodness and Mother Behr's endless forgiveness. Jo treasured their energy, hopes, and trust—and even their mistakes, which only brought them closer together.

It was never a fancy school. It never made them rich. But it was just what Jo intended—"a good, happy, homelike school," a sort of paradise for boys that no one else wanted.

Jo was a very happy woman there, in spite of hard work, much worry, and constant noise. Soon, two little boys of her own added to her happiness, blossoming like dandelions in the spring.

Then Amy and Laury had a little daughter they named Beth. Although the child had her mother's golden hair, sadly she had her aunt's poor health. Fear of losing her was the one shadow in a life filled with sunshine. But love and sorrow helped Amy become more thoughtful and tender, and Laury stronger and more serious. Both grew closer together, as they learned that nothing—not even love—can shelter even the most fortunate people from suffering pain and loss.

There were many special celebrations at Plumfield. One of the most delightful was the annual apple picking festival in October. There the boys played and picked apples all day. All the Marches, Laurences, Brookes, and Behrs brought picnic lunches and helped harvest the fruit.

Five years after Jo's wedding, the trees were ripe with fruit, and the air was fresh and clear. It was a perfect day for apple picking. Everybody was there—laughing, singing, climbing trees, and tumbling down from them.

At four o'clock, Jo and Meg set out a bountiful supper on the grass. The boys were free to eat sitting down or standing up. Some enjoyed experimenting with drinking milk while standing on their heads. Others enjoyed tossing cookies back and forth.

Everyone ate until they could eat no more Then the Professor gathered them together and said, "Let us give thanks in memory of Aunt March, who has made all this possible." The boys nodded quietly, for they had been taught to remember all she had done for them.

The Professor then added, "And now, let's wish Grandma March a happy sixtieth birthday!" Everyone cheered as Demi pulled over a wagon filled with handmade gifts from every grandchild.

During the ceremony, all the boys silently and mysteriously disappeared. But Mrs. March didn't notice, for her eyes were filled with tears.

After she opened the last present, the Professor suddenly began to sing, and she finally looked up. From high in the branches of the trees came the sound of children's voices. With all their hearts, the boys sang the little song that Jo had written, Laury had set to music, and the Professor had taught these "featherless birds."

Mrs. March was so surprised and touched that she insisted on shaking hands with each of the boys. Then they ran off to play, leaving Mrs. March alone with her daughters.

"I don't think I'll ever again call myself 'unlucky Jo,'" said Mrs. Behr, taking her little son's hand out of the milk pitcher. "My greatest wishes have been granted."

"And yet, your life is very different from the one you pictured so long ago," Amy added, smiling as she watched Laury and John playing catch with the boys. "Do you remember all the dreams we had?"

"Yes, I remember," answered Jo. "But the life I wanted then now seems selfish, lonely, and cold. I still hope someday to write a good book. But I can wait. And I'm sure that what I'm seeing and doing now will make my book even better."

Jo glanced from the boys playing in the distance, to her father and the Professor discussing philosophy, to her mother, sitting with children in her lap and at her feet.

"I know I said I wanted fine, fancy things," Meg explained, tenderly placing her hand on Demi's head. "But in my heart I knew I'd be satisfied as long as I had a little home, and John, and some dear children like these. I've got them all, and I'm thankful to be the happiest woman in the world."

"My life is very different from what I'd planned. But I wouldn't change it at all," Amy said quietly, looking at the tiny child sleeping in her arms. "I still hope to be a fine artist. I've begun a sculpture of a baby, and Laury says it's the best thing I've ever done. I'm doing it in marble. So whatever happens, I'll be able to keep an image of my dear little angel."

"Don't despair, my dear," said Mrs. March, as kind-hearted Daisy placed her rosy cheek against little Beth's pale one. "Try to hope and keep happy."

"I'll try, with you here to cheer me up, Marmee. And Laury is so helpful and comforting. I can't love him enough. So in spite of this one burden to carry, I can say with Meg, 'I, too, am thankful to be such a happy woman.'"

"There's no need for me to say it. For everyone can see that I'm much happier than I deserve," added Jo. "We'll never be rich, and Plumfield may burn up any day. For we can't seem to keep Tommy Bangs from smoking in the closet. It may not be romantic. But I have no complaints, and I've never been so jolly in my entire life."

"And I think your 'harvest' will be a good one, too," Mrs. March began.

"Not half as good as yours, Marmee," Jo interrupted. "For here we are. We can never thank you enough for your patience in helping us blossom and grow."

"And I hope that every year there will be more fruit and less disease," Amy said softly.

"It's a large crop," added Meg tenderly. "But I know there's enough room in your heart, Marmee dear."

Mrs. March could only stretch out her arms, as if to gather in all her children and grandchildren. With a voice full of motherly love and gratitude, she said simply, "Oh, my dear girls. However long you may live, I can never wish you a greater happiness than this!"

About the Author

*L*ike many writers, Louisa May Alcott based her fiction on facts—her family, her experiences, and her beliefs and values. The characters in *Little Women*, one of her earliest novels, are drawn almost entirely from real life. As in the novel, Alcott's childhood family was poor, her father was often absent, and the women had to find ways to support themselves. Alcott actually did many of the things she described in the novel. For example, one Christmas day a neighbor asked the Alcotts to come help his ill wife. Just like the March sisters in *Little Women*, the Alcott girls gave up their own Christmas dinners so that their poor neighbors could have a special meal.

Like Jo in *Little Women*, Louisa May Alcott was a tomboy—stubborn, strong-willed, and more interested in books than romance. She once wrote, "No boy could be my friend until I had beaten him in a race and no girl if she refused to climb trees, and leap fences." Unlike most women of her time, Alcott remained unmarried, lived independently, and was financially self-sufficient. In fact, she eventually earned enough money to support her parents, sisters, niece, and nephews.

Louisa May Alcott, like Jo, also had three sisters. Her older sister Anna, like Meg, was a "model" woman of her time. She was a good student, an obedient daughter, a loving wife, and a devoted mother. Unfortunately, her husband died a few years after they were married, leaving her to support their two young sons, Frederick and John. As the oldest daughter, Anna worked as a governess to help support her sisters. As a widowed mother, she worked as a teacher to support her children.

Elizabeth Alcott, like Beth, loved children and kittens, played the piano, and sewed. After falling ill with scarlet fever, she never recovered her health and died in her early twenties. The Alcotts thought of her as "our angel in the house."

Like Amy in *Little Women*, blue-eyed, blond-haired May Alcott loved beauty and art. Her parents supported her artistic talent, and even encouraged her to draw on the walls. May studied art in Boston, and she illustrated the first edition of *Little Women*. With the money earned from its publication, Louisa took May to Europe so she could study art.

Alcott's father, Bronson, was a philosopher and dreamer. He held himself and his family to high—and sometimes unrealistic—ideals. A liberal thinker, Bronson Alcott protested against slavery and sheltered runaway slaves. He lectured all over the country, often leaving his wife and children to manage on their own. Because he did not feel right about charging money for his lectures, Bronson was never able to support his family financially. Bronson also created private schools much like "Plumfield," where he used "shocking," yet progressive teaching methods. He included art, music, and physical education, and favored hands-on learning. He blamed himself for his students' misbehavior. So rather than punish them, he asked his students to beat him instead. He bought textbooks for children who could not afford them. When he admitted a black girl, parents of the other students withdrew their children and forced him to close the school.

Alcott's mother, Abigail May, supported her husband's idealism, but also provided more practical support. Although born into a social class where women never worked outside the home, Abigail (called "Marmee" by her daughters) took paying jobs in order to feed her family. One of America's first social workers, Abigail devoted herself to helping those who were less fortunate than she. A strong advocate for women's rights, at one time Abigail managed an employment agency just for women.

Like her parents, Louisa May Alcott was interested in improving life for women, children, and poor people. During the Civil War, Alcott volunteered as a nurse. Like Mr. March in *Little Women*, Alcott caught typhoid fever and almost died. Although she eventually recovered and returned to her writing, her health remained fragile for the rest of her life. Like her mother, Alcott was deeply interested in women's rights. In 1879, she became the first woman in Concord, Massachusetts to register to vote, and then worked to encourage other women to vote. Like her father, Alcott tried to improve educational practices, which she described in *Little Women* and *Jo's Boys*.

Although her family moved often, Louisa May Alcott spent most of her life in Massachusetts. There she was influenced by the transcendental philosophers and writers who were her father's friends. Alcott loved to read and often borrowed books from the famous essayist Ralph Waldo Emerson, who may have been a model for Professor Behr. Alcott also knew the novelist Nathaniel Hawthorne, and went for nature walks with the author Henry David Thoreau.

Because Alcott's father was more interested in abstract ideas than in material things, all four daughters were well educated, but very poor. As a teenager, Alcott went to work in order to earn money for her family. She read to elderly people, mended clothing, and taught. At age fifteen Alcott wrote, "I WILL do something by and by. Don't care what—teach, sew, act, write, anything to help the family; and I'll be rich and famous and happy before I die, see if I won't!"

At first, Alcott's stories were rejected. One publisher advised her, "Stick to your teaching, Miss Alcott. You can's write." But her parents encouraged her to write, no matter what the critics said. Alcott's first poem was published when she was only 19, followed three years later by a full-length book. Like Jo, Alcott also wrote stories for magazines. Because in those days it was not "proper" for young ladies to write thrillers or horror stories, Alcott published her early work under such funny names as "Aunt Weedy" and "Minerva Moody."

During her lifetime, Alcott published poems, plays, reviews, short stories, and novels—a total of more than 30 books and collections of short stories. Although she often wrote for adult readers, she is best known for the books she wrote for and about children. In 1867, she edited a children's magazine. When her publisher asked her to write a book for girls, Alcott hesitated at first. She much preferred writing for boys, but she also needed the money. Since she "never liked girls" except for her three sisters, Alcott decided to write about her own experiences growing up. She wrote feverishly for two-and-a-half months, and decided to name the book *Little Women*.

Little Women was quite different from other children's books published at that time. Alcott's characters seemed true to life. They had interesting, unique personalities. The women were strong and independent, and Mrs. March raised her daughters without much help from her husband. Ambitious, active, and willing to take risks, the March girls had minds of their own. In short, they did not conform to what society expected of "little women" of the time.

As soon as it appeared in 1868, *Little Women* was a huge success. In the first month after it was published, 2,000 copies were sold—an impressive number at that time. The public then demanded a sequel to the original 23 chapters. Skipping three years in the girls' lives, Alcott wrote about the challenges and choices the Marches faced as young adults. When the next 24 chapters were published only six months later, under the title *Good Wives*, 13,000 copies were sold. Now both books are published together as *Little Women*. Alcott later wrote two additional sequels—*Little Men* in 1871, and her last novel, *Jo's Boys*, in 1886.

Since its publication, *Little Women* has been adapted many times for stage, film, cartoon, and TV productions. There have also been several original novels about the March family and biographies of Louisa May Alcott—some of which have won prestigious awards.

As a woman and as a writer, Louisa May Alcott paved the way for future generations. She was one of the most successful authors of her time, even though she broke from traditional writing styles. She devoted herself to her family, yet pursued her career with energy and determination. In her work and her writing, Alcott dedicated herself to social reform. Louisa May Alcott was born on her father's 33rd birthday, November 29, 1832. She died two days after his death, on March 6, 1888, at the age of fifty-five. Although her life was short, her words and her actions helped shape her world, as well as create opportunities for future generations.

About the Book

"Everyone has burdens to carry," Marmee reminds her daughters at the beginning of *Little Women*. Although she tries to provide them with guidance and support, she also realizes that each of us must "find our way through our mistakes and our troubles."

Throughout their lives, Meg, Amy, Jo, and Beth face various obstacles, challenges, and disappointments—some of which they bring upon themselves. How does each find her way through her "mistakes" and "troubles"? And how do these "burdens" become opportunities to grow from self-centered girls to strong, caring, and productive women?

Meg, the oldest of the "Little Women," tries to set a good example for her sisters. Yet her vanity keeps getting in the way. She insists on wearing fashionable, but painfully tight high-heeled shoes to the Gardiners' New Year's Eve party. But she ends up spraining her ankle and leaving early. She envies wealthy people, and longs for "a lovely house, full of fancy food, pretty clothes, pleasant people, and heaps of money." But spending time with Moffats only makes her dissatisfied with the people and things she used to enjoy. At first, Meg is flattered by the apparent interest these "very fine young ladies" take in her. But later she realizes that they are making fun of her, and gossiping behind her back. After Belle the Moffat dresses her up "like a new doll," Meg discovers that wearing a tight, low-cut dress does attract people—ones who are shallow and insincere. Drinking too much champagne with Ned Moffat makes her "sick all the next day." And trying to keep up with Sallie Moffat makes her deceive and lash out at her loving husband.

Finally, Meg realizes that those people she truly cares about respect her for being herself—an honest, "good and decent" person. She follows Marmee's advice to "accept and live with" her husband's faults as well as her own. She stops being "a slave to her babies," and takes more interest in her husband and the world around her. Together they create a home that other people envy—a good, loving home, "filled with riches that money can never buy." As a teenager, Meg "wanted fine, fancy things."

As an adult, she enjoys the richer rewards of having people who respect, accept, and love her. And she has learned to respect, accept, and love herself—not for what she has, but for who she has become.

At age 12, Amy, the youngest sister, is spoiled, selfish, and conceited. She feels she deserves to have and do whatever she wants. She doodles instead of doing schoolwork, yet complains about being teased for her mistakes. She suffers when an envious classmate takes revenge on her for being snubbed. Yet she vengefully burns Jo's precious book of stories.

Realizing that people love Beth because she is modest and unselfish, Amy tries harder "to think of others, keep cheerful, and be satisfied just knowing she was doing the right thing—even though no one noticed or praised her for it." Aunt March's little ring becomes a reminder to be less demanding, and more deserving of other people's love.

As a teenager, Amy thinks that "the best people" are those with "the most money, status, and refined manners." She tries to win their affection by inviting her wealthy classmates to a fancy lunch. But when only one girl attends, she realizes "that being wealthy is different from being noble or good." At the charity fair, she follows Marmee's advice to "answer meanness with kindness" instead of revenge. In doing so, she honestly earns everyone's respect, admiration, and love.

In Europe, Amy makes the most of the opportunities she's given, instead of envying, resenting, or pretending to be like those who are given more. Unable to afford jewelry, she artistically decorates her gown with wildflowers. She studies and practices art seriously, yet accepts that she may never become a "great artist." Instead of marrying Fred Vaughn for his money, Amy chooses to become "a lovable woman—not a social queen."

After marrying Laury, Amy shares her wealth with others, creating a program for struggling women artists. She works hard to become a fine artist, no longer insisting on becoming "the best artist in the whole world." Amy's love and compassion for others—as well as her self-discipline—make her sculpture even more beautiful. Amy is content to do her art, love her family, and help other people. She comments, "My life is very different from what I'd planned. But I wouldn't change it at all."

As a teenager, Jo is strong-willed, yet sometimes stubborn; honest, yet sometimes insensitive. Though determined, her ambitiousness to "become rich and famous" sometimes distracts her from her dream of writing "something wonderful, so people won't forget me after I'm dead." To become a good person and a great writer, Jo must learn to manage her willfulness, yet live by her principles.

After Amy falls through the ice, Jo asks her mother's help in controlling her temper. She admires Amy's self-restraint, "principle and nobleness of spirit" at the charity fair. But it is not until Aunt March rewards Amy with a trip to Europe that Jo resolves to discipline her "big mouth" and tame her temper.

To have her stories published, Jo learns to compromise with her editors. Yet she learns not to compromise her principles just to make money. Jo's father tells her, "You can do better than this, Jo. Aim high. Always do what's best—not what pays the most." But she does not follow his advice until Mr. Behr points out that writing trashy stories is like putting "poison in candy." Only after Beth dies does Jo write a story that is truly "from the heart"—and one which finally earns her a good reputation, honest money, and well-deserved success.

Jo used to think that self-sufficiency meant doing "everything for myself." Determined to be "perfectly independent," she cuts herself off from other people. But when she asks her parents for help, she becomes much closer to them. As a young woman, she realizes that Beth and Mr. Behr are true heroes because of their compassion, commitment, and "good will" toward everyone. Even "sweeter than freedom" is "the one precious thing" she truly needs—a heart that is "full of love for her."

From a stubborn, angry, uncompromising, fiercely independent teenager, Jo becomes a flexible, gentle, cheerful, accepting, grateful, and kind young woman. Looking back, Jo recognizes that "the life I wanted then now seems selfish, lonely, and cold." She still dreams of writing "a good book," knowing that living a full life will make her writing even better. Having learned to be true to herself, as well as loved by others, Jo realizes that her "greatest wishes have been granted."

Even Beth, the "angel" in the house, has her shortcomings. Although she tries not to complain, she quietly tells her sisters that "housework is the worst work in the world" because it makes her hands too stiff to play the piano. She envies girls who have "nice pianos," and is fearful and shy of other people. But despite her childlike innocence, Beth matures more quickly than her sisters. It is her idea to buy gifts for their mother instead of themselves. She quickly overcomes her fear of old Mr. Laurence, and learns that "love can chase away fear. And gratitude can conquer pride."

Unlike her sisters, Beth does her duties cheerfully and without complaint. She "never asked for anything, because the only reward she ever wanted was to be loved." Once she has her little piano, Beth wishes only that her family be together and stay healthy. Even as her frail body grows weaker, Beth becomes "the stronger one" so she can comfort others.

Despite her challenges, Beth seems "to live in a happy world of her own." She approaches both life and death with hope, courage, acceptance, peace, and love. She tells Jo, "I don't want to go. But I am willing . . . I'm not afraid." Her dreams are realistic and unselfish, and she is content with what she has. Her life, though brief, is so full of "simple, unselfish goodness" that it is "a true success." She hasn't had children, created fine art, or published stories. But Beth finally realizes, "I haven't wasted my life. I've been loved, and maybe I've helped someone."

By the end of the book, Meg, Amy, Jo, and Beth have faced problems far worse than teaching the spoiled King children, going to school with rude girls, caring for cranky old Aunt March, or doing housework. And they have received gifts far greater than new clothes, drawing pencils, books, and piano music—the Christmas presents they longed for as teenagers. Some of their difficulties and gifts come from the outside. But many of their greatest challenges—and resources—lie within themselves.

By overcoming hardships and developing the most of what they've been given, the four "little women" grow into powerful adults. They develop the self-discipline and courage to pursue their dreams, as well as accept their limitations. Strong and principled, yet flexible and kind, they learn to balance work with play, and others' needs and values with their own. In spite of many setbacks and sacrifices, they always remain grateful and hopeful. In short, Meg, Amy, Jo, and Beth take to heart their mother's advice "to do good and be happy."